Done With Mirrors

Sarah A. Hoyt

Copyright © 2026 by Sarah A. Hoyt

Cover Copyright © 2026 by Sarah A. Hoyt

All rights reserved.

No portion of this book may be reproduced in any form without written permission from the publisher or author, except as permitted by U.S. copyright law.

Contents

About Done With Mirrors

Holly Chism

I've been acquainted with Sarah Hoyt's writing for a few years, now. I think I found the blog, first, but only barely. I don't remember if it was *Mad Genius Club* where she (and others) write about writing, or the one where she talks about the state of the world, reality, and how politics intersect with it (spoiler: politics usually has a barely glancing acquaintance with the reality most of us actually live in). I didn't read her fiction for another year or so.

I kinda jumped in the deep end with both feet, too. The first novel of hers I read was A Few Good Men—third in the Darkship Thieves, and read in between naps while I was down with pneumonia. I could barely think, but she pulled me into the story and I didn't have a lot of trouble following the main character around through his life, even oxygen deprived. Dreamed in the world, too—re-watching what I was reading when I fell asleep (and the book landed on my nose).

I've been picking my way through her (frankly incredible) volume of work since. I think some of my favorites have been some of her short story collections.

So. When Sarah recently asked for volunteers to read this lovely collection of short stories...I sat bolt upright with a squeal, (metaphorically) flung my hand up in the air, and started bouncing in my recliner like a demented teacher's pet, going "Me, me, pick me!!!"

And I got to read the collection you're holding right now. Let me tell you, I enjoyed all of them. Each and every one made me feel *something*. Sometimes it was rage, sometimes outrage, sometimes horror. And sometimes, schadenfreude.

If you've read her work, and I'm assuming you have, you're going to recognize some of the worlds. If you've read Baen authors, you'll recognize at least one more, where she'd played in someone else's world with her own inimitable style.

If you read and liked *Darkship Thieves*, you're going to really love "Scrubbing Clean." You're going to hate it a li'l bit, too—what the so-called Good Men do to keep control of their world is heinous, and the way they acquire their tools to do so is, honestly, horrific. Very reminiscent of Marvel's Red Room that turned out the Black Widows.

If you read and liked Other Rhodes, you'll probably enjoy "Dead End Rhodes." But you'll want a box of tissues handy. You know, normally I don't cry when I read, but this one had me leaking for the last bit, and I had to stop reading for a little while. That's called catharsis, and Sarah's a master at it.

There really is a little bit of everything, from science fiction, to horror (zombies! I hate zombies, and hate it more when there's a plausible reason behind the outbreak!), to high fantasy, urban fantasy, noir fantasy...you name it, it's there. And each and every one of the stories is masterfully crafted.

Most of my life, I've read about people and their love affairs with drugs or alcohol: they describe a feeling of floating, of flying, of feeling on top of the world euphoric.

This collection made me feel exactly that. And relaxed. And mentally and emotionally rejuvenated, ready to face the real world (and the dishes, and the cats' litterbox, and the laundry).

Grab a cup of coffee (or tea, or cocoa), snuggle down, strap in, and hang on. You're in for a heck of a ride.

Holly Chism, 2026

WRITING HONEY FALL

HONEY FALL IS ONE of those stories that came out of nowhere. Kaycee Ezell contacted me and said she was editing a short story anthology for Baen and the title was Noir Fatale. And the story was there in my head, complete with the protagonist and the fact it was set in Denver in between World Wars.

Of course the problem was that I knew next to nothing of Denver after World War I. I mean there were bits and pieces I'd picked up from attending lectures and reading books, but I didn't know enough of the crunchy bits to write a story set there. And of course, you say, how accurate did I need to be considering that the story has magic being used on the daily?

Well, gentle – or ferocious – reader: the more fantastic the story the more you have to anchor it in plausible, verifiable reality. It's like this big lie. A lot of truth helps sell it.

So I went for a deep dive on the history of Colfax, specifically, but the story probably would never have been written if I hadn't happened to be on chat with my friend Charlie Martin at the time. Because as I wrote, things came up like "what did a driver's license look like in Colorado at the time?" and only Charlie would happen to have his grandfather's right there, and immediately scan it for me to see.

Another big help was the Forney Museum of Transportation that we'd visited a day or two before by purest happenstance. If you're in Denver, go give it a look!

Anyway, like most stories in this book *Honey Fall* is the visible part of the iceberg. I now have two novels outlined that involve .... Magic space opera is the best thing to call it. In the future of this story, humans go to space and there are at least two loners in spaceships solving crimes in that future.

Will I ever have time to write them? I don't know. We should all hope I live very long.

Honey Fall

It was raining. I could hear rain pattering on the roof, singing along gutters. An unaccustomed sound.

There was an odd smell, a sound of gnawing. And I needed to get out and do—

I didn't know what I needed to get out and do.

I was in a small room. There was a window. Dismal grey light shone through, illuminating a series of hooks on the wall, with clothes hanging on them. I sensed more than saw an unmade bed nearby and a large workbench. Smells were chemical with an undertone of bachelor living quarters, all dirty socks and dust. And I had a run in my silk stocking.

I stared at the stocking a long time, knowing that was wrong. I was not the sort of sloppy dame who wandered around with runs in her stocking.

I became aware that I was leaning against the wall, in an uncomfortable position, my legs splayed out gracelessly. The hem of my skirt had got torn.

It felt as though someone had flung me in a corner of the room like a broken doll. I blinked. I did not remember being flung. I remembered—

There had been a scene with Ale. I remembered that and made a face at it, but I didn't remember what the scene had been about or what had happened precisely. A quick memory of a shot, and of a bullet… I took my hand to my left, under my breast, but there was no pain, and no wound. A dream.

I got up. It's easier told than done. I had to brace myself against the floor, push with my legs, then pull myself up the wall with my hands. And I can't explain it. It's not like something hurt, or like my legs were broken. My body just felt all prickles, like your legs feel if you sit too long.

Standing, I looked around. The room was not familiar. It was a largish bedroom, with a workbench, and the man who lived here must be a natural born slob. The bed was unmade, and it looked like it was never made. There was stuff scattered on it on top of the tumbled blankets. Getting closer, I saw a wallet. Also a broken magician's wand. A rat was gnawing on it, eliciting sparks for every bite, but not seeming to care.

I'd never been here. I was sure of it.

"Honey," I told myself. "You're getting sloppy in your old age. A woman should not be alone in a man's house without knowing the man rather thoroughly, and if you've descended to slobs like this, you've come a long way since Arty."

And then I realized what I'd said, and clutched the bed clothes as memory returned. I was Honey D'Orio, and Arty was Arthur James Arcana, the love of my life. Who had left me, to go chase his dreams-- Well, chase something, at any rate, in Los Angeles. Not that he didn't have reason to do it, since the Pater did not approve. Or perhaps it was more fair to say that Arty did not approve of the Pater, and refused to work the family business like a good little boy.

I let it go. The words came with a feeling of screamed arguments, in which Ale always took his part against Arty, and where Pater for once listened to him. The whole felt not so much like my memories – though I was sure they were in fact mine – but the memories of some other woman, that I'd bought piece meal at a rummage sale.

The feeling of urgency returned, the one that had caused me to wake. I was supposed to get out of here and go get help.

Help for whom or what?

Five long steps to the door, and I found it unlocked. So I was not a prisoner. Help for whom, then?

I went back to the bed and grabbed the wallet, flipped through it. There were two fifty dollar bills in it, which made me cast a look around the place again. A lot of money for the owner of this dump.

There was also a much folded, greasy looking driver's license listing the owner as Donald Griffin. There was an automobile key. At least it looked like an automobile ignition key and the fob said Chevy. I pocketed that. Something nagged me about that license. I'd swear there was something relating to Donald Griffin. I'd also swear I'd never heard his name.

With no idea where I was going or why it was urgent, I opened the door and stepped out.

And into a steady downpour.

Which caused me to blink in confusion. I was a Colorado girl, born and bred, and in Colorado you're more likely to get wet with snow than with rain. But every ten years or so, we had a year where it wouldn't stop raining. Spring and summer come, and it keeps raining. This had that sort of feel.

I exited the house into a garden path that descended in a series of very broad steps among a garden more luxurious than Colfax usually was. There was lush grass and old trees and roses blooming in the moisture.

But I knew where I was and looking back and at the house confirmed it. I was on East Colfax, the street that ran from Denver to Aurora. Twenty years ago or a bit more it had been a respectable street, home to mansions in large gardens, but the wars had taken their toll on everything. Now the big Victorian mansions that no one could afford, like the one that rose in front of me in tones of need-to-be-painted grayish blue, had been subdivided into apartments. From the looks of it, Donald Griffin lived in the cottage at the back, which had probably once been a carriage house, or perhaps a gardener's cottage.

I walked down the path, not even bothering to avoid the dripping from above, then climbed down ten steps to the street level. There was a Chevy parked upfront. It was a 1926 Chevy Landau that had seen better days. Its rear back panel had been shoved in at least once, maybe more, there was rust on one of the doors, and the whole car was in dire need of a paint job.

But all I needed was a car that would allow me to go somewhere where I could think.

Home, I thought. I wanted to go home. Something in me, some feeling, that same sense of urgency that had awakened me protested, but the urgency could wait. I wanted to go home. And I knew exactly where home was and how to get there.

Acting as if the car belonged to me, and I had a right to do it, I opened the door and sat down. There were a gaggle of children playing across the street, and a couple of women, their bags loaded with groceries, walked along the sidewalk talking. None paid any attention to me as I started the car and followed the route I could follow in my sleep.

The Landau didn't purr as I remembered my car purring: my own, beloved Auburn Speedster, painted candy-apple red, that Pater had bought me to celebrate my nineteenth birthday, or perhaps because I'd let Arty go. I still wasn't sure letting Arty go had been a good idea, but at least, dear Lord, I'd got my Speedster out of it.

I blinked unaccountable moisture from my eyes, not sure why it felt like the Speedster was long lost, and took a deep breath, looking up at the grey sky where a couple of broom-flyers sped somewhere, darker against the grey. What a day to be flying. I wouldn't want to try it, not even on the most securely enchanted of brooms. Sure, a lot of veterans flew because they'd done it overseas, but it still seemed like a comfortless form of transportation.

I drove away from Colfax, towards Cherry Creek and the Country Club district. Pater had built the dear old family home less than five years ago. It's an almost embarrassing pile, all golden stone and sweeping European-looking turrets and balconies. I suspected it was his Sicilian grandfather's idea of a palace. The things that get transmitted in the genes!

Because when he'd built the house, he already could see a day when Ale and I would want to move away, and because Pater is unable to bear anyone leaving and going beyond his control, he'd built two apartments into the house, the sort of place where we could live – presumably even after we married – and pretend to be independent.

Mine was around the back, through the terrace at the rear of the house, the same terrace that led to the ballroom where we'd had my come out ball, and where I'd danced all night with Arty, while Ale glowered.

I hadn't realized how late it was until I pulled into the broad driveway and around the house. I could not have known it of course, not with the overcast sky. But when I got home it must have been well past dinner time. I toyed with going into the dining room and apologizing, but I had a strong feeling I should not. I wasn't sure why, but I reasoned that with my impaired memory, it wasn't a good time to buck my instincts. Not that I had much experience with impaired memory, save a couple of drinking binges, one of them the night Arty left. But even that was enough to show me that sometimes, when you couldn't remember, feeling was all you had.

I got out of the car. A man weeding one of the flower beds straightened up and stared at me, mouth half open. Well, he was probably one of the gardeners and wondering what I was doing driving this pile. Let him go on wondering. I ran across the corner of the terrace, up two stone steps, and took the path to the side that led to my door. Then I stopped. I didn't have my key with me.

Well, it wasn't precisely an unheard of predicament. Sometimes purses got forgotten. I walked around the edge, and felt in the flower bed for the peculiarly-shaped stone at the base of the yellow rose bush. The key was there, under the stone, feeling weirdly encrusted with dirt. I couldn't remember when I'd last needed it, but it took me a while to get all the dirt off, so I could put it in the lock and turn it.

The door opened with a creak that nearly pushed me out of my skin.

Inside was ... my apartment.

See, I chose all of it when I was barely fifteen, which will have to explain why it was decorated in tones of silver and green. My wallpaper was a tracery of delicate green branches, and the furniture was metallic silver, elfin, delicate constructions. Pater had laughed that it was not at all proper furniture, but he liked to indulge me.

My front room was a large sitting room with enough sofas and divans for a party of twenty of my closest friends. I walked by the piano and trailed my fingers across the keys, before going to my room at the back.

My room was also silver and green, with a soft green coverlet on the silver bed. Next to it was the most expensive bathroom money could buy. I had to make myself decent before going out.

I didn't realize how bad it was. Beyond the torn stocking there were dirt smudges on my cheeks, and the fact my skirt had collected dust from Griffin's floor. My shoes, too, green patent leather to match my skirt, had become scuffed.

I undressed, washed, and started dressing again, before I realized that my entire room was covered in a layer of dust. It made me uncomfortable, in a way I couldn't explain, but I shrugged. I might have been away for a few weeks, and Pater been busy with his ventures and not paid any attention. Obviously my maid had taken advantage to take a vacation.

Because it was nighttime, and because I had a feeling where I should go, even if not why, I picked a tailored dark green dress, which I wore with my jade beads. At least, whatever I'd been doing with myself, my hair passed muster. Which wasn't a given. Left to its own devices, it grew black and in a riot of curls that my father reassured me was exactly the same as his grandmother's when she was young. Fortunately in the modern era a girl didn't have to sit under that, and I didn't. Instead, I made it platinum blonde and arranged the curls in a stylish fall that blocked my right eye.

The stockings I put on did not have a run, and I picked new heels from the shelf in my closet. Because I had no idea what this was about, I picked my two guns, the ones that Daddy had given me when I turned sixteen, pearl handled .22 Baby Hammerless. One went into my purse, and one into my garter. Because it was raining and the temperature falls fast in the Rocky Mountains once the sun sets, I picked up my fox fur stole, and my seldom-used umbrella. Between the two I managed to stay cozy and warm all the way to the car. And yeah, it was the Landau again. My car might still be in the garage at the back, but I was in a hurry.

I backed down the driveway and drove to The Magic Cat. The Magic Cat was at the edge of the Five Points neighborhood. But it was not colored. Not as such. People of all colors frequented it. Well, mostly the patrons were white and the personnel, including the excellent jazz bands were colored. But the thing was no one looked very closely at you there. It was a place I could both be myself and something more than Daddy's little girl

The parking lot next to it was full, and my car would have passed more unnoticed than the Landau by make and model. But I found a spot all the same, and walked out, Griffin's two fifty dollar notes burning a hole in my dainty purse.

Coming in from the cool rain, pushing open the polished wood doors of The Magic Cat, with the bas relief of a cat in a fedora playing the trombone, felt like coming home more than my apartment did.

Inside, the club was cool but dry, and illuminated by golden-lampshaded lights that gave an impression of a tropical night.

I didn't recognize the band playing, but the notes wound in a spiral of sound around the usual dancers. Well dressed, well-coiffed people. Couples who twirled together in every semblance of a passion not acceptable in public. This, too, felt good. It felt like I'd been away for a long long time, somewhere remote and cold, and I wanted to warm myself at the fire of human passion and familiarity.

Some people looked oddly at me, but since I didn't know them, I assumed they were new. I pulled my fox stole up over my shoulder, as though to protect myself from stares. It hit me that I'd neither eaten nor drunk in a long time, and I was dying for a drink.

I was skirting the dance floor towards the bar when from the other side, the dark space next to the bar, a hand shot out and grabbed my wrist, at the same time a voice said, "Honey."

I turned, ready to freeze whoever had dared touch me with a look, and stopped. "Arty!" I said, half in a shriek.

He let out a surprised chuckle. "That revolting nickname!" he said, as I reached up to save the fur my startled movement had unsettled.

I didn't know what to say, so I smiled and said, "I didn't know you were in town."

"I wasn't till yesterday," he said. "I arrived by train yesterday morning."

"Oh. From California?"

"From Los Angeles, yes."

"For... you're coming back?"

He shook his head but shrugged a little, as if he wasn't quite sure what to say, so I thought maybe he hadn't made a decision yet. "I'm parched," I said. "You must buy me a drink."

The back of my mind was telling me to let him know everything that had happened, since I'd woken up, but I thought I was just going mushy and wanting to unload all my troubles on Arty's very broad shoulders.

He put his arm over my not-so-broad shoulders, and led me to the bar. It was Steven serving the drinks, and he gave me an odd look, then seemed reassured at Arty being with me, and when Arty ordered a bourbon for himself and a Cosmopolitan for me, he just gave us the drinks. Arty paid, then led me, with his arm still over my shoulder to one of the booths.

I sipped at my Cosmo, which was precisely how I liked it with the right proportion of lemon and grapefruit, and wondered if I should eat something, or if I was going to get sloppy. I couldn't remember when I'd last eaten.

Arty took a sip of his drink, and made a face, while looking very attentively at me. He'd gotten older. He was always older than I. When I met him, I was seventeen and he was twenty-five. He'd been in the fourth year of med school when they'd called him for his brief war service as a flyer. Because the moment that John Whiteside Parsons had discovered magic, the army had searched for men who could use it, before the Krauts found it too and used it first. We'd gone into the war on the Allied side, as magic flyers. And it turned out that Arty was chock full of magic, as well as whatever natural brilliance had propelled him into medical school.

He was still looking at me as if I were a very difficult problem he was trying to solve, even as he reached in his coat for his cigarette case and extended it to me. I was happy to see that it was the one I'd given him, silver, engraved with his initials, as I took a cigarette. I let him light it, and blew two puffs before taking another sip of my drink, and returning his serious look.

"I came to Denver," he said. "Because I got this." He reached into his jacket again, and pulled out a postcard. It was one of those they sell at the train station, advertising the newest trains. He turned it over and slid it to me.

The handwriting was crabbed and irregular, and it had been written with thin ink that looked brownish, but it was perfectly legible, "Art, I am in a spot of bother involving the D'Orio family. I don't know what to do, and I can trust no one. It seemed like a good time to call in a favor." It was signed, in a shaky hand, Don Griffin.

"My family?" I said. And to his shrug. "And who is Don Griffin?"

Arty toyed with the corner of the postcard. "Old friend from the war. Same corps. Saved my life. That's the favor he talks about."

"A flyer?" I asked.

Arty shrugged then seemed to think better of it. "I was never a flyer, Honey. Didn't it strike you as peculiar that I would go to California to work in Hollywood? No. My pidgin was always illusions."

Illusions. Look, I'm no strategist, and sure, I don't read all those super-important accounts of the war and analysis of "how we won." But I do read the pulps. I know what illusions mean. They mean spies and assassins. "And Griffin was in the same corps?"

"Stronger than I. He could create simulacrums."

I raised my eyebrows.

"Simulacrums. Creatures called up by magic, who move and live like the real thing, sometimes for months. Useful, when, say, you killed a high value target but you didn't want the enemy to know he was dead or that he had been compromised and escaped to the allies. Anyway, too long to tell you and too technical a story, but he saved my bacon once, in the war. And then he came here, to Denver, partly because I'd told him about it, to make a living as a magician for hire."

"And you kept in touch?" I said, wondering why I'd never heard of Griffin, not once. At least not that I could remember until I woke up in his pad

"No. We lived in very different worlds. I met him once or twice when I-- When we were keeping company, Honey, and I told him about you."

Well, there was a connection between us, though I was not at all sure what it meant. However, this was Arty, and he obviously knew Don Griffin, and the feeling I should tell him everything and fast was powerful enough that it would be hard to stay quiet. So I smoked my cigarette and drank my Cosmo, while around us jazz wound like cool wrap, masking our words as I told him everything that had happened to me today. A woman and a man danced by, her head on his shoulder. Arty and I had looked like that once.

Perhaps it was the Cosmo making me tipsy, as I found myself walking to Arty's car – he'd rented one this morning he said, and smiled when he told me he was doing well in LA though I didn't understand how well he could do in just six months – and driving back to Griffin's place.

It still wasn't locked, and looked exactly as I'd left it, except that the rat had stopped gnawing at the wand.

"What are we looking for?" I asked. I still had the sense of urgency, and it remained unfocused. I'd needed to get to Arty. No. I'd needed to get to someone who could help Griffin, and Arty was one of those people. But other than that I had nothing except the feeling I should... yes, I should be helping Griffin.

"Anything," Arty said. He was going over Griffin's workbench, inch by inch, moving dubious flasks, and rearranging various objects I couldn't identify. "Anything that tells us what he was doing or for whom he was making simulacrums."

"Was he making simulacrums?" I asked.

"Sure," he said. "I recognize the materials. Would your family buy simulacrums?"

I shrugged. "Maybe. You know I don't know anything about Pater's business."

"A wise move, since people who do tend to end up dead."

"Arty, Pater just does what he has to do to—"

"Survive and keep the family safe. Yes. Forgive me, Honey. I didn't mean to start the argument again."

He was still giving most of his attention to the workbench and its paraphernalia, so what could I do? I started looking through the bed clothes, to see if there was anything else there. It seemed weird that Griffin had disappeared leaving behind his wallet and his keys. But there was nothing else on the bed. So I started following the path to the door. Which is when I saw it.

Look, there were other things on the floor, so I might easily have missed it. It was obvious that Griffin was not one of your natural housekeepers. But there, against the far floorboard, near the rat hole was Ale's pen.

I'd have known it anywhere.

Back when Ale was in school and Father still had illusions about being the patriarch of scholars, Father had given him a distinctive silver pen, a thing worked by hand by some craftsman from the old country. It was slick and slim, and it had – I confirmed this as I got closer – Ale's name engraved on it. A. S. D'Orio.

I didn't know what Ale's pen was doing in Griffin's pad, but my first impulse was to hide it and pretend I'd never seen it, because—

I paused. Because I'd covered for Ale all his life, at first hiding his bad behavior from Pater so Pater would not be grieved, and eventually just hiding his behavior from everyone because I didn't want to be associated with a man who had turned out to be a common thug. Yeah, I know. You could say the same of Pater and the family business. But it wasn't precisely that way. The family business had its roots in the old country. It was both vocation and obligation. Sure, Pater lived by crime too, though you might have trouble tracing all his criminal enterprises to him. They were done through flunkies and managers to such an extent that in the end, even the IRS itself couldn't find the connections needed to bring the business down.

Did Pater's enterprise create misery and loss? I didn't know. Ever since I had realized what Pater did when I was twelve or so – and I can't tell you how, except through adding up the hints and stray words dropped over the years – I'd tried to think of it as little as I could. Pater had certainly broken the law during the Prohibition, and I knew there were other things in which he defied the might of the United States of America.

But was it worse than it would have been without him? It would take a better woman than I to know. Arty thought he knew, which was why he'd left me and Denver to go to LA and pursue his idea of using his not inconsiderable magic to create movies. He wouldn't sully his hands with Pater's business.

Still, the one thing Pater wasn't was a cheap thug. He didn't knock women about, abuse prostitutes, or plan hare-brained enforcement expeditions to knock out the teeth of some random man he thought had looked at him funny at a bar.

The thought of hiding Ale's pen, and therefore Ale's potential involvement in this came and went. "Arty," I said. And I walked over and pointed at the pen. I had some idea he might be able to get some sort of emanation or feel from the thing if I didn't touch it. "This is Ale's."

Arty looked over from the workbench, and his eyebrows went up as he stared at the pen on the floor, amid the debris. He flashed a feral grin, "Well, we did know your family was invol—"

"Completely different thing," I said. "If it was Ale. Completely different thing. Ale was a wrong 'un from the beginning, Arty." I looked at his face and explained about Pater breaking the law, but being disciplined and an adult. "Ale is just wrong. He beats women and sends thugs to beat men who best him at anything, from a bet to romancing a girl. My father doesn't know. At least I don't think he knows. I've kept it secret from him as much as possible, but Ale couldn't keep it secret from me, not when we went to the same schools and later had the same friends."

Arty took out the cigarette case and offered it to me first. We smoked in silence a long moment.

"I see," he said. "But you're not holding your peace now?"

"I—I don't know why but I have a really strong feeling that it's important we save Don Griffin."

He nodded. "Well, I certainly think so."

He threw his cigarette butt on a clear bit of floor and stomped on it. I put mine out in an overfull ashtray. I noted with interest that some of the cigarettes had exactly the color of my lipstick around the end. I wondered if I'd known Don Griffin. And why didn't I remember?

Arty had picked up Ale's pen with his handkerchief, put it on the workbench, and frowned intensely at it.

I don't know what I expected. Fire or stars, passes or arcane whispers. I'd seen magic on the stage before. I had some idea what it was supposed to look like.

Instead, what came up was a scene. It was foggy or perhaps just distant. Kind of like what it would look like through a window with condensation on it. Behind the workbench, against the wall, a replica of this room formed. Ale, in his brash finery, expensive suit spoiled by a big yellow-checker tie held down with a diamond tie pin – that boy never did have any taste – was talking to a thin, dark man with sparse hair combed back from his forehead. I knew without being told that the man was Griffin, which made me wonder what exactly had happened between me and him, and why I recognized him.

He was not what I'd expect, not at all. Not my type. And when one thinks of a spy, one doesn't think of a thin, tired looking man. Someone like Arty maybe, but not him.

Ale was giving Griffin a picture, "As close as you can, okay? As close as humanly possible."

Griffin mumbled something about time and materials and how expensive it would be. "And then, you know," he said. "She won't be the same. She won't remember the things the original knew. She won't fool anyone who knew her, not once they have a good look. She'll walk different, she'll talk different. She'll be a different person for as long as she lives."

"Doesn't matter," Ale said. "Not for what I need her. Just being seen around town, and confirming rumors, that's all."

"Well, that... that should be possible."

They were setting a date for delivery. And it was the day after my birthday, on the fourth of July. This confused me for a moment. I thought it was May, maybe April. Suddenly I didn't know what month it was. I'd realized part of my memory was missing, but I didn't know how much of it or what had happened. You know, if I'd used that lost time to take up with the likes of Don Griffin, I needed mental help and would seek it as soon as possible.

"So," I said. "Ale hired Griffin to do a simulacrum, and if I know Ale he probably welched on payment, and chances are that he took Griffin out to the edge of town and had his thugs beat him, and Griffin is now trying to find his way back, footsore and bruised. What do we do now? How do we find him?"

"We," Arty said, going all of a sudden as solemn and serious as a judge, and one of those judges you couldn't buy for love or money. "Aren't going anywhere, Honey. You're going back to your apartment and beddy bye. And I'm going to get some old friends from the corps and figure this out."

"Arthur Arcana, you rat," I said. "You can't do that. This is my case. This is my story. I'm the one who woke up with the feeling I'd got to help Griffin. I don't know why, and I don't know how, but I'm sure I'm supposed to do it."

He smiled a little at my calling him a rat, that weird quirk of the lip he used to give when I railed at him or teased him, but his eyes were dead serious and shading to sad. "No, Honey. You have helped him. You told me the whole story. You brought me here. But this will be dangerous. And there is no way I'm going to drag a dame on this kind of errand."

"But Art, Ale is my brother, and I know his tricks better than you. I know his tricks better than anyone. You need me."

And yet he wouldn't give. He kept looking at me with those infinitely sad eyes. I thought that once more he had seen me as a D'Orio, someone who wasn't fit to keep company with him. He didn't want anything to do with me.

He started to the door, then surprised me by walking back into the room, kissing my forehead with a butterfly kiss, his lips barely touching, "God bless you, Honey," he said. "You're too good, too fine for this. Stay away."

What is a woman to do with that? Once he'd told me I was good and too fine for my family, and he'd walked away and to California, and if this was July or later, he'd been gone for nine months at least. And I still didn't know what to do with that, except one thing: I couldn't let him go. Not now. Not again. Nor could I let him go off to look for Don Griffin, and maybe die alone. I wouldn't lose Arthur James Arcana again.

I should have told Pater that I was out, and endured his temper tantrum, and told him if he sent anyone after Art I'd go to the police with a lot of things I'd deduced about the family business. And then I should have left. By now we'd have a little house on the hills in California, and maybe a kid on the way.

"Well, there is no time like the present," I told myself. I took a cigarette from my own case, and smoked it down to the nubbins, before stubbing it out on the ashtray, with all the other ones with the same lipstick color smeared on them.

By the time I stepped down to the street, there was no sign of Arty's car. I walked in the rain, planning, to a busier part of the street, where I flagged a cab. I used some of Griffin's money to get back to the Magic Cat and Griffin's car.

Me, I don't use magic. Never have. But everyone knows a magic practitioner or two these days. Basic life necessity, right? Even a girl needs anti-wrinkle magic now and then, not to mention getting someone's claws off our best boy's back. If you don't enter in the love philter war in junior high you're a fool. And if you continue it much after twenty you're a worse one, I understand. Not that there was magic when I was in junior high of course.

But I knew magic practitioners, and had heard of others. The one I decided on, more blind instinct than anything else, was Mother Turner, down by the Cathedral.

There's a welter of little houses down there, a colored neighborhood, and Mother Turner was colored. A middle aged woman, of vast proportions, she was the matriarch of a large and respectable tribe. It was a point of pride to her that one of her sons was a bellman at the Brown Palace, and two more worked for the railroad. But she'd run her foretelling and fortunes business long before Parsons had made magic a scientific reality. And I'd consulted her now and then. Nothing much, mind. I knew better than to use magic in love. Except when it came to Arty. I had no brain at all when it came to Arty. Just a blind yearning to be with him, a loud feeling I belonged to Mr. Arcana.

Mother Turner had been straight with me about that too. I remembered the talk after Arty had left, about how I had to choose, and how it wouldn't do to run after a man. And she'd refused to bring him back to Denver and particularly into Pater's business. "No, missy," she'd said. "That I won't do because making a man come back against his will is worse than killing him, and making a man participate in crimes against his will is against God's law."

I respected her more for it than if she'd given in. I parked the car in front of her door, and walked the little path to her house. Her roses, in the handkerchief sized yard, were full abloom.

The door was opened by a young woman in a severe skirt suit, who gave me a tiny smile, before whispering, "Miss D'Orio" and stepping out of the way to let me enter a tiny, oppressively clean living room.

She then walked through an arch to a hallway, murmuring something about "telling mother."

I didn't know if Mother Turner was her mother or her mother-in-law, and suddenly it occurred to me, more urgently, I didn't know if Mother Turner was even awake. I'd been so taken with my ideas, with the need to not let Arty go, I'd forgotten it might be dinner time or later. Certainly, it was full night outside.

I was relieved when Mother Turner came back with the young woman. She had obviously been awake. She'd also obviously been cooking, judging by the apron she was removing as she walked towards me. "Now, Miss D'Orio, it sure has been a long time," she said, handing the apron to the younger woman, who then vanished back into the back of the house. "Sure has." She extended her hand to me, then frowned a little when I shook it, and a little more as she looked at me. She muttered "Oh, my," under her breath, and sat down on her sofa, while gesturing for me to sit. "I see you're in trouble. Tell me your story, Honey. Just tell me."

So I told her. From having decided to let Arty go, to the things that had happened today since I woke in that closet. Because I'd worked with Mother Turner before, I didn't even hold back that Ale was a bad 'un or that he was involved in this. One had a feeling she had to know already.

After I'd stopped talking – and I must have talked a long time, because my throat hurt – she looked at me a long time. She whispered something about not knowing what to do, then she asked, "What would you have me do, Miss D'Orio?"

I shrugged. "Something to find Ale, maybe? Or Griffin, wherever he has him? You see I feel I must save him, and also I understand what Ale thinks and how he works, and Arty doesn't. He doesn't. I'm afraid Arty will get hurt."

Mother Turner took a deep breath. "Very well," she said. "I can make you a charm to find your brother. But you must do me a favor in the meanwhile."

"Find you something of his?" I said. "I was afraid—"

She shook her head. "No. Not that. That won't be a problem. I have a way. No, Miss, I was wondering if you'd eat something before you go, because I can see you haven't eaten in a while."

I'd like to say no, but I was starving. While Mother Turner disappeared into one of the back rooms, the younger woman brought me rice and beef stew, and then, afterwards, a pastry dusted with powder sugar and a cup of coffee. I felt a new woman when Mother Turner came back.

The charm she'd prepared was a little bit of string, which rose like a charmed snake, and pointed in a direction. "That's where he is. Just follow it. You'll find him."

And then before I left, she touched my shoulder. "God Bless you, Miss D'Orio. You'll need a lot of courage."

I thought so too, and it would help if my stomach didn't feel like jelly. But damn it, for all of Pater's failings, he'd raised me to be a lady. And a lady doesn't let a man who she's fairly sure loves her go and kill himself out of being chivalrous fool.

I set the thread on the dashboard and followed its pointing as much as the roads allowed. I got gas when it became obvious we were headed out of town and North. And then, in the dark, in the narrow mountain roads, I followed the thread.

It took me ever higher, and then down a road that, honestly, was more of a goat track, or likely a mule track, used long ago by miner's mules.

Even that ran out, and I grabbed the thread and my purse and continued on foot, cursing myself for seven kinds of fool for not having changed shoes. At least I was going to face death dressed to the nines. It might be some kind of consolation.

The track descended the rock face, in a narrow, winding path. And down below, almost like a ghost, I saw something shine. It appeared and disappeared depending on how the rain drove it, and maybe on someone moving it.

Getting closer, I saw it was the entrance to a mine. Colorado is full of abandoned mines. Some played out after the gold rush, when it became too hard to extract what precious metal remained in the rocks. And some... well, some were silver mines and still full of the metal, but silver price had fallen too much to be worth working.

They usually had romantic names like The Lucky Strike Mine, or The Lost Hope Mine. This one could be any one of them. I approached cautiously. So Ale was here. That almost for sure meant Don Griffin, or what remained of him was here. Good.

At the door, there were two sentinels, I saw. One was fully visible to me as he was holding aloft a lantern, which must be the light I'd seen. Behind him was another man. I knew them both though not their names. They were part of Ale's entourage, his goons to do with as he pleased, and they dressed in a cheaper version of Ale's finery: dark suits and screaming ties, and almost for sure fake jewelry.

The guy who wasn't holding the lantern told the other, "Stop swinging it around fool. As well hang a sign saying we're here, and you won't see anything more than light reflecting on the rain."

"But Ale said—"

The other guy cursed. "I don't know who Ale expects will come in this rain and the dark. If they come it will be in the morning, and the little wimp magician will be done and gone well before then, and us too."

"There were those headlights!"

"Yeah, but they stopped somewhere up there. Probably some miner's shack there."

So, there was that. The little wimp magician must be Griffin. And it hit me they were probably right at that. He'd be done and gone well before Arty got here.

Which left me.

Well... it was raining just enough and they were far up from the cave enough that I might be able to squeeze behind and into the place. But not with my heels clacking on the rock.

I removed the heels, leaving them without remorse by the side of the path, and walked on, in my silk stockings, which were going to have far worse than a run in them.

Down the path, stopping every time I loosened some gravel, or made something fall, and around the two goons peering blindly into the falling rain.

And then I was in the shaft.

It was dark as the devil's toe, a winding darkness. I put out my hand, to feel the wall, and walked following it a good hundred feet, before I heard a bellow from up ahead, "No, by God, she's not a real person. She's a damned simulacrum and you'll give her to me, you little shite."

Another voice answered, one with whining overtones.

"I paid! I paid good money," Ale bellowed. Hard to miss my brother's dulcet tones. "And you'll give her to me. Or you'll stay in the anti-magic cage till you die."

I walked along the wall, towards the voice. As the wall turned – the tunnel turned, I guess – a sort of greyish light filtered in. It let me see a rough hewn tunnel, turning gently.

I followed it as silently as I could.

From the end of the hallway came Ale's voice, and then another voice, murmuring, pleading.

As light became brighter, I knit myself with the wall and slid along it. My dress would be a loss too, and my fur already was.

I couldn't track every word that came from down the hallway, but I could hear the gist and it was this: Ale had paid Griffin to build a simulacrum of some woman, which Griffin had then refused to hand over. Griffin kept insisting his creation had a soul. I wasn't sure what that meant, or how it would be possible. I also didn't know why Ale wanted a simulacrum of a woman. It had been bothering me since Griffin's place. Except perhaps he wanted to hide the fact he'd knocked one of his women around, by having an unmarked duplicate show herself?

I finally reached a point in the hallway from which I could see a round chamber cut into the rock. Down from that there would be more galleries. But this chamber had a lantern hanging from a hook on the timbers bracing the roof, a table and two chairs.

On one of the chairs sat Ale. He sat with the chair reversed, his chin resting on the back. There was an ashtray on the floor next to him. It was full.

On the table, on a cage that looked made of wicker, and looked exactly like something you'd keep a canary in, sat a man. I knew it was Griffin. I'd have known it was Griffin, even if I hadn't seen the summoning at his place. What surprised me was the sudden rush of need, the desperate need to free him, to let him work, to—

I had my gun out from my garter before I realized it. I was always a half decent shot. And I didn't know how one shattered a magic-dampening cage. I knew such implements existed because they were always a plot device in the pulps. But in the pulps usually the hero broke them with his bare hands, or unlocked them or something.

Well, breaking it with my bare hands was likely to chip my nail polish. And besides, I didn't even think. I had the pistol out, and I pointed it above Griffin's head in the cage. And I shot.

The sound was deafening in the mine, and Ale got up, his hand going to his gun, as he turned to where I stood.

"Honey!" he said. Then stopped. His mouth quirked in an unpleasant smile. "Damn, that's good," he said. And turned to look at Griffin.

I looked too.

For just a moment I thought that the cage hadn't broken, that my shot had gone wide. Then I realized that the very top piece had fallen. And the next minute there were a dozen of me all around saying, "What do you mean, Ale?"

Ale looked around, he looked back at Griffin, but the cage was empty and the magician was gone.

"You little shit," Ale said. "I'll shoot every one of you."

And then he started firing wildly.

I don't remember shooting him, but I remember his looking very surprised, then falling. I remember the running feet in the hallway, the shouts, of "Honey," in two voices I knew all too well.

And then there were Arty's strong arms around me, and I was leaning into him, and I felt cold, really cold.

"Stay with me, Honey," Arty said. "Stay with me."

But I faded into darkness.

#

I woke with all of them around me. My father, and Arty, and Griffin.

Pater was saying, "So it's not my daughter?"

And Griffin was saying, in his whining, apologetic way, "Well, it is and it isn't, Mr. D'Orio."

I flowed in and out of a dream hearing bits and pieces: simulacrum, ritual on my birthday. "Sometimes the soul gets captured is what it is. And there's no law about it, and that's the truth, Mr. D'Orio, but I didn't feel good giving her to him for who knew what purpose, while it was a living mind and soul in it."

I thought *Me. They're talking about me.*

I shivered, ice cold, and slipped away into a dream where I was just a magical doll of sorts, and no one cared. And woke up again, to, "She disappeared almost a year ago." It was Pater, and his voice was sad, slow. "I thought she'd gone to California, to... I thought she'd gone. But I investigated, and no one could find a trace of her, and I said something to Ale, and I guess he got scared."

"Yeah," Griffin said. "He just wanted her to be seen around. He wanted people to know Honey D'Orio was alive and well. That's all I know. But it... she had the memories and the thoughts. And Jesus, as you see, she bleeds red."

I opened my eyes and there was a lot of red, over my clothes, and over Arty's hands, and over the hands of a man I recognized, through foggy vision, as our doctor.

I fell into a dream again. I wasn't real. I wasn't even real. I was a thing. Which is why when Griffin was captured, my mind was the easiest to reach, to send an instruction to save him. He'd made me.

It took a week to be on my feet. They found her, meanwhile. They found me, I should say, in one of the deep dark tunnels at the back of the mine. She'd been shot, wearing an evening dress and dancing shoes. Ale shot her in the parking lot of the Magic Cat. And he hid her in the mine, whose name, fading on a board by the entrance, was "Honey Fall."

Pater didn't have the body transferred to the family crypt, though he had a priest come and bless that forgotten tunnel of that lost mine.

He was changed. Pater was. Arty had gotten to him, when he'd realized what was going on. He figured only my father could stop Ale. I'd managed that well enough, but I couldn't make Pater as he'd been. He'd lost interest in the business. He'd lost interest in everything except visiting me every day of my prolonged convalescence.

It was December before I was back on my feet. Apparently, a body and a soul is a body and a soul, even if a body started out as a simulacrum. It takes the same time to heal. It works the same way, as both Griffin and the doctor explained.

"That's why Mother Turner wanted you to eat," Griffin had said. "Simulacrums that are just simulacrums, just dolls made of magic can't. She sensed you weren't that. You moved like the original. And you had thoughts of your own, even under compulsion. She wanted to make sure."

That had been months ago, and I'd been spending time in my – in my original's – apartment, in bed and sitting by the window, while a professional nurse looked after me. Arty had returned to California. He said he was building a studio, and couldn't leave it for that long. I'd had two postcards, one showing sunny Los Angeles, another an orange grove. He'd only written "Wish you were here" on the back both times.

I'd seen pictures of him in the magazines, with this platinum blonde actress who was the big star of his new movie.

Then it was a week to Christmas. Snow covered Denver in sparkling jewels. The house and gardens had been lit.

"I want you to come with me to the station," Pater said, coming into my room, where I sat on a chair, re-reading the glossy magazine with a picture of Arty and the blond.

"Darling," I said. "It is very sweet of you, but I'm no longer five. I've seen the Christmas lights downtown many times before. It doesn't excite me."

"Minx," Pater said, but said it approvingly. "I want to take you to the station. There's a young man coming to town to ask you a very important question."

I dropped the magazine. Tears sprang to my eyes unbidden. "Arty? Daddy, I can't."

"Why can't you? Seems to me you should have married him when he first asked and told me to go to the devil. Well, there is no dynasty here. I'm letting everything go, winding up all my affairs. You two go out, and I'll come and join you when I can. It's time I lived in the sun."

"But Daddy, you forgot. I'm not the real Honey. I'm a body built who knows how, and a captured soul. What if it all stops working tomorrow, and I die?"

Pater patted my hand. "Then, my dear, you're exactly like the rest of the human race. You might as well make the most of it."

So I did.

Writing Scrubbing Clean

Scrubbing Clean is set in the world of my Darkship Thieves series, the one that started with Darkship Thieves, my Prometheus Award Winning novel.

In the original books, the Scrubbers barely appear except as enforcers of the tyrannical rule of the Good Men who rule Earth.

But of course they're humans, and they have a history.

Scrubbing Clean

My first memory is of a snowstorm. Of standing out on a snow storm, crying. In my mind's eye, I see myself clearly and with perfectly detached vision, as though I were someone else, far away. No. As though I were a child who died, somewhere far away.

In a way, you see, this was true.

Because I had no memory of that child. I saw her clearly: blond hair, well cut, and a lacy nightshirt, insufficient for the cold of the snow storm howling round her. She was maybe three years old, plump and pouty, looking like a child who'd never been punished, never felt discomfort. She was howling with outrage as much as with cold. It's like a hologram in my mind, but I don't remember being her.

I remember the creche: the regimented rising and walking. The whippings. I do remember the whippings. They could come for any reason at all. For being two seconds late on the synchronized rising-hygiene-dressing; for showing discontent at anything; for not performing adequately at a task. For me though, I remember years of whippings when I simply wouldn't obey. Just wouldn't. And they'd beat me till I did.

They beat me past the tears and the anger, the fear, the lack of confidence. They beat me, they thought, until they had a completely obedient meat robot.

But that wasn't what they really wanted. The girls they broke that way were disposed of early. For other purposes. But some of us needed brains.

It's always a bad thing when the Scrubbers come for you. I should know. I was one for most of my adult life.

What it means is that the Good Men, the fifty men who rule the world between them, have decided that you're a bad, bad person and should be destroyed. No. Should be made not to exist.

I was sleeping in a room of convenience in Deep Under.

It's kind of hard to explain Deep Under these many years later. It consisted of an area in Syracuse Seacity which was, perhaps intentionally, really hard for the law to reach.

It was under the biggest park on the island, the Hanging Gardens. I don't know which Good Man had thought it was a good idea, but it doesn't much matter. After all, they're all one and the same. On a vast expanse of the seacity – the operative word here being "city" – the Good Man had ordered columns embedded into the base of the island, and over it constructed a vast shelf or tray, which was planted with trees and flowers.

The fact that it had instantly plunged the buildings underneath in darkness meant nothing for Good Man Sinistra, ruler of Syracuse.

Though it might have worried him later. You see, the space blocked out was eight blocks square, with a main street. And as a space it was almost impossible to access, since one side was blocked by the spider: a long-dead automatic unloader, on the docks, whose humongous arms had been officially halted by decree centuries ago. The space between them was enough for a broom or a very small flyer to pass through, but passage was not safe except for the most apt of riders or drivers. At any moment, pieces detached and fell from the broken machinery, or an arm moved randomly with the wind, and someone got hurt or killed.

The other entry was on either side of the desalination plant, where there was about a one-person-width opening between it and the columns.

There were other entrances, mind you – sort of – in the alleys between the buildings at the end of each block. But those alleys were really narrow and often blocked by loading docks. Remember, this had started as a working part of town, composed of warehouses.

So that was Deep Under, and it was safe if you were hiding. Sort of safe. Ordinary police wouldn't go there. But the Scrubbers did. The Scrubbers went everywhere.

I woke up at the first sound from outside the room. It was a scraping that wouldn't have alerted anyone else. But I was fully aware of it, and awake, rolling off the bed, and sliding over to the wall as silently as possible. Not fully silent. That's impossible, despite Scrubber training, as incoming had just proven. But their noises should cover my noise well enough.

I slid to the wall, knit myself with the shadows, and stayed still.

The door slid open, and three bright burner rays cut the bed to pieces. Per protocol.

I didn't move or make a sound. I'd rejected the idea of opening the window and getting out before I was even fully awake, because if I had gone that way, they would have known I'd evaded. And they'd come after me. The only way to get rid of Scrubbers on your tail – for a moment, at least – is to kill them all. Depending on how good they were and how much trouble you are, there's at least half a chance that whichever Good Man put them on your tail will decide maybe you died before you shot the last Scrubber and at least pretend to let you vanish. The only other way was to reach rebel territory. Which is what I was trying very hard for.

Not that there was much hope. Not for a runaway Scrubber.

This bunch obviously didn't take into account the fact I had the same training they did. Four came into the room, since the bright rays cutting the bed showed them it was empty.

That's when I moved: I cut the four in the room, and before the ones outside could react, I dropped to the floor, looked around the corner of the door and cut them down too.

I dropped three credigems by the last corpse. The people who owned the hotel would have to replace the bed and get rid of the bodies, and I was sure it wouldn't come cheap. The credigems were, of course anonymous.

I couldn't hear anyone down the corridor that approached my room. I'm also not stupid. I would not use the grav well to go down. There would be Scrubbers waiting on the next level, and likely one by the main entrance as well.

So I listened at the door to the next room, used my training and some devices I'd kept from my former life, and opened the door cautiously. Still heard nothing. Gave my eyes a moment to adjust to total darkness. The bed was empty. Because I'm not stupid, I looked around the room, which, like mine, was bare except for the bed.

I closed the door, opened the window. Like most places in Deep Under, the room had a balcony. And I had my broom. My old Scrubber broom, with the brains beaten out so it wouldn't track me. And I knew how to fly it, of course. There hadn't been room for failure in training.

My broom was three feet long, one foot wide and cylindrical. It was designed to be small enough to be clipped to a belt when I was not riding it. The antigrav unit powering it was the best in the world. The steering were mere buttons embedded in the front of it. I'd been trained in them. But it had no oxygen or mask for high altitudes. I was supposed to carry those.

I considered briefly going back to get them from one of the dead Scrubbers. But going back risked capture. A false step, and I was afraid I'd pay for it. But there was nothing to do now but head towards Olympus and hope I'd make it. I might or not, but I would at least try.

And how had I got here? From faithful Scrubber to being chased by them.

Well, it had started in a seemingly innocent way.

They say the lower ranks of Scrubbers are drug addicted and conditioned, so that they do everything by rote, without thought. This might very well be true. I wouldn't know. I never even commanded a group on a mission, though I'd received briefings from such.

Oh, I was not one of the big brains in planning, either. Never aspired to it. As far as I understood they never left the compound. I liked leaving. I liked the world outside, the sun in the sky, the look of the cities with people fully busy. The strange shops and little establishments. The large houses. The seacities, each different, each surrounded by the sea. The continents where many barren areas remained from the turmoils.

They were not things I could readily imagine, and so I liked to see them and marvel at how strange different areas could be.

Look, I had no memory of living in the real world among real people. I'm not sure we even really believed in real people.

We read their bios before missions, and sometimes I lay in bed at night and tried to imagine what it would be like to be out there: to live a life believing that I was more or less free. I tried to imagine growing up without the training and the beatings. Without discipline, without mission, without purpose. Without pride.

I imagined what it would be like to live with parents, to be trained – to what extent they were which was not much – to perform some work, to get married, to have children. To sleep at night never knowing that Scrubbers moved in the dark and eliminated those who threatened the Good Men and their three hundred years of stable rule. The three hundred years that separated us from the turmoils and insanity.

The only thing those late night imaginings ever brought me was a sense of emptiness and lack of purpose. We called those people "ants" and the world outside "the ant farm." And to us they appeared exactly like that:

countless interchangeable units, moving busily and aimlessly and sometimes becoming very agitated, but wholly separate from us, real people.

And then as I fell asleep, I had the image of the little girl in insufficient clothing, crying and pouting in a snow storm. I had the sense of a large house behind her, and the feeling that it was on fire, but she never turned to look, and there was just that feeling of orange reflections in the snow, the remembered smell of smoke.

But I never wondered about it, because whoever that little girl had been, whatever her life had been, I felt as though I had been rescued from that formless existence to be a real person; to be who I was.

And who I was...

I'd been identified early on as assassin material. I didn't work well in groups, and I was smart enough that I could be counted on to kill someone and make it look like natural death. Kill someone and have it pass unnoticed by everyone that an assassination had taken place.

Poison, sometimes. But not always. Sometimes it was easiest to make it appear like an accident, or a sudden death. And I could manage it. Every time. Because I had been trained rigorously for years and years.

It started with a dossier, a brief explanation of why this person needed to die – in my moral universe at the time "because Good Man so and so said he did" was enough – and my reconnoitering the location and making my plans.

That was the important part. Carrying them out was almost anticlimactic.

And on that day I was told that I needed to stop Doctor Braith Cooper from defecting to the rebel seacities.

This was a new wrinkle in the briefings before a mission. There was a rebellion, though I wasn't exactly sure what it involved. The Usaian religion had been mentioned in one of the briefings, but in a discussion between the two men briefing me, and I wasn't precisely sure what it had to do with the uprising.

I knew only vaguely that there had been wars between Good Men and their vassals before, but none rising to this, with several seacities and territories declaring for the rebels and the world commerce and law disrupted to such an extent that new turmoils were feared.

One thing I didn't understand, but was explained. If they knew Doctor Cooper was in danger of defecting to the rebels, why not simply arrest him, or perhaps arrange to blackmail him.

Why would it require my services?

As a professional, I was allowed to question, but not to refuse, mind you. But as a professional, and having done my share of assassinations, I was allowed to offer alternatives, not just in methods, but to the idea itself.

Once or twice, in the past, after examining all the circumstances, I'd suggested blackmail instead of death. Or as it was known in our field "a diplomatic solution."

I was told that the problem was the doctor was the head of a group of indeterminate number, all serving in the houses of Good Men and all holding secrets as to biology and treatment which should not be divulged to the masses. And it was impossible to trace the full extent of the network, but Doctor Cooper was the spearhead, and also the only one with contacts in the rebel cities. If he were to die suddenly, and seemingly of natural causes, it would probably all be allowed to fall to pieces, for a while at least. And give the Good Men the chance to crush the rebellion.

At that point I assumed they had intelligence they weren't sharing. And I started making my plans.

Everything available on Doctor Cooper in public archives showed him to be about my age, an expert on reproduction – which surprised me as it didn't seem to be the sort of thing that the Good Men were interested in – and married. He had three children. The holos of him looked somehow familiar, but I couldn't tell why. I would need to meet him, anyway, by accident, and that might allow me to get some idea of why I felt as though I knew him.

At any rate, I had no friends outside the Scrubbers. No, correct that, I had no friends within the Scrubbers either. At some point early on I'd decided friends were a waste of time and a risk. That was after the second time I got denounced for having book gems and a gem reader hidden in my bunk. After that, I'd given the others a wide berth and they'd given me a wide berth. At any rate, it was far preferred that assassins have no friends.

But what I meant is that I had no friends in the outside world, so it was unlikely that I'd balk at doing what must be done to keep Doctor Cooper quiet. If it was deemed necessary and would restore and prolong peace, it was worth it.

Eventually, after collecting all the information on him, I flew out to view his place of residence.

Like most of the upper servants of the Good Men, he lived in a mansion. Though he was attached to Good Man Stian Holgersen, of the Seacity of Hoy, he'd been granted permission to live in the northern European territories that had been reclaimed from war damage.

The areas were pleasant, islands off the northern area of Europe. I wasn't sure – ancient geography was not my forte, and no one had ever required me to know it – if it was in the area once known as Great Britain, or the other islands.

They were now cultivated almost like gardens, since the climate was too cold for serious agriculture, and most of that could be got from elsewhere in the world, and only the top servants of Good Men were allowed to live there.

Which also meant I would stick out like a sore thumb. Give me my kills in well populated areas in cities teeming with strangers; or in the wilds of the American continent, being reclaimed for agriculture, where I could always claim to have been scouting a place for a farm and talk to realtors and maybe go talk to my mark in order to determine his weaknesses.

But there was no help for it. I dressed in a colorful broomer suit, padded and insulated against the speed and the heights of flight. And I put oxygen tanks and mask on. All of which would help me not be recognized. Which was important in case they saw me in the vicinity of the house later.

And you're probably wondering why I'd put on a colorful suit before going flying about in normal areas, areas where brooms were forbidden means of transport.

Well, various reasons. One of them was that despite the prohibition there were any number of broomer lairs in various parts of the seacities and continental areas. Almost all the broomer lairs wore a variation of black for their brooming leathers. Well, except the Lavender Buzzers, and the least said about them the better. I'd once been contracted to kill their leader in the most embarrassing way possible that could still pass for natural death. It wasn't a memory I relished. I don't kill innocents for no reason; I don't play with my kills; and I don't embarrass my targets. For good and sufficient reason, I'd violated two of those in that kill. Maybe all three. I'd never been sure the man was half as dangerous as my superiors maintained.

So wearing colorful leathers kept me from being identified as a broomer. The broomer lairs should be forbidden, anyway. And shouldn't be tolerated. I had heard that years ago – fifteen or so – a group of Scrubbers had been sent out to a broomer lair and killed everyone there and made the bodies disappear. It was a rumor among Scrubbers, and I'd overheard it as part of a conversation. I didn't know if it was true, but I hoped so, because most broomers are dangers to themselves and others, but mostly to themselves. You can't ride a broom anywhere near populated areas without being attacked by some idiot broomer who decided that you look like their rival broomer lair invading their territory.

The other part of it is that I could be as colorful as I pleased and fly in the face of local law enforcement because the built-in transponder on the broom transmitted sequences that told local law enforcement it wasn't worth their lives to investigate.

And I used brooms by choice, because their being, nominally at least, illegal meant that there would be no record of my arrival anywhere, and nothing that could be traced.

Normally Scrubbers didn't bother hiding too much, but my branch did. It was best that no one even knew that I existed.

It was a lovely day out. Late spring, and I flew beneath the cloud layer. The sea sparkled silver-green. There were a few pleasure boats out. Few enough flyers that none of them flashed lights or acted like they thought I might be someone brooming away from an accident.

The sea smelled of salt and everything was beautiful in the garden. Approaching the island territories of Hoy, I crossed paths with another broomer, and tensed, particularly because he – I think he was a he – was wearing black leathers. But we were flying close enough he could flash sign language at me, and he asked if I needed help, obviously having taken me for someone that had escaped a flyer in distress on a broom. I flashed back that all was well, and he didn't – to my knowledge – follow me or care who I was
.

At any rate, there was nothing identifiable about me, with the hood pulled up hiding my hair, and the oxygen mask hiding my features. The most obvious thing he'd remember was my leathers, in bright rainbow colors, and the leathers would be disposed of by end of day.

Dr. Cooper's mansion was on the edge of the island, facing the ocean. It sat atop a cliff, but the area on which it was located had expansive lawns, a rose garden – on the edge of the property, facing the cliff and the sea – and a semi-circle of pine woods behind that gave it the impression of being carefully nested in an embrace.

Something about it tickled the back of my mind, but I couldn't say what.

I flew around it, noting there were two dogs on the property. I don't like working at houses with dogs. They can get hurt.

Look, I'm not sentimental, but my trainer early on said that we all need to have our internal stopping points, and as I said one of mine is not killing innocents. Dogs are by definition innocent, and I don't like killing them. I'll do it to save my life, but as with the thing with the Lavender Buzzers target, if I have to it will break me a little.

So I decided the kill wouldn't happen or be set up at the mansion. For some reason this gave me a great feeling of relief.

I flew around a couple more times and headed back to regional headquarters.

That night, without warning, I dreamed of being the little girl crying in the snow.

The dream was intense and more detailed than it had ever been before.

For the first time, too, I was aware of being the little girl. It wasn't just like looking at a holo. I could feel the snow beneath my feet, and flakes clinging to my shoulder length air. I could feel my throat raw from wailing. I could smell the smoke in the air, and the sting of it on my eyes, and I felt afraid, very afraid.

I didn't know where Daddy was. Or Mommy. Or Braith. They'd disappeared. And there were sounds of flyers and sirens, and I was afraid.

I knew without turning around that the mansion was the one I'd flown over on the broom that day.

I woke up in a foul mood.

There have been questions raised in the past about my mental stability. Even for a Scrubber who worked in assassination, I was unusually solitary and it worried my superiors.

They might or might not have understood my need to have no friends. Whenever someone forced tests on me, sooner or later it came down to my unusually high levels of paranoia.

But I was still efficient. I could still do my job. So, no one had tried to pull me from the work. At any rate I didn't know what that would mean. I had a vague idea it might very well mean being pulled off the world of the living, permanently.

Still, that was not the important point. I suspected it would come anyway. Yes, I know that when we asked we'd been told that some sort of retirement waited us, but I'd never believed it. Not after the things I'd seen and done.

But I'd never before started coming unglued at the seams. And this was coming unglued at the seams.

I was sure that for whatever reason my mind had decided to juxtapose that mansion with my memory of toddlerhood. And I wasn't sure why, except that I'd always had the impression there was a mansion behind the crying little girl and now my mind kept insisting the sea had also been nearby. Only I wasn't sure I believed my mind in any of it.

I woke up in my normal room: a closed-in cell with one bunk, a desk with a computer for research, and a door to a tiny fresher. I didn't keep anything else in my room because it wasn't needed. Whatever I needed: clothes, shoes, cosmetics, weapons, poisons, I'd ask for, and it would be delivered in minutes.

One thing I could do, but rarely bothered to, was call up a false window on the wall above my bed which I could request to show me any place in the world.

I rarely bothered to request it for pleasure, but now, glaring at the grey ceramite wall, I sighed, and said aloud "Window." And then the coordinates of the Cooper mansion.

It appeared on the wall as though a window looked down on it, and as it must look at that time of day.

It was night, near dawn – I should check the time, as I'd thought it was morning, and we were at the same general longitude – with the sky a deep dark blue shot through with pink glowing bands near the horizon.

The pine trees swayed in a gentle wind. I could hear—distantly – the sound of waves and the barking of dogs. There was a light on in the bottom floor.

Unbidden, my mind told me that was the study, and conjured up an image of a room lined with books, with a big desk in the center, and of walking in, seeing everything at about my eye level.

I said "Window off."

I was going insane.

Briefly, I toyed with the idea of going to my superiors, requesting a meeting, and telling them I couldn't do this. Not this job. Not this particular job.

But if I did, it would mean counselors at a minimum, poking and prodding and looking in my head. I wasn't sure what they'd find in there. And worse come to worse, they might very well decide that I was ready for the recycle bin, whatever they called it.

No. I'd go on with my plan.

And the plan was to fly to Hoy and intercept the good doctor, accidentally on purpose in the vicinity of his job.

If it didn't work, I could always arrange to get temporary credentials that would allow me to go into the laboratory where he worked and meet him there.

But—

Accidental meeting on the street was better. Or ambushing him at the place where he ate lunch.

No, not ambushing him in that sense. I hadn't even decided how to eliminate him, much less been ready to do it. I'd have to gain familiarity with him and come to know him to the point I could arrange his death with no surprise to anyone.

I flew in by broom, landed in a deserted area of Hoy, concealed my broom and broomer's leathers in the back pack.

Under it, I wore a colorful loose skirt and a frilly white blouse, the sort of thing a day-tripper might wear.

Not that Hoy had a lot of tourism. Not like Shangrila or Liberte or others of the very old seacities where people obsessed with the Fish War, or other ancient history, might come to gawp at decaying structures.

But that was not the point. All the seacities get traffic of strangers, either come to visit and see what it's like, or come to sell something, look for work, or another normal pursuit.

Enough traffic that I'd pass unnoticed, unlike in the territorial enclaves.

Hoy is actually a pretty seacity, built in circles around a central sculpted mountain, itself rising with spiral terraces to the top and the mansion of the Good Man. All the buildings are in deep clear colors, mostly blue and green, but with the occasional yellow.

The terraces are big enough for houses with gardens, and I momentarily wondered why Cooper didn't live in one of those, with the other favored retainers of the Good Man. But I didn't care, or not really. It was just that part of me would rather not go back to that mansion. But then again, hopefully I'd have no reason to.

I'd get to know Cooper here, after "meeting accidentally." And hopefully I could eliminate him here.

I'd identified the fourth circle layer as being the one in which the lab and hospital the good doctor worked at was located. So I headed there. I found the entrance to the building in which he worked. And I loitered more than I should have.

There were some shops around there, and I flitted in and out of them looking at things, always careful to make sure the things I was looking at faced the street, so I could keep an eye out for Cooper.

I think I stayed too long and was too obviously not buying, from the looks the shop keepers gave me, but at least none of them demanded to see the inside of my backpack. Not that I had anything there but a broom, but all the same....

Finally, I gave up and started walking down a narrow road between two sets of colorful buildings to the diner Doctor Cooper preferred.

It was an expensive little establishment, called Hungry Mouths, and it had real live servers. That part was a problem, maybe, as I didn't want my description to come out in any possible reports or research afterwards. But that was unlikely. And anyway, I hadn't any official existence. One of the reasons they said never to bother to wear gloves was that our DNA wasn't on record anywhere. Or not as that of anyone living, as far as I understood.

Anyway, I started down the little alley, with the idea that Hungry Mouths would be to the left and backed up to a rose garden, when it all went wrong.

I heard a sort of strange gasp behind me, and then the steps accelerated, and someone overtook me, and turned around to stare at me.

"Coral!" he said. And then again. "Coral."

I had no idea at all who Coral was, but one thing I knew for sure. The man facing me was Doctor Cooper. This is not how I'd planned to meet him.

For once, my normal reactions were fine as I stopped dead in the street and said, "I have no idea who Coral is!"

"You're Coral. You have to be. We thought you were dead. I thought you were dead."

My mouth was unaccountably dry. My palms compensated for this by sweating like fountains. "I have no idea what you're talking about," I said.

He was silent a minute, then said, "Please come with me."

I should have refused. We had procedures for when a job was blown. And the one thing I was absolutely sure of was that this job was blown. I should have run from there, gotten all the way back to headquarters, told them the job was blown and I didn't understand how.

But I didn't.

Instead, I followed Cooper, as though it were some sort of compulsion, to the Hungry Mouths, where he called a blond waitress over and said something. My heart was beating so fast I could not hear him properly over the drumming in my ears. But I think he said something about a private area.

We were taken to the back to a small room. It was a pleasant little room, the sort you probably could rent to have a tryst in, only I didn't get that feeling out of Cooper at all.

We sat down at a table and ordered. I don't know what I ordered, because I don't remember reading the menu and have only the vaguest of memories of talking to the wait person.

I know that when it came it was a sandwich, but since I never took a bite I don't remember what it was.

"You're Coral. I'm sure of it," Cooper said.

I cleared my throat, mostly because it was too dry and tight to talk through. "Who is Coral? Why do you think I'm her?"

"I don't think," he said. "I know. And Coral was my little sister."

I couldn't speak. I had the memory again, firmly, in my head, of the little girl standing in front of a burning mansion, crying crying, until a pair of hands grabbed her, covered her mouth. And then the crying was done and I didn't remember anything else. Until the creche.

"My name," I said, carefully, "is Cori." As I said it, I realized how close the name was to Coral. And it might very well be as close as a three year old could come to it.

He shook his head. He was fumbling with something in his wallet. I wondered if it was some sort of weapon, and almost shot him right there, but before I could, I realized he was extracting little glass squares. Holo keepers.

Cooper pressed the first one just so, and a little image projected above the square.

It took my breath away. It was me. Me, the little girl in front of the mansion in the snow. Only there was no snow, but there was an older boy, who was, unmistakably, Cooper.

"I'm six years older," he said. "My sister Coral.... There was a fire. Father said it was something to do with work. I don't know what it was. But there was a fire. And people came. And Coral disappeared. We always thought she'd burned to death in her room at home. The home where I live in, that is. It was rebuilt, and I inherited it from my parents."

"I still don't know—"

He shook his head. "No. Listen, look."

Cooper pressed the other little square of glass and the image above was of a couple. And the woman looked almost exactly like the face I saw in the mirror every morning while brushing my teeth.

"That's my mother," he said. "And you're my sister, Coral Cooper. What happened to you? Where have you been? How come—"

He stopped because I was crying.

Look, I don't remember crying. The only thing the word crying conjures up is the image of that little girl, long ago.

It is possible that I did cry, the first days or weeks or months in the creche, but I don't remember it. Not at all. I remember punishments, but I remember taking them as one should, with clenched jaw and unfocused eyes. Crying never does anything but make them feel you're soft and they can do worse.

But now I cried, and I couldn't stop.

I mumbled through my tears that I needed to go to—

He gestured vaguely towards the area where I imagined the freshers were. He looked bewildered and, fortunately, he didn't follow me.

I didn't go to the fresher. Instead, I left the Hungry Mouths and hit the round running.

At first I thought I'd go to headquarters, but as my feet slowed – having climbed three or four staircases – somewhere around the eighth level of Hoy and near a bunch of public buildings, it occurred to me that several things had changed:

First, I was absolutely sure Cooper was right. I was his long lost sister. The only alternative would be to imagine that somehow he was a counter operative and very well briefed. And even that would not explain his having that holo. I'd never told anyone about my dreams. Not even the counselors. I'd always had a sense that these were, if not dangerous, intensely private.

Second, that I couldn't go to the headquarters and research the Coopers of past generations and find out what had happened. That fire had the hallmarks of a punitive expedition. Had Cooper's father also been intending to defect, or perhaps been involved with a subversive movement, but too precious and important to discard? It sounded like Scrubber work.

I probably could tell if had been Scrubber work from public documents. Which was good because:

Second, I could not go to headquarters to research this. Not if it had been our work to begin with. I couldn't imagine why in the seven hells of the ancients someone had assigned me to this case of all cases. I didn't think they were laying a trap, though of course that was always possible. But traps weren't laid involving outside people. And Cooper wasn't one of us. His surprise in recognizing me was absolute.

I've been trained in finding information, and places where I can find information. It's my job. Well, it's my job before I kill people, at least.

And I had credigems. Lots. I always did when on a mission.

But I also had a broom which would track all my movements.

So, I backtracked down to the level the lab was in, and found a public locker. I rented it for three hours, and locked my broom in it. Someone might notice I wasn't moving, but it was unlikely. They'd think I was standing somewhere in cover, watching the lab. If they thought of it at all. I had some latitude when working on this phase of a kill.

Then I went two levels lower, to buy a used reader. The sort that could search public records. And then I tracked way up near the palace of the Good Man, into a copse of woods where I sat and searched.

The history wasn't complex. It was heartbreaking, and might have been even if I didn't know what happened to Coral.

Dr. Mark Cooper, my father – how strange those words sounded – had been a doctor working in reproductive medicine, just like his son. Why that was a function for trusted servants of the Good Men, I did not know.

There was not in the public record any indication that he might have wished to defect, or perhaps betray the Good Man. There wouldn't be.

But the fire of unknown origin that consumed his mansion was a typical Scrubber intimidation maneuver.

Doctor Braith Cooper, my brother, had two children. A boy and a girl. I could suddenly remember playing around the mansion, with my older brother, and I could imagine—

I went back. I went back to the lab. There was a young woman at the entrance. She smiled vaguely at me, and looked not at all surprised when I told her that Dr. Cooper's sister was here to see him.

Yes, the mission was blown to orbit. But that didn't matter. Not now.

Braith came from inside almost immediately, looking startled, eyes wide. "I'm glad you came," He said. "I thought—"

"There's an emergency," I said. "Come with me. I need to show you something."

He went with me. I thought that he'd have been very easy to kill. But I don't kill innocents, and I was starting to think the only non-innocent in all this was me.

I led him to the rose garden. It was deserted at that time, and it was unlikely that someone was listening there. I set an erratic walk among the paths, and I spoke softly.

I told him who I was and everything I remembered. When I told him that the Scrubbers wanted to eliminate him and everyone in his network before they defected to Olympus, he made a sound, but other than that he said nothing, until I was done.

Then he said, "You're going to kill me?"

"Don't be stupid. Why do they want you dead?"

He laughed. "I have some.... Genetic secrets of the Good Men. Things that aid in their reproduction."

"What? Don't they reproduce like other people?"

He laughed again, but there was no mirth. "They're not normal people, Coral. That's part of it. Do you remember the history of the Mules?"

"They didn't teach us much history, but something... Weren't the Mules bio engineered, just before the Turmoils started? Something.... They were created to be very intelligent and made rulers, and that's what destroyed Europe? Oh, and they were all male and couldn't have babies with human women, which is how they got their nickname."

"Yes," he said. "That. More or less. But-- I know they say they went to the stars, but it's not true, you know? They, or some of them, stayed behind and changed identity. And became the Good Men."

"Impossible," I said. "Three hundred years of peace and prosperity!"

He laughed. "Yeah. I used to believe that too. But lately real news has started to leak through, because of the rebels. I think now that they just control information better. I'm not absolutely sure they haven't made blunders almost on the order of destroying Europe."

I felt my hair rise. "So, you thought..."

"I'd leave. I've always had a bad feeling about the fire in which you—In which we thought you'd died. I thought Father had been doing something they didn't like."

"Almost for sure. It's the right modus operandi."

"I see. Well, I was afraid they'd do that again. This—"

"Yeah," I said. "Perhaps because of the rebels, they view you as a bigger danger. Listen, Braith, go home, collect your wife and children. Remove the tracking device on your family flyer. No, I'm serious. I'll make you a drawing of what it is and how to remove it. Then fly for Olympus. Don't try for a clever plan. At this point your best chance is just to fly in."

"But I have people waiting who—"

"Can you contact them from there? You can't contact them if you're dead. And as you said, rebel coms get through."

He was sweating. His eyes were wild, but he said, "Come with us."

I shook my head. "Not yet. I have some.... Scrubbing to do."

I went back to headquarters. Very fast. Had to do it before they figured that Braith was gone.

I was let in with no problems. My room was the same.

The first thing I did was crawl under the desk, remove a panel on the wall, and remove the tracker on my system. It wouldn't alarm immediately, and I wasn't going to stay here very long.

I looked up the Cooper fire. All was as surmised. Then I looked up my own file, and realized why they'd slipped up and assigned me this case. I was registered as Cori Coon. A mistake, I'd guess. Though I'd long known that children of those assassinated were often recruited. It was easy. They were never looked for.

But in my case-- I wouldn't speculate. It didn't matter.

Instead, I took the people responsible for planning the Cooper fire.

I know it's stupid, okay? They were just doing what they thought they had to do. But I'd killed enough innocents that killing non innocents might atone a little.

Not that I killed them. Let's say there are substances you can use that will drop the person of a heart attack in a day or two. I had some put by – never trust on having to ask for stuff like that. Of course I had a stash. In the backpack with me – and there were three beds contaminated at headquarters.

And then I left. In a nearby abandoned platform, the sort erected in the twenty-first century to cultivate algae, I beat the brains out of my broom. I mean, I didn't damage any of its flying, but with a rock, carefully, eliminated the tracker.

Afterwards I set off for Deep Under, where I bought a disposable com. Braith had given me a code to call. I called it and sent "?" and received "Olly Olly Oxen Free," which we'd agreed would mean he'd gotten to Olympus, and was safe.

And waiting for me.

But the night was dark, and I needed to sleep some hours. Olympus on a broom is not impossible, but it would take seven or eight hours. I'd probably be better off stealing a flyer, and not right then. Besides, I thought I was safe.

Having left the hotel behind, I flew through Deep Under, and out through the dock loading robot that the locals called the Octopus.

Luck favored me. Nothing fell on me though some pieces of rotted machinery fell close by as I flew out.

I could have stopped to steal a flyer. I could. But the sky was starting to paint pink, and the flight to Olympus on the broom sounded lovely.

No, I don't know if it's possible for something like me to change. I don't know if I'll ever be normal. One of those 'ants' with normal lives.

But Braith said that risking my life to save theirs was a good start. And maybe it was. He probably would disapprove of my killing in revenge for the fire. Or maybe not.

I had no idea how a normal person thought or felt.

My whole life I had been the instrument of a corrupt state.

I didn't know if that would ever scrub clean.

But I meant to try.

WRITING LAST CHANCE

BACK BEFORE MY SONS moved out – which is closer in time than it seems, since they both lived at home through college, to save money – we had four writers in a house. This meant you would find the most interesting research books in the bathroom, or on the coffee table, or on the kitchen counter (unexpectedly and with no explanation.) Non-fiction books, I mean. The fiction ones were usually on Kindle, at least in the last ten years.

I'm fairly sure I didn't buy the book on paranormal research by the US army. I'm also sure when getting up ridiculously early after a sleepless night – I'm given to inexplicable bouts of insomnia -- the book was sitting at the table, looking all innocent. (You know to this day I haven't asked the boys which of them had left it there, or "Psychic Discoveries Behind the Iron Curtain" (which was also there,) or in heavens name WHY? Though from the tone of it, I'd guess it was younger son and he was pursuing some strange idea.) Anyway, I ended up reading that book over successive cups of coffee, while the snow fell relentlessly outside our Castle Rock, Colorado home, until the sun came out and people started moving around.

Coincidentally this was the day I was invited to an alternate history science fiction anthology about Weird WWIII.

Well at the time, in addition to my fiction work and my blog I was writing three or four articles a week for PJM (it helped put the boys through college.) So I really didn't have time to research some complex military snafu that could have resulted in WWIII.

And I had read that book. The result follows.

Last Chance

It was starting to snow as I drove past Silverthorne.

And I had no idea why I was even in this road, or why I had to drive to Meeker, Colorado to go hiking.

Twenty-two years of a blameless life as a city-boy, thriving in Denver, between bookshop and café, between job and apartment, why the hell did I start having insistent, persistent, vivid dreams about going out to hike? And why did the hike have to start in Meeker?

There were hundreds, perhaps thousands of trailheads closer to me, north and south. And for that matter, as much as it will shock the tourists, no, there was absolutely no law that made native Coloradans have to hike. Or ski, for that matter.

As I said, I was happily urban, not given to fantasies about the great outdoors. Hell, growing up in the Colorado Springs suburbs had been bad enough. Back then they still gave us pamphlets on what to do if we met a bear coming back from elementary school and – believe it or not – it wasn't "put your head between your legs and kiss your ass goodbye" which even at ten seemed to me to be the only realistic response.

Sure, urban environments have threats too, I'm just more confident in my ability to kick the ass or a pushy homeless druggie than a bear.

So, again, why the hell was I headed for Meeker – named after a famous dead-in-a-massacre government agent –as the snow started to fly?

I turned up the heat in the car, glad that I had an SUV. Sure, it was a Honda pilot more than twenty years old, and the only reason I owned it is because you have to be crazy to drive a compact in Colorado. You end up stuck between SUVs and can't see ahead of the two or three tall cars blocking you.

I'd bought good boots, and a decent jacket, so there was that. But I remembered all the TV features and newspaper reports about newbs and tourists found frozen in their cars in the back of nowhere, and I really wondered what the hell was wrong with my head. Except that at some point it's easier to give in, to do what your subconscious is obsessing about, than to fight it. *Which I suppose must explain all the people who finally give in, cut up their neighbors and stuff the bits in plastic bags,* I thought, as I passed a convoy of trucks doing well under the speed limit. And it wasn't precisely fair. It wasn't as though I was cutting up anyone or stuffing them into anything. I was just going to Meeker – of all stupid places – and taking a little hike, and then probably holing up for the night some flea motel while a blizzard howled outside, before returning to Denver and never again doing anything that stupid, ever ever again.

As with skiing – bunny slope, and major spill at the age of five – I'd be able to tell anyone who asked if I hiked "Tried it, didn't care for it."

I was busy being pissed at myself, so I don't know how far past Silverthorne I was when the car stopped. Look, it's not like the landscape is particularly inspirational, okay? I know for a while the road wound up around amid mountain slopes, with houses a distant thing. And then I was driving through a series of small towns. Between them there were... ranches and entrances to ranches.

As I said, I was too busy being mad at myself, and not paying a lot of attention, and it wasn't until the car suddenly and completely lost power, that I became aware of where I was. And where I was happened to be in deep dog shit. I mean, there were ... ranches nearby, or at least there was a metal arch saying "Last Chance Spread" in cut out metal letters, next to some cut out shapes that were boots or cacti or something. And there was just enough space for me to coast my car to that on residual motion. It was almost timed, I swear, because it came to a complete stop just short of the opening, which led to a path.

And I started cursing softly to myself. Because that's where this crazy and sudden need to be out in nature led. I was just lucky if it didn't end up in rattlers, like all those school trips when I was a kid, that seemed to take us to some park or other full of signs saying that we should be careful not to disturb rattlesnakes. Those usually ended up with me holing up in the school bus with a book, refusing to go out, and resulted in another phone call from the school to my bewildered parents.

I looked dubiously down the path, past the arch, and decided that it was the best part of valor to call triple A or something. Because if I had a ranch like that, in the middle of nowhere, I'd shoot up anything that came up the path uninvited, be it man, bear or rattler.

So I pulled out my cell phone.

And it was dead. As dead as the car. The screen just reflected back at me, and granted it would have made a handy hand mirror, which unfortunately was not what I needed right then.

I was glaring at the path – which led on past a hillock and some trees, with no house in sight – and thinking that at least bears and rattlesnakes would not be out in the snow, when a man came walking out of the trees.

He didn't seem to be carrying a weapon. And what the hell, he was likely to have a phone, right?

So I got up, pulled on my insulated jacket, and started down the path towards him, doing my best to look like "See, I'm just a stranded guy, and definitely not a rattlesnake pretending to be human" impression.

As I got closer, I saw he was probably my dad's age, or a little older, with a long white beard, and the sort of look of a guy who doesn't bother overmuch with haircuts, because he doesn't see anybody much.

"Car trouble?" he shouted, as he got within shouting distance.

"Yeah," I said. "And my phone isn't working."

"Mine just went out too. Happens, 'round here."

Which of course just filled me with no end of thrills.

He was close enough now to see what he looked like. I mean, really looked like. Well, sort of like a tanned, leaner Santa-Claus with very blue eyes, and a look of puzzled helpfulness. He extended his hand, "Joe Brand." I shook it and said "Mike Grer. Anything we can do?"

He shook his head. "Nah. This stuff just happens round here sometimes. My dad used to say that it was some kind of government experimentation. That or UFOs. Except we never saw any UFOs." Pause. "Of course I never saw much in the way of government experimentation, either. Could be something having to do with the ore around here. Anyway, it usually stops cars and phones for a few hours, and then it all starts up again. You can stay in your car and wait, or you can come down to the ranch. There's a group of travelers, there, waiting it out."

Look, I'm not horror-movie deficient, okay? I know as well as anyone else that this type of situation ends up in chainsaws and one last girl running down the road towards the highway, just before the madman with the chainsaw cuts her down. And I'm not a girl. On the other hand, I grew up in Colorado, and it was snowing, and I – like an idiot – hadn't thrown a couple of thermal blankets in the back of the car driving out.

Besides... well. Besides this old guy didn't feel threatening, and he was probably easier to overpower than a bear particularly than a bear would be if I were still an elementary school child.

"You're more than welcome to stay," he said. "Shouldn't be more than a few hours."

"I don't see any other cars," I said, as a last protest, in case, you know, this would be enough to make him confess to having chainsaws hidden somewhere.

He shrugged. "The path is slightly downward. If you end up staying any time, it's easier to come and push the car to this area just past the trees where the others are. Just in case some truck isn't affected and crashes into you."

Made sense, though, "You mean some cars aren't affected?"

"Nah. Never understood why. Though the phones will be affected."

Okay, so worst case scenario, I could hitchhike a passing truck. So... why didn't I? Why walk down the path with a total stranger?

I don't know. Like the idea of going to Meeker, it was the sort of compulsion that made no sense at all to my rational mind. Which I supposed is why, even to myself, I was sounding like a total lunatic.

I'm not normally given to irrational compulsions or following them. And, just to get it out of the way, no, it's also not mandatory to toke in Colorado, and as a rule, I didn't do it. Mostly, honestly, because even smelling the stuff made me clog up and have trouble breathing, which had been some issue since legalization.

Anyway, I didn't seem able to help myself, so I followed the guy down the path. I felt a little better when I saw a bunch of cars in the clearing past the trees, and none of them with obvious blood stains or chainsaw dents.

The ranch house was sprawling and made of logs but with enough windows and stuff that it had obviously been built in the last twenty years. Inside the front door was a living room filled with people – none of them obviously chainsaw-wounded – who stopped talking when we came in.

"Mike here got stranded, just at the entrance to the ranch," Joe Brand said. And the people in the room laughed and sympathized.

There were four men: Paul Jones, from somewhere in Denver, Jordan Gutierrez from Boulder, Josh Beranger also from Boulder and Ken Scotti, from Colorado Springs. Three women: Marianne Smith, from Boulder, Kathy Pines from Colorado Springs, and Jill March from Denver.

They all looked... well... normal. Except that Josh had a man-bun and I had the impression his jeans and t-shirt were designer. And Marianne was dressed in new-revival-Earth-Mother style, with flowing colorful skirt, and a sort of peasant blouse in something shiny. Which was completely explained as it emerged in the desultory conversation in the first few minutes that she owned a New Age Store in Boulder. Which, it seemed to me, must be some kind of achievement in fluffy-headed crystal-and-curse thinking. Or at least it was mere minutes before she was talking of the ley lines around here, and how they had made our cars stop.

I noticed – because I notice these things – that our host wasn't taking part in the conversations, as we tried to figure out what had happened. I also noticed that most of the people – Marianne excepted, since she apparently had friends in Steamboat Springs – were not used to driving out this day, and had done it on a whim. And judging by the haunted look in their eyes, I judged that "whim" meant compulsion.

Which made it all the more interesting to me. Weirdly not even Marianne admitted to that.

The rest of the situation was pretty normal. Joe provided us with coffee. After about an hour, when phones still didn't work, and with the snow piling up outside, I went with the guys and pushed my car into the parking area.

When the phones still didn't work at dinner time, Joe brought out ham, and vegetarian soup – for Marianne, who was a vegan – and then we sat around the dinner table, talking.

I don't remember – which is weird, because I notice these things – who first brought up ESP or the psychic forces used during the Cold War.

"It's a joke now, or we think it's a joke," Joe said. He was leaning back and smoking. He'd asked our permission, and honestly Marianne was the only one who'd gotten upset at it, but even she wasn't brazen enough to tell our host he couldn't smoke in his own house. Josh had pulled out e cigs, immediately after. "But the seventies was a really strange time. Sometimes I wonder – doesn't everyone? – how we got here from there. Psychic powers were just assumed to exist and work. If you go back to the science fiction of the time, they're part of it. It was assumed they would be part of the future."

"Because they are," Marianne said, with a bright smile around the table. "If the government didn't suppress the knowledge, we could have free energy from the ley lines. When the Earth changes come, some people are going to be very surprised."

"Well, yeah, that," Joe said, once the silence had gone on for a while. "The thing is that what the Soviets were experimenting with was more like mind-control at a distance. We've got to the point of laughing at the idea that the government could control your actions, and there's talk of chips and stuff, but the Soviets claimed they could control people, at a distance.

You know, like if you can control the mind of the person pulling the lottery balls, you can pull certain numbers? That type of thing. Supposedly they controlled all sorts of people, including people in our government."

Paul laughed. He was a little older than us, and might have been born in the seventies, though I doubted even he had been conscious of what was going on then. "But that was all nonsense, wasn't it? Mostly because people were doing a lot of drugs."

"Maybe," Joe said. He stubbed his cigarette out on an ashtray he'd set in front of him, and lit another, taking a deep pull. "Maybe it was. But back then the American government was threatened enough by the reports, and maybe by... well, maybe by some successes they were sure enough there was something in it that they started a program called Stargate."

"Like the TV series?" Jordan asked.

"Well, this was before that. Well before that. But yeah. I always wondered if someone in on that brainstorming session was involved in the original Stargate. I mean, putting it in a military base and all."

"Didn't they close it because it had only a success rate of something like fifteen percent," Jill asked.

"That's what they said."

"Well, they closed it," she said. "And they never close any government programs for lack of success, so it must have been something special in the way of failure." She was slim, with short hair, cut in a way that made it seem to shimmer and move under the lights. I wondered what she did for a living. None of us except Marianne and Josh, who was a barista, had volunteered that.

Joe smiled. It was a very disquieting smile. "And perhaps you should ask yourself, given that we still have a strategic helium fund, why precisely Stargate was discontinued."

Jill opened her mouth as though to protest, immediately, then frowned and was silent.

Marianne smiled and said something about the Galactic union of minds, and how mundane people tried to thwart it, but I could tell from Jill's frown that she was battling the same thought I was.

Why would a government that never closed anything down have closed down the program of psychic research.

"I read up on it, once. There was at the end of a book on psychic discoveries in the Soviet Union, which I think came out in the nineties? Something about how it hadn't actually been closed, and someone wrote an expose on it, but then it was hushed up? He was a drop out of the program or claimed to be."

But Joe was looking into the middle-distance, his eyes strangely cold, bleak, "I think," he said. "That Stargate is effectively closed, in every possible way it could be. But perhaps not... because it didn't work."

I had no clue what he meant, and he didn't explain. At that point, Jordan pulled out his phone and checked it, and it was still dead, and then we all checked ours.

"Well, you're all more than welcome to stay the night here. We have plenty of rooms. Dad used to rent out rooms to hunters, and then when he went to the nursing home and I came to live here, I stopped doing it. But we still have the rooms."

It was snowing outside, the flurries looking like big feathers and coming fast and furious. Outside the door, the path was obscured in a glittering blanket of snow.

And the weird thing wasn't that he had the rooms. It's that the rooms, to which he led us down a hallway, were clean and the beds freshly made. I did some amount of living with roommates in college, okay? I know what places look like when they haven't been cleaned, and this is Colorado. Dust gets everywhere, even on made and unused beds.

But the room I was led to was spacious, with a big king size bed, that looked like it was made of tree trunks, a style that, in Colorado, is used mostly for people who rent rooms to tourists. Or of course, to people who are tourists and furnishing their vacation house.

The rest of the furniture followed the theme. There was a painting of tree-covered mountains over the bed, with a rutting elk in the foreground. Or at least I think it was a rutting elk. It didn't look like your common run of the mill deer, which, yes, we did encounter often enough in our suburban neighborhood in Colorado Springs when I was growing up. There was a very large dresser, built on heroic lines and probably supposed to hold on Titan clothes or something. It held a large-screen TV, but all the TV showed was snow. Which was weird. I mean, I could see something disrupting the cars and the phones, but surely that same thing wouldn't disrupt cable. And if something stopped all electrical works, then it would stop the lights, too, no? And the heating. The house was obviously heated. None of this made sense.

What made even less sense is that when Joe brought me into the room – with all the others following in a gaggle, as we all went from room to room – he said "This is yours Mike. And in the closet, there are some clothes that should fit you. Dad always believed in having pajamas and a change of clothing in every size, you know for emergencies, and these should fit you."

And it wasn't just that they fit me. That would be strange enough. Really? They'd had rooms equipped with clothes in every size, but one size per? It's that the two changes of clothing – jeans and a shirt – were exactly what I might have bought.

Even weirder was that in the bathroom there was a plastic-sealed toiletries kit: toothbrush, tooth paste, comb shampoo and soap. And that the plastic was stamped in very faded lettering "United States of America."

I mean, maybe that was just a "made by"? Who needed to have the country in a toiletry set?

But I put on the – fit just right – pajamas and went to bed.

Yes, before I did, I did drag the very heavy bedside table in front of the door.

But the window was locked and had a safety bar that simply wouldn't allow it to be opened from the outside.

I did a circuit of the room, examining the walls, and I really didn't see any way that there was a secret passage. So there was a good chance that for all the weirdness, it would be a good night, with no incidence of chainsaws.

And tomorrow I'd get back in the car, start it up and go back to Denver, because it was quite obvious that whatever the hell else was going on, I was not made for hiking or the back country of Colorado. My Rocky Mountain High – with no hint of pot – could be just as profitably achieved in Denver.

I went to bed, having looked in the dresser drawers – empty – and in the bedside table – which contained just an SAS training manual.

And woke up almost immediately.

Joe was standing by my bed, which was outright impossible. I'd made sure that the room was sealed, and he couldn't come in.

On the good side, he wasn't carrying a chainsaw. On the bad side, he was wearing a suit and tie, which looked incongruous with his long hair and beard. The Santa Claus eyes shone with a fanatical gleam.

I tried to sit up, but couldn't. It was like I was paralyzed in place. Some part of me insisted I was just dreaming, but it didn't feel like any dream I'd ever had.

"Of course, Stargate wasn't disbanded, not as such. It was... eradicated."

I wanted to ask by whom, but couldn't move my lips. Which was just as well, because apparently now Joe Brand could understand thoughts without my saying anything.

"I was recruited into it right out of college," he said. "Early seventies. I was studying mathematics, and when the CIA approached me, I thought, well, why not? It was part time work, and I was having trouble enough paying my tuition then, not that it was anywhere as bad as it is now. And I saw it. One thing I'll say for crazy David Morehouse and his book: he was right that the success rate was far more than 15%. A lot of spying and influencing went on. And we countered a lot of it from the Soviet side.

"Of course by the time Morehouse wrote his book he didn't realize that he was being influenced by the Soviets to write it and that the whole purpose was to discredit the idea that the project had ever happened. Much less of what had happened to it."

"Happened... to... it?" I managed to say, my voice sounding distant and somnolent.

Joe smiled as though I'd pulled a particularly clever trick. "The Soviets happened to it, of course. End of 78. We didn't know it, but what they called their influencers, their... mind control people, really were so much better than us. All those fluffy empty heads – a lot like Marianne. Don't protest Marianne – who went to the Soviet Union and came back very impressed with their psychic developments were right. They were much, much better than us at that stuff. I guess when dealing with a human trait that isn't easy to pin down, is erratically transmitted to offspring, and difficult to track down, it helps to be a totalitarian government that can separate kids from their parents, and force reproduction between strangers." He was quiet a while, and as much as his words seemed to approve of such methods, I could tell by the way his eyes glittered that they made him mad. "Which is how they assembled a cadre of ultra-powerful mind-influencers and won the Cold War."

Despite my stunned state, a laugh escaped me. "The Soviet Union hasn't existed since 1991. If that was winning..."

"Someone, I can't remember who, said that the devil's greatest trick was convincing people he didn't exist. The Soviet Union might not have been the devil, although there are people who'd say it was, but the trick is probably about the same."

I decided this was the weirdest dream I'd ever had. Particularly since as Joe spoke next, I started seeing the scenes in my mind.

"One day, out of the clear blue sky, I woke up as the only member of Stargate who knew what had happened, who remembered our success rate."

In my mind, a young Joe – his hair cut, his face shaven, wearing a nice suit – went into an office to find everyone packing up. A jovial older man said, "Well, it never worked, and it's a good thing they are releasing us from this. I'm going to go back to school and get a doctorate. What are you doing?"

And I saw Joe, paralyzed, confused, thinking none of this made sense.

"It took me years to figure it out," Joe said, standing in the middle of my bedroom. "Years. Their biggest trick was to convince us they didn't exist. Everything you think you know about the Soviet Union is a lie. They still exist in all the essentials. Did it bother no one else that their leader is a KGB man?"

I thought it had bothered a lot of people. My dad still went on about it.

"Of course, of course it is. Their organization still exists. It just went underground, at the same time it controlled all the opinion makers in the West, every journalist, professor, everyone with authority."

I wondered if they'd had that much power, why they hadn't invaded.

"Because they couldn't. They didn't quite have the power to influence every person on the street, and make them docile. And you know what Americans are like. Let's remember the Soviets broke their teeth on Afghanistan, against illiterate peasants equipped with outmoded weapons. They knew they couldn't dominate Americans in the open, even if they deprived us of our leadership." He gave a chuckle. "Probably worse for them if they deprived us of our leadership because we're all individualist hot heads. But that's what they set about changing, here and in Europe.

"They took control of those who could, and changed our education, our news, everything they could. They raised two generations now, in the belief that socialism and communism isn't a bad thing. Did it never make anyone think that after the mass-deaths it caused in the 20th century it was a strange thing that our supposedly brightest thinkers were all willing – nay, eager – to give it another try?"

In my mind, I saw something... blue glowing tendrils, reaching into the minds of the people, making them suddenly preach communism to school children, talk about the glories of socialism. I saw the New York Times writing with nostalgia of the USSR, talking about how their space program was superior to America's.

How hadn't I thought that was strange? It had seemed... normal.

"People get feelings that something isn't right, but they don't know what to do with it," Joe explained. "It is no coincidence that while embracing a love of socialism, people talk of being woke, of being part of the resistance. Their subconscious is yelling warnings at them, but they don't know what to do about it."

The images in my mind – some kind of powerpoint. If they did this at our business meetings, it would be far more interesting – were of masses and masses of robot-like people repeating things that they'd been taught by others who were controlled, even as their minds tried to rebel.

"Took me decades to find the right people, the ones with the power to combat the Soviet Union influencers. Now I got you all here, I am going to do something. This should activate your psi powers. It might not, of course. I haven't been able to practice. All I could do was save all the microfiches of years and years of research."

In my mind, the young Joe packed his car with cardboard boxes, all while smiling and saying things about how he'd brought all his paperbacks to work because it had been so boring. His co-workers looked worried but said nothing, because of course, they'd stopped believing there was research worth saving or hiding.

"I studied them. I practiced. And I think when you wake up you'll be – all of you – fully activated influencers, as strong as anything the Soviet Union had. Had because their new generation isn't as strong.

"They have carried the pretense to their own people, and while they have, still, a lot of power, they don't have the kind of power that can force breeding. Or kidnap children from their mothers to train at an early age. Their best ones have died, aged out. Their new ones are half a dozen and not as strong as you are. With you, I'll be able to rip the veil of delusion from the world.

"The people who have been mind-controlled will know it. And we'll have a chance to fight back. From here. From Last Chance Ranch." He smiled, disquietingly. "Now sleep while I work. You'll wake up with a headache."

I woke up with a headache, the sort of headache you get when you drank way too much and it was cheap booze. My stomach wasn't affected, but my head pounded with a sort of dull ache, increasing and dulling then increasing.

There were other things. It seemed to me that thoughts that weren't mine swam in my mind.

It was like waking up and finding that your underwear drawer has been rearranged, only no one could have got in. You feel uncomfortable, disquieted, but you're not at all sure that any of it is true.

I stumbled to the bathroom, and pissed, and stood at the sink looking at myself in the mirror. My eyes were bloodshot, and there were dark circles around them, as though someone had punched me. I remembered everything the night before and clearly. I believed it, what was more.

I not only believed that Joe had been some sort of presence – astral presence – in my room. I believed what he'd told me too. But I didn't like the idea that he'd... what? Manipulated me into driving out to hike somewhere past his ranch. I'd bet he had arranged, somehow, for the phones and the engines not to work, too.

I couldn't just that let stand. Could anyone?

I checked my phone. It was still dead. But perhaps his control had slipped on the cars? I mean, he wouldn't think of us getting out of there and driving out, right? Not with the snow, and not with this headache.

The house seemed silent. I put my clothes from the day before, unblocked the door and sneaked out to the hallway, and out the door to the parking lot. Snow crunched under my feet, and was up to my ankles.

The car was as dead as it had been yesterday.

When I came back into the house, Joe peeked out of the kitchen. "Good morning," he said. "Coffee?"

"I need a shower," I said, grumpily.

"Yes. It should help with your headache."

It did help with my headache. When I came out and back to the kitchen, this time dressed in clean clothes, my teeth brushed with the weirdly patriotic toothbrush, Joe had eggs, bacon, coffee and toast, all of it set out on the counter as a buffet. My fellow stranded travelers all looked like they had the twin of my headache, and were eating silently. Only Marianne looked perturbed. The rest looked, I'd say, more angry than worried.

We were finishing breakfast – I was on my second cup of coffee – when Joe came out and talked to us. "You don't have to do anything," he said. "Though I'll caution that because you are here, and they will find out you were here, you might be targeted by retaliation from the Soviets. But you can help me now if you wish."

It was Josh who spoke up, and I think he spoke for all of us when he said, his eyes squinted in the "headache pose," "Whatever. As long as you make our cars work afterwards."

Joe didn't even try to deny it. He grinned. "They'll work."

So we gathered in the entrance room on sofas and Joe said "Take my lead."

How do I explain what happened next? You remember how I thought I saw blue mist reach into the heads of every influential person in the west?

Well, now we were aloft, in a form like fog. Joe was there, and he pointed us at the problem.

There was... or at least I saw, mentally, a large, dark smoke octopus floating over the world, reaching into western countries.

If you think of the whole sequence as an animated movie "Seven against Cthulhu, you won't be far off.

At first we attacked the tentacles. Our hands like blades, we cut at it, but for every tentacle cut two more was born. And now they were reaching into us, trying to get to our heads. Which is when Marianne – Marianne, whose astral presence, looked like a little anime girl all hung with crystals – gave a war cry and said "we have to kill the mind."

She flung herself against the main part of the octopus, the place where a red dot pulsed. We followed. Jill, a beautiful anime-girl had, from somewhere, procured a shiny white sword. I'd guess it was a sword of the mind. She plunged it near the dot.

I tried to follow and was grabbed and immobilized with a tentacle, that suddenly grew a head like a rattlesnake while the rattling was heard.

I think I was paralyzed for a moment. But you have to understand, I hate being lied to. I fastened my teeth around the snake's neck. There was a cartoonish look of surprise on the snake-face, and then I was free, spitting out what felt like venom, and flying to where the others were attacking the brain of the octopus creature. I dug in, with my hands, which had grown claws, and started pulling out handfuls of stuff.

The others were there, biting and kicking and stabbing. Marianne was crying as she did it, and some of them were screaming. Some looked wounded and bruised. I'd guess while I was captured so were others, but we were fighting, and we were winning.

Suddenly the thing convulsed. There was a shriek like a dying bird. Tentacles flung about. I felt myself swept, but a hand grabbed my wrist. "I have you," Joe's voice said. "I have all of you."

The room looked the same when we came back from the mental battle. We didn't look the same. Around me, everyone had aged ten years in minutes. And Joe was on his phone, talking in guarded tones.

He looked up, as a few of us tottered to our feet. "The White House—" he said. "The president will want to talk to you. All of you." He sounded hoarse. "Every participant in operation Last Chance."

"But we're free to go now?" Paul asked.

"Yes. If you want. They shouldn't be able to retaliate. Not right now."

I took a deep breath. My mouth felt burned. I stumbled down the hallway to the room, not sure I was in any state to drive. In the room, as I collected my things, I turned the TV on.

The leader of the house minority was on. I won't say she wasn't as shrill as she had been, but she was saying things I couldn't have imagined before, "For the last few decades in this chamber, I've said things and supported causes that were against the interests of the United States. I was the manipulated puppet of the enemy. Today I'm here to remedy that. To tell you—"

I turned the TV off. I bundled my clothes under my arm and trudged to my car. I had just turned the ignition on when my phone pinged with a text. "You won't believe who just committed suicide. He said he had woken up this morning, convinced he was a Soviet Puppet all these years. What the hell is going on?"

The text was from my friend Rick. We used to shoot the breeze and discuss politics.

But I felt as if I were bruised inside my head – no, inside my soul – and I couldn't find anything to answer him with. I suspected in the next few days everything would come to light. People would know.

What would this do? To myself, to the nation?

I didn't know.

The phone pinged again. A look sideways showed the sender of the text as the President of the United States.

There would be time for that. Right now, driving through the Colorado snow towards Denver, I drove through terra incognita.

Who knew how things would change? The future was something I couldn't even imagine, now that we'd won the Cold War. Or was it still a cold war? World War Three, I guessed.

It had been the last chance, the most improbable of dice throws.

Seven against the behemoth, and the seven unequipped and ignorant.

But Americans always do well against long odds and in strange circumstances. And knowing the devil is there is better than closing your eyes and pretending he no longer exists.

We'd won this one.

Tomorrow and the day after, and all the ways to forever, we'd win the rest. One by one.

Now we were masters of our own mind. The future was ours to make.

Writing Great Reckoning In A Small Room

I was very ill when I wrote *Great Reckoning In A Small Room.* If I hadn't been, of course, I'd have remembered I'd already written a story by this name. I really have to stop undead-stalking Kit Marlowe. I mean the man has been dead for centuries. It's in poor taste.

Anyway this is one of those stories that revealed itself step by step and I didn't know what I was writing till I did. And what worries me? I'm not sure this is fiction. I mean general worldbuilding. None of us writers are sure this is fiction.

Great Reckoning In A Small Room

Of all the private investigators' offices in Imago, she had to come into mine.

Okay, you're going to say, of course she did, Kit, you're the only private detective in Imago. Where else would she go?

Yabut—

Look, a man shouldn't complain, but it really wasn't fair. She was long and lean, with blond hair that looked like spilled moonlight caught up in a kind of bun thing, with sticks stabbed through, and falling in little bright rays here and there, down her back and shoulders, and little tendrils dripping down the front of her white blouse and over two softly rising mounds, not excessive but impressive. Down from that, a tiny waist cinched into the band of her short skirt. I don't know if her waist would fit in my hands, and I wasn't in the mood to get stabbed trying to test it, but it looked like it would. Under the short, slit skirt, her legs were encased in silk lace, some chiaroscuro pattern of climbing ivy. Her shoes were pointy and shiny and balanced on quite unrealistic stilettos.

And she was a muse. Which was the unkindest cut of all.

Oh, technically so was I a muse. Very technically. But I wasn't stupid. And I saw trouble when it stared me in the face.

Which brings me to the most unfairest part of all: Her eyes. They couldn't have been some reasonable color like blue or green. Heck, I'd have taken violet, that color beloved by the muses in the fanfic quarter.

But no. They were liquid gold, this side of amber, like old single malt spilled over ice and held up to the light in a spotless glass.

It was evening, and the sepia toned light seeped in slashes through the blinds in my office window. I'd just finished the paperwork for my last case and filed it – one of these days I need to figure out how to get a secretary, I do – had locked the file drawer, retrieved my wallet and gun from the desk and slipped them on, and was about to put my coat on.

I had evening plans, though nothing much. A vague idea of hitting up The Heartbreak on the corner for their steak sandwich, and maybe seeing if Pinky and Baltazar were around for a poker game. You know, normal downtime after a case.

The tap tap tap of her heels on the old oak boards of my floor called my gaze, and there she was. Standing just so as though she'd arranged herself artistically to catch the light of the blinds just so. Hell, she might have. Muses are like that.

"Mr. Marlowe?" she said, and that was almost my undoing. That voice, low in the throat, just slightly scratchy, like smokey honey edging into a purr. Don't question it. I know I'm mixing senses. But trust me, it is what it is.

"Yeah," I said, my patter failing me, my mouth suddenly dry.

She raised an eyebrow at me. "He said it was you, but I didn't believe it. The eyepatch completes the image though. I have to ask, is it real?"

I reached into my pocket for my smokes. Look, that's the one vice I brought from my human life. Much grateful for cigarettes, though. A pipe is all very well and all. Still have one now and then at home. I mean, this is twenty-first century pipe tobacco too, not the moldy sweeps of a drying house that I could afford in Elizabethan England. So, all very well, but nothing beats the convenience of the little packets rolled in paper that you light with a lighter. Fire in your pocket at will. I'd think it was magic, if I'd been transported from my mortal life to here, without seeing what happened in the world in between.

I took a cigarette from the silver case – gift from a grateful client, and what a piece of—Never mind – and lit it with silver lighter, ditto, looked her in the eye and said, "Oh, it's quite real. Cotton. Not even custom made. I buy them off a shop a block from here."

For a moment my effrontery stopped her. "Not the patch," she said peevishly. "The injury it hides."

"Yes. Real. Quite." I didn't feel like adding more, and I certainly wasn't going to add a peep show. It was sealed, unless I needed it. But a Muse would know what she was looking at. And I don't reveal weapons till they're needed.

If I did, I wouldn't have survived hundreds of years in the business.

She looked annoyed. Not angry precisely, but annoyed, which was interesting in and of itself, because Muses.... It's not so much like they get angry easily, but more like they have two speeds. They are all cloyingly seductive, or screaming in your face and threatening to cut you if you don't do what they say. Makes living among them interesting, mind.

Am I that way? I don't think so. Mind you, some people – modern authors, honestly – say I was that way while human. But I don't think so. I remember being human and the days that weren't lived – if you pardon the expression – on the edge of the knife. The day to day. You have to be able to call up other emotions to deal with those.

I blew smoke into the air. Perfect rings? Nah. I could do them, but why bother. "So, did you come here to ask me if I'm really myself or just impersonating me? To check on old injuries? Or to comment on my sartorial taste in eye patches?"

She clicked her teeth together once. Either annoyance or I'd given her a case of the shivers. "No, Mr. Marlowe, I've come to ask you to lay down your life for a friend."

Well, that was new. Refreshing. After these many years, you don't see much that's new in the business, honest. But there was only one small snag.

"You've got the wrong man. I'm not the least bit like the one who said it. I'm no longer human for one. Though truth be told—" I was not going to be drawn into theological matters. Look, as a human I'd been rather drawn to high church, smells and bells and the ceremony. But my father-- No. We won't talk about it. The man I was is dead. Or if not dead, as good as, which is the same. "Never mind." I blew more smoke. "Thing is, I don't have friends."

"Ah," she said. Her gaze followed the tendrils of smoke, unrolling in the light from outside. I should turn on the office light, but that would only encourage her to stay, and I was starting to get a feeling I wouldn't like what she had to say. Either she was wrong, or this was going to end badly. Memories half forgotten, lost in the transition when brain matter followed the knife out of my ruined eye, tried to flood back, appropriately chopped and sliced. A young man my age, but oh so different, a smoky tavern. Bawdy songs and sweaty hand clasps, and earnest conversation about the craft, the craft, the craft.

He didn't mean witchcraft. That would have been safer. Alas for both of us.

I'd thought him dead, and wondered if he was. I'd always had an odd feeling about him. Like.... More than one writer in a single body and lifetime.

Never mind. It was over four hundred years gone. And the chap was almost certainly dead.

But he was the only one I had ever called by the name "friend." Then, as now, I had acquaintances, associates, interests, honeys, dolls and .... Other coarser links. But friend? No one had called me that. I'd called no one else that. And he'd started it.

She took a deep breath, "He said you would say that. And also that he was dead. But he wanted me to deliver a message and then said maybe—" She shrugged. "He still said you wouldn't do it. The situation is—" she waved a hand as though she lacked the words, but there were spikes and blood in those gestures, somehow. "And you might well die. Be finished. Whichever applies to you now. Which he says he couldn't ask you. And he knows. So he said to ask you but to let you go if you would not with his blessing, because...." Her eyes rolled slightly up as people do when trying to recall something. "He said to tell you that when a man's verses cannot be understood nor a man's good wit seconded with the forward child, understanding, it strikes a man more dead than a great reckoning in a little ro om."

I wanted to laugh. I might have cried, given a small push, but what I did was let out a weird sound, between a gasp and a squeak, which frankly embarrassed me, and to cover it, I said, teeth in my words, "Oh, really? Not something from Gentlemen of Verona? Will, I'm disappointed in you. Quoting yourself and not sharply."

She didn't acknowledge I'd spoken at all. The amber eyes were staring ahead, sightless. "If you cannot. If you will not, he says you're free and to tell you that he understands men have died and worms have eaten them, but not for love."

I bit the tip of my tongue and tasted the iron of all-too-human blood. Let's say I didn't have many defenders, in my human persona, nor many epitaphs, but that one had been given and freely. And he'd had no idea, then, of what I'd done, nor that I was still alive after a fashion.

In fact, I don't know when he'd discovered that. Or if he had. I still—

I didn't understand where my friend was or what was happening, or how he could still be alive in his all too human frame, but one thing I knew for certain sure: He needed me, and I'd have to answer.

I'd have cursed, honestly. Good curses, dirty and profane as they had them in my birth time and place. But there are predicaments that are beyond swearing. Though I'll say this was only the second I'd encountered.

"You've delivered a lesson, Mistress. Do you have a name?"

"He calls me Nan."

Well and of course he would. "So, Mistress Nan, you've delivered a lesson, question and answer, but what you've not told me is how this is more than to my purpose nothing. Where is Will? Does he live still? And what in the hells of the forgotten can I do to rescue him?"

Her eyes flashed dark and light, as though the reflection of light from the window moved, and then she looked up, disarming, clear, "You can dive into the hells of the forgotten."

I physically scrambled back without realizing it, till my wall stopped me. It was a good solid brick wall. In need of painting.

"I'm not—" I started. Everything in me wanted to scream: I'm not going there. No.

I'd dived into it, once. Once only. On the way to undying. Once was more than enough. Everything in me tried to escape, even if the only way out was through that brick wall.

But—But—

Ah hell. Men have died and the worms have eaten them. But not for love.

I took a deep breath. Till now. Aloud I said, "Give me a last cigarette, and I'm willing. But I'm afraid you'll have to lead. I've forgotten the way."

She slit her eyes at me, till the lighted not-amber shone between impossibly long lashes. Did she look like Anne Hathaway? I wanted to know so badly I felt like the question hung over my head, like one of those thought bubbles in old comic books. And I was not going to ask. Not of her, and on my soul not of him, if-- when I met him and he could talk.

"I only want to know," I said, conversationally, lighting a cigarette from the end of the other. "If we can get there tonight. For tonight, I'll be bound to the task. But another minute, no." It is important to set boundaries when dealing with muses. Slaves learn, you know, the way to cut the collar.

She cackled. "King and Queen of Cantelon, How many miles to Babylon? Eight and eight, and other eight Will I get there by candle-light? If your horse be good and your spurs be brightHow mony men have ye? Mae nor ye daur come and see."

And on that she revealed herself. The old ones always do, and speak in half unintelligible poetry. Where had Will found her? And why him? I would keep a close eye on her, too. She was here on his behalf, maybe, but the ancient ones have strange ideas of what is to your benefit. What I knew for sure is that this was going to involve horses. And the horses of this kind.... You know the horses of the night. Nightmares.

This was just going to be a wonderful trip. Strip me naked, dip me in candle wax and light my fuse. I was in for an ardent time. Possibly terminally so.

And yet, there are bonds that can't be broken, and obligations that call across the worlds, aren't there? He'd almost died to allow my escape from my rapidly ending mortal coil. As Atropos stood, her scissors already opened over my dingy spool, he'd stolen it, and helped me put another in her grasp. A life for a life. It was always so.

And a life for a life meant I owed him a life.

I wanted to spit, but I dropped my cigarette and stomped hard on it. The landlord will sigh and erase the mark. "Great reckoning in a little room."

"Isn't it always?" she said, sarcastically.

*****

Outside my office it was raining, the dreary rain called "mizzle" that feels as though the sky were sweating. It haloed in shining rings around the street lights, as if a giant spider had trapped every point of light in the landscape.

I tilted my fedora so the brim covered most of my face – or the shadow of it did – even if it left that uncomfortable drip down the back of my neck, seeping into my coat and shirt. Look, it's best that some people don't immediately recognize you. You can't do what I do without making enemies. And some of them have as little sense of humor as a literary novelist.

Why do I live in the Noir District, you ask? Wouldn't it make much more sense to live in the Elizabethan district?

Ah, no. Look, I love the colors and the madness as much as the next man, but it's not that far away. I can take the street car to the end of Noir, then walk a dozen blocks, past the quay and the taverns there – though I rarely make it past the taverns there. Some parts of my reputation are true. And others grossly exaggerated – and find myself in the old familiar streets, crunchy and fragrant and busy. Did I say fragrant? Let me repeat fragrant. And I don't mean that in a good way though the word is pretty. Stinky or odoriferous are not as pretty, and more descriptive. But *not as pretty* disturbs me. I was a poet once.

In one or the other way, the Elizabethan Division, which bleeds ever so slightly back and forth across the Tudor Division and the Regency Quarter, because no one knows history anymore, reeks. Then there's elves. It would make you weep, but I have met elves drinking in the Mermaid. As I live and breathe – still despite it all – have muses and authors of the present day no shame? There is a Fantasy Quarter for a reason.

At any rate I will cut this short without giving you the full map of Imago, since the night is young but it will age like milk curdling in the oven, and the muse with me is intent on taking me to hell and back. Well, I hope and back. I don't think she cares.

I live in the Noir District because it is clean enough, convenient enough, I find the sepia toned light restful, and I like the fact people and muses mostly leave you alone. Take now. Everyone was hurrying home under the mizzle, wrapped in their raincoats, sometimes holding umbrellas over their heads.

Oh, there are stories at every corner, and more if you care to guess. A man and a woman walking too close. The sound of a gunshot from one the tall brick buildings. The howl of police cars.

And that's the other reason I'm here. I'm a muse. Every century or so, I have to find a poor sap and inflict myself on him or her. It's written in the rules. It is you might say, the bill – or as my friend Will would say, the reckoning – for this life. Last time I did so was in pulp days. I won't name my charge. Think on it, though, and you'll work it out. It will come to you .

Nan walked ahead of me, tic tic tic of stiletto heels on cement. I could have caught up with her, but I was sure she was the type to enjoy being ahead. And besides, you know, it was good to have someone to hide behind if an all too known menace jumped me.

We got to the corner, and she put her hand out, casually. A taxi, all yellow and black, slid up and stopped. She opened the door, and gestured to me.

I'd been wondering.

I mean, look.... So the geography here is strange. And sometimes we grow whole districts. Noir, was an outgrowth of pulp, and the two bleed together, but the whole area is one of the newish suburbs of Imago. A hundred years old, or little more. Nothing to the older ones, where men – and women, and sometimes even muses – fear to tread.

Go venturing into the real ones, where memory loses its surety and words themselves become something strange and slippery, and—

Well, and you'll be in the Hell of the Forgotten. The undiscovered country, from which—Will sure did talk purty, didn't he?

Anyway, you could take the bus anywhere in Noir. And there were other conveyances.

But no bus or train, nor gig, nor carriage nor conveyance, nor even magic wand or one of those gleaming spaceships that they have over in the science fiction quarter will take you where we needed to go.

And I'd wondered if she was going to clamp her hand – or her teeth – on me and drag me screaming, step by step all the way.

Well, that was answered. I slipped into the cab. Horses can take other forms, and I wasn't sure this was better than a bolting steed. I had about as much control. It was cleaner than any I'd seen in reality, though there was a bullet hole in the window, over which something had been taped. But it smelled faintly of fish, and I didn't need the glance at the cabbie's license, clipped to the dashboard to know the name would be Charon. I eased back and relaxed against the upholstery. She'd have the two coins for each of us. That's what muses did.

And yes, if you are going to ask, yes, Charon was broad shouldered, dark haired, and his reflection in the rearview mirror: prominent nose and dark eyes almost lost under prominent brows just about screamed Greek.

He drove like a crazy person through the streets, which fortunately were at that time almost empty of traffic and whose pedestrians stayed on the sidewalks. I'd like to say that Nan made me feel comfortable, but she didn't. She sat in perfect pose, legs crossed at the ankle, not a hair out of place. An odd scent came from her.

Look, muses – the real muses, created as such – can smell like anything. Any flower or spice. Each of them has a peculiar scent unique to them. But usually, yeah, flower, spice, ocean. This one smelled like fresh baked bread, which caused me to give her the wary eye. What kind of muse does that? What kind of attraction? But I knew.

"How can Will be in the hell of the forgotten?" I asked. He had died – or I thought he had. It can be complicated with writers – and everyone in the world still read him. Everyone still talked about him. He was not forgotten. Though sometimes, not particularly well understood. And the opinions about him—

She shrugged. "He was caught in the trap. He'd left enough of himself behind."

And that was all. I wasn't sure I fully understood what she meant. He'd never been there. Not as I had. He'd almost fallen in. But not really. I felt a sudden tightening at my gut. "Was it in saving me?"

She shook her head. "Hamnet."

Hamnet. The all precious son. Will, who was a broad minded man, who loved his wife and spent hours extolling to me the virtues of his "broad hipped Nan" who was older than him, and also wiser, and he who delighted in his Susannah and his Judith, had one son, whom he loved. For his son's sake he dreamed of success such as the son of a small town merchant didn't often have. He dreamed of a crest. He dreamed of a large house. And he'd set an entailment so his son inherited all the riches.

Only Hamnet had died. Which I'd only found out in the twentieth century, long after Will himself had died. I remembered feeling a pang, thinking that must have hurt. But that was all.

I hadn't looked before, because that would hurt. In fact, even here, in Imago, I'd stayed away from the Elizabethan side, save for some rare, sodden evenings.

There are things that are too real and too painful, no matter how many jokes I make about the stink. There are things you don't touch because the centuries don't erase the flinch of the torn flesh, or perchance worse, the torn memories.

I fidgeted with my cigarette box in my pocket, and contemplated the hip flask in the coat pocket, but didn't take it out. Instead, I looked out the window, while the landscape outside had changed, as we skirted out of Noir and into.... I don't know. We momentarily drove through a forest road pursued by a giant dog with luminescent eyes.

I still didn't fully understand how from losing his son to death, Will could have tumbled into the hell of the forgotten, but...

I see I'll have to explain the world of muses to you. Or perhaps not the world of muses, as there is no such thing as a separate world, or else there are many, infinite, touching only as though a panel made of wax, sometimes melting enough to be permeable, but really separate.

In these separate worlds humans live their ordinary mortal lives, never guessing that there are other worlds of humans, side by side, some with humans so much like them that they're really the same save for normal differences, and some so different that—

Well, never mind. I called them worlds, but they're really not. They're all one world. You have to forgive me. I'm a shoemaker's son from a time and place in which you could imagine a clockwork was an accurate representation of the solar system. And that it all might in fact be run by clockwork.

So, endure with me, if my images and explanation are less than apt.

Imagine then this endless set of ... variations of reality, all separated from the other by a thin sheet of wax.

Most mortal men go through life, beginning to end, beginning of time to never ending eternity without ever deviating from their little assigned path. And most that cross from one to the other, be this because the wax melted enough, or simply because for one moment they leaned enough upon the wall to leave an imprint, are never aware of it.

In that other world, where they exchanged places with their own selves there – there is a balancing. Perhaps why people say if you see a doppleganger you will die – life will be the same, except the red coat is blue in that one.

There are occasionally and more noticeably in the more .... regimented, or perhaps recorded world since the twentieth century people who disappear and show up, with no possible explanation. Started before that, though. The man who walked around the horses and was never seen again.

Children who show up in a place where they could have not have got to, and who belong to nowhere. Cars which disappear ahead of you on a highway with no turnoffs.

Those are rare enough they are forgotten. Swept aside. Explanations are made. That never happened. Or else, of course, it was misreported.

But they do happen. Rarely.

So, then again, what with muses? What with Imago? What with those others we catch glimpses of now and then and which our ancestors thought were gods?

We were now driving through a small American town, and you'd think we were in literary or perhaps period fiction, except that we passed a sign showing a white haired gentleman and words extolling the Colonel's fried lizard parts. I smiled to myself. Well, of course, if you were going to take this road in Imago, best find the way worn for you by one of the writers and his muses, long ago.

"I believe that you'll understand when I get you to him," Nan said. "Getting you to him is the first and necessary point."

I nodded once. Seemed reasonable. And also like something no one should ask of me, but yet inevitable.

So... Muses. No. Then again, first writers.

Rise above the many realities separated by sheets of flimsy and pliable wax which we'll call the world. Above, and above, till you're staring at the whole thing from an eminence.

Now. Imagine thought as wire, fine and silvery, and imagine that it crisscrosses realities, forming lines and patterns. Ideas will appear from one world into the other where they make no sense.

Or events will happen more or less the same, because the thought and the cognition from the other world is there.

If you wish, think of it as the tool artists use, to copy a drawing. Where at one end is the pencil that traces it, and at the other, sometimes at quite a remove there is another pencil that, by following the movements, recreates the drawing.

At any rate, there are, in each reality, people who whatever reason are at the intersection of a lot of wires. Their thoughts extend through many worlds, and the realities intersect in their minds.

Those people are generally howling madmen. Or if you prefer artists. It is not a joke that throughout the ages and whatever you called them, bards or prophets, dreamers, muse-led, there was a significant intersection with losing control of your life, with being eaten in some way from the inside.

Those whom the gods love die young. All that rot.

And the idea exists, in many cultures, because it's broadly true. That is the unfairness of stereotypes. They're stupid and wrong, and often evil. But also very often, in broad strokes, they are true.

It is hard to live there, pinned at the intersection of many worlds, your thoughts wandering about without your permission, till you know the story of this one and that, and things that make no sense in your world. None at all. But you know them. Are acquainted with them more than with mother or father, sibling or child.

Their thoughts are yours in the dark of night, and you wake up praying a prayer for their safety, even though you'll never meet them in the flesh.

For writers, but also for musicians, haunted by music never heard, or for painters, who see so clearly what never existed, it is possible and in fact probably likely to go insane. To lose track of who you are in the babble of voices, until you run about disordered, unable to do the most elementary things in life.

So then there are muses. I don't know where they came from or if they were created. As a species I mean. I don't even know how individual ones were created, truth be told. My own origin story is not normal. If indeed anything about me was ever done in the expected way.

I said or implied that muses are made, not born, but I don't know for sure. I only interact with them fully grown and in Imago, where I often am not sure who is the creator or the created, the muse or the character.

For all I know there is a part of Imago where a mom muse and a dad muse live in a perfectly normal house, with a vast brood of little muses, by the side of their muse neighbors.

I looked at Nan and the mind boggled at the thought. I don't think so, but it is possible indeed.

At any rate I don't know where the first muse came from, or what caused her – or him – to appear. It is possible they are related to the shadowy Others, the ones who move between realities with no compunction or stop. The ones who—

Well, we don't know much about them, save that people of long ago – I think as we drive past a place, I hope in fantasy land where a barefoot congregation gathers around an altar with a masked priest. There is a human shape on the altar – thought they were gods, and sacrificed to them, sometimes to draw them near. Sometimes to keep them away. Both with indifferent rates of success.

Or perhaps the muses created these humans. If indeed artists are human. Self to the contrary. They do behave to them like shepherds to sheep. Or slave owners to slaves.

But they keep them sane. Or at least alive. Just like the shepherd keeps the sheep from the wolf, till it's time to shear it.

The muses direct and focus the creator and bid her or him or it – never heard of an it, but there's many things I've never heard of. Perhaps cats or worms have their own bards – create a certain thing in a certain way. And they will chase the poor creature down and pin it, as though it were a butterfly, could it still live with the pin driven through its solar plexus, stuck for once in place, but perhaps displaying its brightest colors.

It might be simply because human minds – no, human bards – create and build Imago, the imagined reality – or I should say the different reality – where muses dwell. In self defense, the muses would want to control it, just like humans try to control the course of the river on which they depend for their crops.

There is an idea that sometimes comes to me in the middle of the night, on nights I'm alone and staring blind at the ceiling, that perhaps – perhaps – it is not just Imago that these dreamers build, but all reality. That by some peculiar grace of the Creator, in His image and semblance, these human minds create and expand the realities, kept separate by wax.

It doesn't matter as those are infinite, and verification impossible. Except perhaps for the Creator. Or the Others.

For the muses, the effect on Imago would be more immediate, and require more attention.

And so muses move between the human realities and their own, in their own free to be more at ease, in the human world, sometimes passing as human themselves, but rarely to their.... Clients. I almost typed victims.

Outside, we'd now entered the shadowed road again, and this time the pictures I caught outside were not—

Remember the caves at Lascaux? I visited, once, shortly after they were discovered and open to the public. I recognized the muses handywork, in the vibrancy and life of the offerings. Some poor caveman labored over those, or maybe many primitives, by scant light, doing what they did because the images must be gotten out of his or their heads, so they could sleep at night.

This area of Imago looked like that. It was all sketches in ochre and kohl, in sudden flashes in the car's headlights, so you could not tell if the vivid semblance of a horse was racing, or the light just made it appear so.

"Not long now," Nan said.

Outside the drums started. There was an atonal singing with it, something like the buzzing of insects, turned to the human voice.

On the way to the hell of the forgotten, you go down and down the unknown paths, before writing, before language, and then just before. Before humans perhaps or even just before human rationality.

I don't know if you go far enough if you'll find yourself underwater, surrounded by the chemical exudations of amoeba-like beings who speak that way. Perhaps. Or perhaps only humans. But I've never gone that far.

I've gone as far as I have, and that's enough to be difficult making it back.

The drumming and droning singing faded away, and we were driving in a deep fog that writhed at the windows.

Suddenly the car stopped.

Charon turned back, startling me because his eyes had the unfocused look of those long-blind.

"This is where it ends," he said. "No further."

I opened the door, started to get out, and realized Nan was still sitting, prim and proper, her legs crossed at the ankle, her hands held together in her lap, her look bland.

"Aren't you coming to guide me?" I asked.

She shook her head. "From now on, you go alone, Mister Marlowe."

I blinked at her. "But how will I find him, much less free him?"

She smiled a little. "You will.I have full confidence in you."

I opened the door and got out, cursing softly. Always beware of muses having full confidence in you. I'd had a muse once.... And I am one. If you trust nothing else, trust this.

Outside. I want to say it was cold, but it wasn't. It's difficult to feel cold here, because frankly there was not much of anything. One of those things that my pulp-era writers kept talking about was the cold of space. There is no cold in space, because there's not much to transmit the temperature to your skin. Not that this will make much difference to you, since you'll probably pop or boil or something in your own blood, since there isn't anything around you and the lack of pressure—

Kind of like here, only it was more pressure, here.

Way more pressure. As I walked past the driver's window, Charon reached out through the open window, and grabbed my coat sleeve. "Remember the *no look back*, right? Very important. *The no look back*."

I didn't protest. *The no look back* seems to be really important, from Eurydice to the Old Testament, to ... My life. Where nothing can be won by looking back. And yet, I always did. At least I hadn't turned into a pillar of salt. Yet. Maybe.

It was, sensory-experience wise, kind of like walking in fog, without the cold and the wet.

Just.... Walking through what seemed to be clouds of fog, in this case interspersed with what seemed to be vague forms, perhaps people, perhaps animals, not fully visible.

I never fully understood what this level of approaching the hell meant, except perhaps the stage of development of the human mind where humans didn't have any kind of thoughts, and just went around going "oooh. Kind of tree."

I walked on anyway. I remembered this. Though it would have helped if I had some idea how long I'd walked and past what.

So I can't tell you how long I slogged on. But I did hear a noise to my right and moved that way.

After a while I saw it, but I didn't know what I was seeing. Through the not-fog a knot of ugly and dark showed, bits here and there, enough for me to piece together that there was something menacing with overarching wings out there. Okay, as more bits appeared and vanished in the fog, a lot of bits, I thought there was a lot ugly and big wings out there. It came with noises. A noise like wet umbrellas poked into someone's ear.

No, I didn't want to go near it. Would you?

And to be fair, I couldn't really remember what had happened to me in this place. I suspected there was intended forgetfulness at work. But maybe not. Maybe what I remembered was all it was for me. It had been a flash, plunging in, then a sense of searing pain, and then.... The exchange was made, and my eye sealed. And then I had to make it back. Only there was no going back, except to Imago, though the despond and the pain. Because there is no return. Only a life for a life. Or.... Not.

I hadn't thought through this. A life for a life.

But I got nearer, nearer, nearer, and suddenly the fog cleared and there was—

Oh, you think Prometheus, he who gave humans fire, and was condemned to spend eternity as a Liver Restaurant for Eagles had it bad?

We should all be so lucky.

Will was the centerpiece. He was staked down, though I couldn't see with what. Some kind of spears? Through his feet and hands, pinning him to the rock-like ground.

Around him were... call them eagles. Or furies. Or.... What will you. I'd never seen anything like them. They were human sized, with proportional wings. But they were no bird – or human – I'd ever seen. They looked like they were made of rags and despair. Of all the fears and darkness distilled from all the lonely midnights, all the cold and the self-doubt, dredged through despair and utter denial, through impossible odds and broken dreams.

They flapped their wings and lowered their beaks and....

It was his heart. Or maybe not his heart as they pulled out long pieces of what looked like blood sculpted words, and swallowed them in messy gulps, only to dive down again.

Will-- He looked like he did when I met him. When we were friends. And if you think that I'm referring to him as some lover's dream, you have been watching too many movies. Young Shakespeare, my own age, born my own year, looked at least ten years older. Always. He looked like a young and promising merchant, with a receding hairline, and fine lines on his forehead from spending the night worrying over the ledger books.

Only it was not the ledger books. It was the words and the stories, the wires that intersected in him, the muse that whispered eternal verse to him.

Unlike mine who was – who knows why – a male psychotic, obsessed with blood and mayhem and dragging my soul along between revulsion and anger, his was a sweet creature, who, in her female form, the roaring boys of the low taverns we frequented called "the Swan."

When Will was writing, his eyes lit up. Not literally but with the fire of passion.

I don't know what he and his wife got up to, in that second best bed of which he joked – the first best bed being the one they'd bought for their first born Susannah, that she'd take with her when married, he said – but he couldn't have looked more passionate more intense, more full of desire and joy than he did over the manuscripts late at night, slinging one more line at me, and rounding it out with one more set of perfectly rhythmic imagery, and laughing at me for being tone deaf, he said, and missing the full music of the words, and coming in clanging when it should flow. And me reminding him that I'd invented the form. Iambic pentameter, my creation. And him laughing and saying that I'd only done it because I needed a crutch to lean on.

He wasn't utterly wrong at that.

But now, his eyes were dull, though they flinched, with each blood-soaked word string pulled out of him, each long drawn-breath, each painful piece of his heart and mind and soul.

He didn't scream though there was that feeling that he had done so a lot, and the ghost sound of the screams that no longer echoed rent the air.

His hair, what remained, was pasted down with sweat and blood.

Then he saw me. His eyes fastened on mine, and his lips shaped my name.

The creatures turned. What were they even? Was this what the Others looked like in their other form? Was it a perverted sort of Others. Or was that what the Others looked like at home, when indulging in a little blood sacrifice?

I remembered a sentence, from Will about my then muse, "Never trust anything that feeds on blood."

And then I was running, while they rushed me. Five against one. What are the odds? But God Bless Smith And Wesson, who worked to make men equal.

I'd been in fire fights before, only this was not a fire fight. Only I had the fire. I drew while running, and shot without much preamble. One fell before he knew he was dead. Or rather he burst in dark ominous smoke that smelled of death and poverty.

The others were on me then. One on my right, one on my left, the beaks through my arms forcing me down. The pain was odd, detached, clinical. The beaks felt cold, like ice and death and eternal damnation. A life for a life. Was only fair.

The gun in my hand felt heavy. I was almost all the way to the ground, where they would pin me through and to the rock. Number three and four were coming at me from the front. Long blood soaked beaks at the ready.

Will was thrashing. I saw one of the lances go flying through the air. The one that had been through his right wrist. It was a quill, I thought with shock. Made of metal, man sized.

I heard sounds of exertion and in between my approaching executioners, I saw him pull the quill from his left wrist and toss it aside.

Then while he freed his feet, the two standing creatures, one and two, tried to force me to the ground. I was resisting, though I don't even know w hy.

A life for a life was only fair. It was a bargain that had been struck before I ever came here.

Number three leaned in, and his beak would pierce my chest, and while he did this, I'd be helpless and get completely pinned on the ground, and then Will could escape and—

But you see, there was a gun in my hand. And I'd used a gun before to get out of straits. I guess it's something you never forget. An habit of mind and body.

Before I even thought the muzzle went up. And never mind that it hurt like hell to move my hand up against the beak through my forearm. I made sure Will was not in the trajectory of the bullet. Well, you never know, do you? But he was nowhere to be seen, and must have run, like the sane man he was, to Nan – either of them – and safety.

I pulled the trigger and blew the ugly beak-like thing away, and the blood-spattered face it was attached to. Number four leaned in towards my gun hand.

I blew his beak away right as he opened it. And then the head for good measure.

I could feel blood pouring down my arm, under my suit and shirt, and I thought that I knew how this ended. The other two would still force me down, and these would regenerate. It was what happened here. There was a sense of having heard the story before.

But by damn, Kit Marlowe would go down fighting, and not like a willing victim in a blood sacrifice.

I lowered my head, I lifted my left hand. I pulled the eye patch off. I turned my left eye on the creature holding me on the left.

There was a moment of startled surprise, and then bizarrely human – but dark, so dark – eyes opened wide, in shock.

Then it made a sound like *caw* but prolonged and drawn. And the force of a hundred winds pulled it in, shredding it in pieces, and pulling it into my eye, where it would burn and vanish.

I know. It shouldn't work but it does. You know, at that moment, when the muse and I exchanged places, he to my mortally wounded mortal body, me to his damaged but immortal muse body, the wound Will had given him with his quill while rescuing me had transmuted. It had become something primal, complete, a conduit back to the beginning, where everything got consumed and reapportioned in fire and chaos. Which is why I wore tasteful cotton eye patches. What an inconvenience for every day life. And imagine looking in the mirror while I shaved.

I felt my other arm go free and in shock almost turned. But I've spent four hundred years managing the thing, and slapped my hand over my eye before turning to see....

It was Will, with one of the lance-like quills, through the creature's heart.

I gave him a weak smile, and covered my eye in the patch, again.

There was blood running down my arms, and he was all over blood, though it shouldn't be disappearing as though it were being erased, like imperfect words upon the page.

"I didn't know if you would come," he said, his voice hoarse, as he offered me his hand, which I clasped.

"I didn't know if I would come," I said. "But Nan came and got me, and reminded me of the epitaph you wrote for me."

He looked embarrassed. “Ah, oh, that. It was all nonsense.” He made a voice as though mimicking the gossips of the time. “Killed in a fight over a bawdy love.” He shrugged.

“But no one else defended me, Will, only you.”

His hand clasping mine was strong and warm. I pulled away. “We’d best get walking. Any idea of the direction?”

He pointed. “I must go there.”

I couldn’t see anything there, but I went along to be companionable. After all, the important thing was not to look back.

“So, Nan is your new muse?”

He hesitated. “I don’t think so? Only I think my words are done. I was—” There was a silence. Looking at him – not even slightly back, unless you take that as meaning that I was looking at his past – I saw that he was flexing his jaw, a gesture I remembered when something upset him. “I called out of my need, and she’s a muse. She was shaped by it and came, all comfort. But I needed another muse to escape.”

There was a cackle as if a sob were caught at the back of his throat, and turned into mirth. “I see by your garb you have lived....” A jaundiced eye over my apparel and he added, “I hope centuries past all I know, so I will say that I think at this moment my body is wandering alone in the rain, after a visit with my friends from London in a tavern in Stafford on Avon.”

“I... Heard,” I admitted. “I heard that at fifty eight you’d wondered in the rain and caught pneumonia and died.”

He shrugged. “You know, I think so, and yet it was all so long ago, too.” He pointed back, but didn’t turn. “They were devouring my words, my thoughts. I only sometimes remembered who I was. And Nan cried when I didn’t recognize her face.”

I’d heard of that, and I’d heard that theory too, for his death. But Lord what a way to go. Bards. Cursed one way or another. Look at me.

“Nifty weapon, the eye,” Will said.

And we both laughed.

And like that, ahead of us, in the fog, a great light shone, and a young woman, with a young boy child pressed against her side, leaned out and called, “Will, where have you been?”

Time is flexible and strange where it intersects with Imago. Time, I’m told is a function of the human mind.

Nan was older than Will, their children grown – their daughters, the son they had lost – when he died. And she presumably followed after. But I had no doubt I was looking at his heaven. That was Nan and Hamnet and I doubted me not the kitchen would have fresh baked bread and wholesome home brewed ale, and a cozy fire.

"I am home," he said, and his eyes sparkled again with the love and life I remembered. "I am home, Kit. And you're welcome in."

"Ah. Not yet my friend." Perhaps never. I was too good for hell, too ill for heaven, and perfect to solve the passion crimes between humans and their muses. Someone has to be on the side of humans.

He clasped my shoulder. That contact somehow was more than I'd ever got from ever so skilled a doxy, ever so willing a honey.

What sense does it make, except that I had only one friend, only one person allowed past the hard shell in which I'd encased myself to avoid breaking?

"When you are ready," he said. "Remember you're always welcome with us." And then he turned and walked into the house. Nan gave me a lingering look before closing the door. And she was Nan, yet no muse.

The other Nan was waiting, out by the cab, which turned to be ahead of me, in the fog. Don't explain it. Directions make no sense in the hells.

We rode back in silence. I presume she paid the drachma.

Back in Noir, under the spider web-lights haloed in rain, she said, "You know, I am minus a client, and you are still a poet."

I laughed and kissed her, a hard kiss on those perfect lips. "I was a poet. Now a muse. But mostly a gumshoe."

She gave me a dubious appraising look, and for a moment I thought she was going to ask about Will. But she didn't and we parted on good terms.

I walked under the rain to the corner bar, just in time to grab a sandwich. Beef on rye and a passable beer.

Sooner or later Pinky and Baltazar would show up, or another of the fellows for a round of poker. Muses sucked at poker, and it paid the rent.

And sooner or later another case would show up. I hadn't even gotten paid, but it didn't matter.

The reckoning was finally done. Will to his reward, and I to mine. I was at peace.

Men have died and the worms have eaten them. But not for love. For love, it's better to live.

WRITING HORSE'S HEART

WHEN I WAS A young writer, knee-high to an ink blot – or if you prefer, 28 years old, when dinosaurs roamed the Earth and mammals were thought-forms with no physical existence, after older son was born, I had written eight novels set in Elly (the world of *No Man's Land*) and tried to submit them to uniform rejections. (They would be deep prequels to that world, if I rewrote them now, set around 500 years before in the historical time referred to as "The war of the magicians."The last rejection informed me the editor thought the book was well written, but she hated the world, the characters and the plot. This, you could say, is when I cracked. I realized for the first time it was not my skill but the story itself. And I didn't know how to change the story so people would accept it/read it. It was too long and too confusing. There was too much world. (This year, mumble mumble decades later, I published the re-written first novel, in three volumes as an indie work. There might have been no way to modify it so trad pub would swallow it.)

But... well, it was the first of many *Annus horribilis* that appear to randomly fall into my life. The particular *Annus horriblis* started when our new son for whom we'd waited six years (infertility is like that) was born and I found out husband hadn't been paid by the startup he was working for – so he could work from home and look after me while I had pre-eclampsia – for six months. We'd been paying our Visa with our Mastercard. Of course he quit but there were no jobs to be had. And when he found a job it was in Columbia, South Carolina, where the house we could afford to rent had no air conditioning. Also, I was still recovering from pre-eclampsia and my mind wasn't right.Also (mumbles) it's entirely possible I'm a little weird.So I wrote this entire fantasy novel about spirit-aliens who attach to certain humans and give them magical powers. Those humans have to perform animal sacrifice to feed the creatures. And it's all set in a proto-Greek reality (which is a parallel world, as you'll find if I ever write the novel.)Again, the novel kept getting rejected, and I couldn't figure out why until I read the opening with a horse sacrifice, at a conference, and an entire amphitheater of 100 plus people stared at me in horror. "Why are they killing the horse?"And so into the drawer the novel went (It also was 600 thousand words long, so.... Chances of its selling were always low.) until it was bothering me enough that I had to write this short story.There will be a novel.... Eventually.

Oh, yes, additional funny: after that novel my husband (and later the kids, who learned it from him,) referred to my beloved Denver, Colorado as "Denre by the sea." Because all three of them are deranged, that's why.

Horse's Heart

Horse and Bull save us from night everlasting and ice eternal.

From ice, night, and nothingness, Horse was spun, and Horse's hooves ignited the stars. From the fire in Horse's heart Bull was born, and in the plenitude of his might, Bull gored Horse. From Horse's blood gods were created, from Horse's life gods drew their power, and in the fullness of time, the gods killed Bull. From Bull's blood men were born, and from Bull's spirit fyhis was given them.

Life from death. Death from life. The goddesses of each are twins, never parted.

The stranger came into Denre on a windy, wintry afternoon, with the dark grey clouds above rent and driven by an angry wind. The sun that now and then pierced through had a drowned quality, that made the scene look like something misremembered, something lost in the mists of time and never fully captured in painting or poem or ballad.

The city, as he saw it from the beach, standing next to the pounding grey-green waves, had that quality too: the steep-roofed buildings overtopping the stone wall bleached by encroaching salt.

As he looked, for a moment, the sun gilded the roof of the Lord's house, and a smile twisted the man's lips in something not at all denoting of pleasure. "Denre beloved of Horse," he said, as though reciting something learned in childhood. "Sweet Denre by the the Sea."

Where he stood, he could have chosen to take the gently curving path from the beach up to the city's main gates: the way taken by merchants and visitors who arrived by sea. He looked at it a long while, but then continued, instead, by the sea shore, his bare feet digging into the cold, wet s and.

To be fair, he did not look like the kind of man who should enter a city – no matter how prosperous or how poor – by the main gate. Though he held his sandals in his hand, they were the kind any fisherman might wear. And though a cloak draped around his head and shoulders, falling in negligent folds to his ankles, it was a dark and dingy garment, rent at the bottom in a way that denoted much wear or hard times.

Had anyone been watching, they might have been struck by the fact that though he moved like an old man, his face, now and then semi-uncovered by the wind was that of a young man, either in his thirties, or in his twenties, if he'd lived a hard life.

He stopped where there were marks of boats that had rested on the sand and been pushed out to sea, and shaded his eyes with his free hand, looking out at the water, as though wondering who'd take sail boats out in such weather.

Then he continued walking, till he came to the rough steps carved up the side of the cliff. They'd been there from time immemorial and had once admitted menials to the confines of Denre House. Since the fall of the family, they were used by peddlers and low-status visitors to enter the city without going via the main gates and inviting question about their business and why they were there.

Judging by his clothing and the labored, slow way the man climbed, it was entirely possible that he had come to Denre to become a beggar. Which meant that had any inhabitant seen him, he'd likely have laughed and said good luck finding a stray crumb of bread in Denre these days.

But there was no one at all on the beach, or the stairs, or even keeping token guard on the arched opening in the walls above.

So he walked up the steps unmolested. When he was halfway up, rain erupted out of nowhere, wind driven, lashing at him and soaking his wrap.

The Temple of Horse had seen better days. It had once been the centerpiece of the city of Denre, back when the House of Denre had been the second in the kingdom of Areva, its Lord important and revered, and the town itself a center of trade with Susapeta.

A vast building of stone covered with a facing of marble, it boasted a colonnaded portico, which led to a sacrificial chamber also covered in marble and ornamented in polished brass. The altar was vast, circular, and set on a raised area, up a set of steps.

None of it had collapsed, and there was nothing at all a casual visitor could have pointed at to indicate disrepair or neglect. It was more like the people who were supposed to shine the brasses and scrub the marble had vanished. Also the braziers burning around the altar must have been fed with inferior fuel, as their flames wavered and flickered, more blue than bright.

The two priests and one acolyte laboring at the altar looked like they'd seen better days. The men were too gaunt, their hair white, and the boy was too thin, looking nervy, his black hair caught back in a straggly pony tail, his tunic much mended and in dire need of a wash.

As for the colt lying on the altar, two problems would strike anyone familiar with the rites of Horse. The first was that the animal wasn't flawless, but a scrawny creature, looking like it had some disease of the skin. And the second was that they had drugged the animal. This was obvious by the way it lay sideways on the marble altar, unable even to lift its head, though it attempted several times.

Even so, they had tied its forelegs and back legs with sturdy ropes, and the older man, the principal priest of Horse, Akakis, kept saying "mind the legs" to the acolyte as, his own hands trembling, he poured the sweet wine over the stone blade.

A poor sacrifice, and he knew it too, this wild colt, caught outside the city, without its dam. It would probably have died anyway, without being dragged to the temple for sacrifice.

The year had been too wet, too cold, the harvest too late, and the wild grasses upon which the wild horses fed had barely started to sprout when they had died, yellowing on the field, and turning rank and spongy. The wild horses were starving, and either the mare had abandoned her foal to save her own life, or the colt was one of twins, and abandoned as it couldn't be supported in such cold year.

It mattered not. Akakis knew only that the foal had life. Uncertain, vacillating light, like the sacred fire in the bronze receptacles, but life nevertheless and much needed to bolster the power of his failing fyhis. Their failing fyhis, he corrected. They must make sure all their fyhis were fed before the battle that was to come.

He closed his eyes, trying to still the trembling in his arms and hands, as the hunger of his symbiont communicated itself along his arms, demanding, craving food.

Go too long without feeding and the fyhis started feeding on the host, creating wraiths. Which was part of the reason they were in the fix they were. All those noblemen cast down, exiled, pushed away from any chance to feed their fyhis. All the men that the mad king had sent from their lands—

He didn't want to think of them, though they'd been sighted by the patrols of boatmen sailing too close to the coast, trying to spy the oncoming threat. Kyrva... No, he wouldn't say of Denre, not even in his own thoughts. Kyrva might be the old Lord's son, but he'd been left behind, raised as one of the urchins of the village by his old nursemaid. And he was an invaluable scout, fearless. *Possessed of a laughing demon,* his nursemaid and adoptive mother said, but it was no demon. It was simply that he was much what the old Lord had been before the king's edicts. He was also, probably, should the new king restore the rights of the dispossessed, the Lord of Denre. The oldest boy, Telbar, had been sold into slavery, and though they'd sent scouts the length of Areva they'd never found him. There was a good chance he was dead. A slave that harbored fyhis was a liability for the host.

The other boy—Akakis opened his eyes briefly, to look at the acolyte, and whisper, "Teryon, mind the legs."

He recalled the message again that Kyrva ... not of Denre had sent, loud and clear, mind to mind, an extravagant waste of fyhis power in these lean times, *There is an army of wraiths descending on Denre. They're being sent forth by the Susapetans to destroy us. To take us, so they can take the land with no battle.*

An army of wraiths. If it were an army of mortal men, they'd fight with spears. Even if they had scant warriors and the fishermen had been too hard pressed fishing to defend the walls. But an army of wraiths must be fought with fyhis. He lifted his knife even higher, and said, quickly, "May Horse accept the life, and return it."

The knife of polished obsidian flashed in the insufficient light and slashed at the Horse's throat. The animal made a weak sound, not quite a whinny, and then—

With his fyhis sight, Akakis could see the uncertain light of the colt's life-force flare above the body, then break free. And he could feel his own fyhis in its normal form, like a tiger made of blue light, reach for it with claw and tooth. He was just telling himself that he must share, he must let the other two—

His hesitation and control delayed his fyhis a few seconds. Which was a few seconds too much. A famished fyhis leapt on the altar, his form visible only to those who also bore fyhis symbionts, but since those were all the three present, there was a scream of consternation from the two priests and devotee as the lean, vacillating fyhis reached with sharp claws for the life.... And took it.

For a second, for just a second, Akakis raised the knife, bristling with anger, and traced the pale link of light between the fyhis and his symbiont.

He'd have sworn they were alone in the temple, he and his brother priest Myriar, and the boy Teryon. But now he saw there was a man well at the back, knitting himself with the shadow of the wall. The man was almost-ragged, dressed as a beggar or a supplicant.

Akakis's voice trembled with frustration and hunger – and where they'd find another horse to sacrifice, he didn't know – as he said, "You, the stranger! You, fyhis thief! Who are you, and by what right do you steal that which is Horse's."

The man had collected the fyhis to himself. The beast was now invisible, but there was something like an outline around the stranger, enough to see that despite his clothes he was well built. And as he stepped forward – though anyone who had seen him earlier would be surprised at the sureness of his step – there was something familiar to his movement.

He pulled down the hood of his cloak, revealing dark, wavy hair pulled back, and the eyes he lifted to the priest were dark intense blue and almond-shaped, a distinctive shape he was used to seeing in the tapestries and frescoes moldering in the house of the Denre Lords.

Of course, it meant nothing. That hair and those eyes which were so distinctive of the house of Denre had been passed, over the three thousand years of the family's hold on the region, to many a byblow. You could see them in many a vendor in the market stalls on trade day, which explained how they'd managed to hide Kyrva so neatly of course.

But all the same Akakis's voice had a less accusatory tone as he repeated, "Who are you?"

The man cleared his throat, and the first two words came out hoarse, as though he'd been unused to speaking, "I am," he said. and then his voice gathered strength as he added, "Telbar of the house of Denre, the house of Horse. None are more entitled to the fyhis force than I."

At this Teryon made a strangled sound and spun around. And in that minute, Akakis, who was ready to ask for proof, to demand that the man show a sign of his ancestry, of his legitimacy, and that he was in fact the lost heir, was caught by the similarity in the two faces: Teryon, barely fourteen, a downy hair just coming in on lip and chin, and this man, mature and fully formed, his face tanned by the elements. But the nose was the same, and the lips, and the eyes that dropped at the corner.

The sad Denre eyes, grieving for Horse himself.

Akakis was suddenly shaking with something more than his fyhis hunger. He still didn't know where they'd find the way to feed himself or the boy or Myriar, not to mention Kyrva. As the only fyhis-bearing men in Denre, they must be fed so they could defend the city.

"My fyhis was barely restrained from devouring me. I thank you for the life," Telbar said, evenly.

Caught between ancestral respect and confusion, Akakis bowed, quickly, almost reluctantly, but disciplined his voice to say, "I am glad that we have-- I'm glad you've not become a wraith, but we are facing an army of wraiths headed this way. And we have no one to combat them, except.... Except you, and I don't think."

"I know," Telbar said.

"But but... milord you are proscribed. You are denied entry to the city. All of your name were barred from Denre by King Dracar and I-- None of us... Our feeding your fyhis, though unintended is a crime against Areva and its kings."

Those very blue eyes looked back at him unperturbed, the urbane voice said once more, "I know." And then with a flickering look at Teryon, who looked as though he'd been poleaxed and remained, mouth partly open, staring. "And yet, you have my brother, and you have not turned him out."

The priest opened his mouth, intending to claim he didn't know who the youth who was his acolyte might have been or what his parentage, but the stranger chuckled, a deep chuckle in his throat. "Do not worry. Dracar is deposed in Areva. His nephew Tuoranel reigns in his place, and he's my comrade at arms. It is by his order that I am here, to resume my house and my family and leadership of Denre. I am here to hold the frontier against Susapeta and against the wraiths."

"Well!" the priest said, "And how do we know—"

In that moment, the stranger's mind touched his, impelled by their fyhis. In his mind, clear as day, he saw a youth, not a stripling, but probably not twenty yet, standing in front of the gilded throne of Areva and giving clear orders for "Telbar, Lord of Denre" to have this and to hold that, and to "guard our border."

The vision was so clear the priest almost bowed to the crown-bearing brown haired figure. In fact, as his liege-lord's power withdrew, he was still wide eyed, holding his breath, struggling to bring himself under control. When he managed words it was to say, "Milord, I don't know if you realize what you are saying. Of all the men and women of Areva, all those who were fyhis bearing, your uncles, your great uncles, your cousins, were expelled with your father. If their bodies live still, they are likely part of that army of wraiths bearing down on us. There is only the three of us and you milord and... and Lord Kyrva." He saw the man smile at the name. "I do not know how we can hold the wraiths back, much less the Susapetans behind them when they come."

The man smiled. For a moment there was in his expression something of Kyrva's laughing demon, but also something of his father, Lord Euridir of Denre as he was, a haughty lifting of the eyebrows, a certainty in the eyes. "You know very well how to solve all this Akakis. And you must do it."

"Milord! It will be no use without the ring."

But the man moved his hand from under the fold of his cloak and held it up, showing the darkened gold circlet and the blood red stone on it. It was a ruby, Akakis supposed. Or at least he had always supposed before, but the legends called it the blood of Horse and said that when Horse had taken human form to sire his son, the first Lord of Denre, he'd left the ring with his concubine to give to the boy.

That was as it might be. Before these disturbed times, Akakis, though he believed in Horse as a metaphor, and knew, of course, that the fyhis which was Horse's gift to mankind, allowed those who bore it to perform miracles, from teleportation to communication mind to mind, from shielding to causing explosions. But secretly he had always thought all that talk of gods coming down to mingle with mortal women and of the House of Denre being descended from the god of life himself was all very well, and no doubt worked as propaganda for Denre. But really. It couldn't be believed by any rational man, could it?

Now he wasn't so sure. But he was sure of one thing. "The ring was on your father's finger when he was dragged out of the town by the king's forces, after your lady mother was... after she was killed." He remembered what had happened before the killing, and the screaming of the beautiful, noble lady before they'd given her mercy. And probably so did the newcomer. Teryon remembered nothing, and Kyrva might or might not remember, but this man had been twelve. He must have heard and known what it meant.

If he did he gave no sign. He looked, perhaps, a little colder, a little more distant. "My father gave me the ring," he said.

And at that moment Akakis realized that boys of twelve sold as slaves into the court of Areva probably knew all too well what such screams meant. He had heard of what went on in Areva, and that was before the king had decided to consolidate his power over the land and destroy all the old houses. And then what the man had said reached him, and he said, almost weak with relief, "Lord Euridir lives? He is—"

Telbar shook his head. "No. Lord Euridir does not live. He is, as you surmised, a wraith."

A moment of unease and confusion and Akakis said, "Milord, are you saying that your father's wraith...."

"Yes, that is precisely what I am saying. Now, will you give it me or not?"

Akakis hesitated. Teryon, who'd been silent till then said, in a voice that was more breath than words, "Sir, sir, we must—"

Akakis could sense in Teryon that if he were not to accede, Teryon would. Not that he blamed Teryon. Sure. They had raised the boy as though he had been a foundling, left at the temple, but someone had told him the truth. Denre was a small town, and had been a fiefdom of the same family from the beginning. Or close to the beginning. *Before the stars were fully ignited, Denre was Horse's.*

Still he wasn't sure. If the ring had come from the wraith, what was this man? No fyhis-bearer could come too close to a wraith and not have his own fyhis devoured by the soulless man and becoming a wraith like him.

"I was one," Telbar said. His voice sounded almost hollow, distant, as though he were trying to remember something in the distant past, something that didn't quite make sense.

"One?"

"A wraith," he said. "But when the ring was given me, I...." He passed a hand across his forehead. "My fyhis recovered. I don't know how. I just know it recovered, and then I found my way here, ahead of them. They—They ask only mercy. They wish to be defeated. If we can do it."

"If I give you Horse?"

Telbar laughed. It was a strange sound, because he did not look at all amused or pleased. "Even with Horse," he said. "It will be difficult. The-- It will be difficult. There are many of them. Which is why you must give me Horse now. Right away. Because it's not just fyhis that must be fed. What I've seen of Denre tells me its people are starving. The battle will take everything we have. Everything. And we have only a few hours."

Akakis blinked, as though wakening. There was that. In a few hours the wraiths would be here. And as things stood no one would survive in the town. It would be ten thousand souls destroyed, devoured. Those who had no fyhis would be corpses, those who had fyhis would become more wraiths, to join the wandering army and attack the next town, and the next, as Susapeta swept behind them, their Lords well protected by their own fyhis shield, to take it all, till Areva itself was taken, and every last one of the subjects of the once proud Arevan confederation destroyed.

What did it matter if he gave the sacred pendant to this man, who was probably Telbar of Denre but who might not be sane – because what man would claim to have been a wraith and have returned from that place that was worse than death unscathed? – to attempt to set things to right before the attack.

What was the worst he could do to the people of Denre? Kill them? Make them wraiths? Well, that was going to happen anyway.

Akakis turned, faint with hunger, shaking with the hunger of his fyhis.

In time immemorial – the legend said – when Horse himself had given the mother of his child the ring ornamented with his blood, he'd given the temple he'd established in Denre the carved medallion of his likeness.

The ring passed to the oldest son of the house, usually named Telbar. But the blessing of the temple was necessary for the son to become the true Lord of Denre. And only the true Lord of Denre could command the seas and the land here around, and ensure the nets were full, and that the trees bore fruit. And that wild horses of the right kind were available for the sacrifice.

He looked at what remained of the poor, abandoned colt, and almost absently, stroked its matted head.

Then he stepped away, around the altar. The pendant of horse always returned to the temple when the Lord died or lost his power. It was something he'd always thought was a long-set spell created by some old priest's fyhis.

Now he went to the place where the pendant had been, these sixteen years, in a niche in the wall, protected by a heavy stone lid, which took the fyhis of the principal priest of horse to open.

His fyhis was so weakened that for a moment Akakis thought he'd not make it. Then he reached with hands, as well as with fyhis, one assisting the other, and the box slid open.

The pendant was ancient, very ancient, of ivory turned almost golden with age. And for its age, it was carved with immense care and exactness, a depiction of Horse's head, the mane flying, the eyes, suggested in carving, seeming alive. It hung upon a leather cord.

Holding it in his cupped hands, Akakis walked back. He did bow when extending it.

And in the next minute, he had to catch his breath and remind himself that there were no miracles.

As Telbar of Denre took the pendant and tied the thin leather strap around his neck, something like a light flew from ring to pendant and from pendant to ring, and it seemed to him that Telbar grew stronger, straightened, and that the voice in which he said, "Send men to the North Entrance. There will be horses. Bring them here," sounded like his father's voice when he gave orders.

He sounded more normal as he said, "I don't suppose we can open my house? I need clothes. And I would love a bath."

It was that reassurance of normalcy and humanity that made Akakis fear less for what he had done.

The house of Denre wasn't a ruin, which had shocked Telbar. It meant that villagers had come in there, covertly, in secret, and frankly at risk of their own lives, while the family was gone and proscribed. But then the people of Denre had housed and hid his brothers. That he and his sister had been sold into slavery, and all the rest that had happened couldn't be held against them. He knew how the emissaries of the king had held everyone in fyhis thrall, even the priests and noblemen. There was nothing servants or merchants, farmers or fishermen, no matter how loyal could have done.

But the people of Denre came back, behind him, as he went from room to room of the abandoned house, avoiding only his mother's room, because he remembered. He'd not seen anything, but he remembered. The screams, the smell of blood. The rooms would have to be cleaned and set to rights, if they'd not been yet, but not until he married. If he married. If he survived today.

What he'd told Akakis was the truth. The ring and the pendant would allow him to feed his people, both body and fyhis, but he knew the hunger of the wraiths, and how many there were. How many able bodied men remained in Denre? And how could they fight?

Somehow, without his giving any orders, his servants – or he supposed the descendants of his father's servants – had come in, led him to the master's room, filled a bathtub in the adjoining bathing room, laid out a fine, if everyday and ornamented tunic which must have been his father's.

For a moment, for just a moment, Telbar felt tears prickle behind his eyes, realizing that his people had been starving, and yet they'd not looted his house nor sold even the possessions of a family they presumed as good as gone. He suspected, should he look for them, all the jewels would still be in the strong house. Devotion like that wasn't rational. But it did move h im.

By the time a young man came running into the Lord's room, Telbar was dressed, shaved, his hair oiled, his tunic falling gracefully around the sturdy leather belt.

The young man was red-headed and green eyed, and his features reminded Telbar of his sister, Phillida, whom he'd left in the court of Areva. "Kyrva?" he said, half laughing, despite the sting in his eyes. Kyrva had been six, a laughing child, who used to follow him around and imitate everything Telbar did. Now he was a man, sturdy, with overgrown red hair and a beard. But the eyes were the same. He wore a much mended tunic, folded on the top in such a way that it left the right arm free, in the manner of fishermen. He also wore sturdy sandals, and his calves were white with salt. He and Teryon had been out of Denre with their nurse when the royal troops, all fyhis-bearers had come. Telbar never knew if they had escaped. Ti ll now.

The green eyes looking into his filled with tears, even as the mouth opened in a smile. "Telbar. By Horse's mane. Telbar! We thought you dead."

Telbar smiled, "Sometimes I thought myself dead." He did not add that sometimes he wished he'd been, until he'd been sold to a humble potter and his wife, who'd freed him and raised him as their own unaware of what had come into their house. And even after, when a raid had killed his foster parents, and he'd found himself in Susapetan hands. It turned out Susapetan princelings didn't treat their slaves better than Arevan courtiers. Only differently. Someday he might tell Kyrva or he might not. Someday he might tell him how Phillida had found him. How Phillida had conspired with the nephew of the king to depose the tainted regime from the throne of Areva.

But not now. Now he must call food and horses. "Go to the men, the—the fishermen and tell them put to sea. There will be fish. Then return. I will hold off the sacrifice till you do."

In the end, there was not enough space to feed the people – and they looked just as ragged and weak as he had thought – and they'd laid the tables out in the market place, as fish roasted. And horses, too, once the fyhis had fed on their life force.

He'd not let them serve wine. "No, there will be time for celebration, later. Now the wraiths."

The wraiths were a ragged army, but they were many, and their smell and the sense of their hunger traveled ahead of them like a cloud.

The smell came from their being unwashed. These creatures who had been humans never bathed. They lived on what they could find. Telbar had seen them fall upon a flock of sheep in a field, while the shepherd ran away.

Telbar shuddered. He did not remember what he'd done, nor who he'd been while with the wraiths. While he was a wraith. His time hadn't been long, as he'd tracked it afterwards. Only a few days. But he was glad he didn't remember roaming the country side, his mind empty, his soul lost.

He still didn't understand the miracle that had called him back.

He'd woken, like a child wakes in a strange place, surrounded by wraiths, with a large one keeping all others away.

It had taken some effort to remember the face of this wraith as that of the father he'd lost so many years ago. His father's wraith had kept all wraiths away and held something out to him, glistening red in the sullen moonlight: the ring that contained Horse's blood.

On the ramparts, having ordered the doors closed and barricaded with barrels and the remains of the tables, Telbar paced. He wanted to lead a group against the wraiths. No. He wanted to lead a group against the Susapetans who drove them. But though he'd dressed in his father's armor—light sheets of metal with leather sandwiched between, molding to arms and legs and chest and hips, the rest of the men were poorly protected. And they were even more poorly trained.

Kyrva, he thought, had some idea of how to fight, and Teryon might have. Their father's erstwhile master of arms, now a humble shepherd, had nonetheless seen that the sons of the Lord had some training.

But it was still not enough. And besides Telbar bore the ring and the pendant of Horse. Perhaps they would fall to Kyrva, if Telbar died, but he couldn't be sure. After all, the king had a choice as to the ring, and the priests of Horse as to the pendant.

Though one or the other might incline to Kyrva, if Areva were in turmoil and invaded, who could tell? And only the Lord in possession of the two could command the wild horses, and only he could – at least at times – call the fish to these increasingly frigid shores.

Barred from fighting, though carrying a sword against any invader who might get in, Telbar had armed his people, but more importantly, he and Kyrva and Teryon, and the remaining priests of Horse had built a blue wall of energy with their recently fed fyhis. The wraiths could not penetrate it. Though as Susapeta pushed behind they had to go somewhere.

At first they milled, between the two living walls of power, not moving, then little by little, they started.... Disappearing.

On the walls, Telbar felt Kyrva come up behind him. "What is happening?" he asked, wild-eyed. "What is happening to the wraiths?"

"I don't know," Telbar said. "I think it's Father."

"Our Father?"

"Yes, he is a wraith but an unusual one. I'd fallen-- I cannot explain it to you, but I'd become one of them. And then I met Father. He retains his memory, though he's a wraith. Might have been the ring that kept him, all that time... He lifted his hand. He gave it to me, and with it, my fyhis returned to me, and I was whole. I walked here...." He paused. "I don't know what he's doing, but I think it is him. See that figure that moves amid the wraiths? I think that's him."

"It was so long ago. I barely remember. Telbar, why did the king of Areva... How....?"

"Human sacrifice. It gives power, such as even horses don't give. They were gorging on it. The noblemen tried to rebel, but... They were put down by the superior human-fed fyhis of the king and his courtiers. Our father and others were sent to exile, barred from feeding their fyhis till they became wraiths."

"But Tuoranel of Areva managed to rebel? I heard he's the new king."

"It's a complicated story. One Phillida will tell you if we win, when we go to Areva. Which I think we must do, because I believe Tuoranel means to marry her."

"Oh." Kyrva paused. "If we win? Look, the wraiths are vanishing."

"Yes, but behind it comes the Susapetan army. How long do you think we can survive in here, without being able to send out the boats for fish."

"Oh."

Kyrva watched as the wraiths disappeared. The Susapetan army was behind them. They'd meet shield to shield, and even from a distance, Telbar could tell, and knew Kyrva could tell that the Susapetan shield was stronger. "I don't even know, Telbar said, "That we can hold off their shield. They might break through and slaughter us all."

"Do they also use human sacrifice?"

"I don't believe so. At least I never saw it when—" He stopped as that was neither the time nor the place. "But there are just too many of them."

The roar of the Susapetans was now audible, deafeningly louder, louder than the sound of the sea.

"Telba!" Kyrva said, calling Telbar by his childhood nickname. "I have an idea."

Telbar looked. Kyrva's eyes danced with mirth. "We have some goats." And impatiently, to Telbar's blank look, "I can rig poles and lanterns to their horns. I say the goats, because we don't have that many cows and also it would be harder to take them down the steps to the beach."

"Why would you take the goats to the beach?"

"We shall take the goats out now, before the sun rises. In the dark, it will look like some of us – perhaps the most important among us – are escaping. If you can thin the shield a little, to appear like the fyhis-bearers are leaving? The Susapetans can take the path up the cliff and lay siege to the city. Or, if they think all left behind will be defenseless if they—"

"Go to the beach and capture the fyhis-bearers and those who might be of use to the king of Areva, and command ransoms? They will take the path around instead. It doesn't matter, they'll think they can always come up here afterwards and take the city. And they'll be on the beach, and defenseless."

"Yes."

"But Kyrva, can you return?"

"Oh, I'll return."

"Not as a wraith?"

The green eyes laughed at him. "I'll do my best, my lord Denre."

And he'd left, calling to him some of the fisher boys, his foster brothers.

Moments later, the goats moved down, the lights on their horns making a bright spectacle on the sand, approaching the boats.

The Susapetan shield broke, as their fyhis-bearers rushed to the beach, to capture hostages.

And while the best and bravest of the fighters, led by Teryon, who showed his age was nothing to his bravery, went the other way, from the high side, separating them from their army, and laying into them in the darkness, with shield and lance and sword, and whatever implement the locals could lay hands to, Telbar and Akakis and the other priest joined their fyhis.

It was difficult work, and unpleasant, to send the fyhis out as a killing power, a ravening beast of energy that burned everything in its path.

There were screams of men and horses till the field was a vast abattoir, a place of bones and horror.

The smell of their death rose to the sky, and it would be so easy, Telbar thought, so easy to avail yourself of their life form. He wondered if that was how the former king of Areva had fallen, after a battle.

But then he heard in his mind, as Kyrva called, "Telbar, Telbar, help."

He heard frantic urgency in the call.

He followed the message blindly, forgetting his temptation. And yet in the following of the request there was another temptation, another thing he should not be doing. The Lord of Denre should not throw himself into the fight and risk dying. He should not...

Before he could help himself he was running down the steps, as he had when he was a boy, the son of the house, running down the steps to see the fishermen pull in the catch, or, on rare occasions, his father return from Areva, sitting very straight on a much better boat, his cloak pulled around his broad shoulders, against the wind from the sea.

There was a trick to running down the use-polished, fine sand covered steps.

Impossible not to slip, but there was a way of catching the slip before it became disastrous, and righting yourself, then slipping again, then catching yourself once more, so that you arrived at the beach with a slide upon the sand, and then righted yourself too.

Falling into the instinctive rhythm, Telbar had the fleeting thought that he must look like a child running to play.

But on the beach below, the smell of blood hit him, coppery and sharp.

Men moved around in the semi-darkness upon which the light of the goat's lanterns served only to cast horrendous shadows.

The party of Denre was victorious, that was easy to see. He recognized the profiles of Teryon and his companions, fighting, seeming unarmed, while the foes being slashed and falling wore the blunt helmets the Susapetans favored.

Teryon must have used his fyhis to disguise them until it was too late and fallen upon the Susapetans before they were detected.

A frantic look around, and then he recognized Kyrva's silhouette, out by the boats. There, by the light of an errant lantern on the horns of a bleating goat, Kyrva fought two opponents.

One of them would be Kyrva's size and probably his age, but the other was a giant of a man, with pale hair illuminated by moonlight.

That glimpse sent a chill into Telbar's blood. In a moment, he saw his adoptive parents' home blazing, taking what remained of them and their possessions, while he was chained at the back of a slave hunter's train.

This... man, the Susapetan prince Salahan had come deep into Arevan territory, with an armed escort and taken peasants and potters, mothers and maidens. He'd chained them together and made them walk, over frozen ground and slick, to the slave market in Susapeta.

Telbar? Telbar he'd kept for himself, amused at the idea of a slave with fyhis. He'd kept Telbar's fyhis starved, and for a crumb made him beg and perform. He'd made Telbar serve at table, and clean the stables, and anything that occurred to him. Fortunately he lacked the imagination and the inclinations of the Arevans, but making one perform for the necessary bite of the life energy to keep from turning a wraith was the same, no matter what the performance was.

For three years Telbar had served, before finding the opportunity and despair to run into the night. To risk becoming a wraith.

And now here stood the man who had made him beg, who'd made the Lord of Denre behave like a slave indeed. And he was threatening Kyrva.

Telbar might have tried to scream the princeling's name, but what came out was an incoherent scream of rage.

Salahan turned, nonetheless, leaving Kyrva still fully occupied in fighting the younger opponent, but maybe, Telbar thought, with that part of his mind that could still think, this would allow him to win free.

For a moment Salahan looked surprised, then when Telbar lifted the sword to strike, he fell into form, interposing his shield, with the figure of the lion upon it.

Telbar's sword rang upon the shield like a bell tolling.

And then Salahan laughed, "Why, if it isn't the potter's brat," he said. "The slave boy." Salahan made a swipe with his sword at Telbar, a lazy one, probably thinking him wholly untrained. Telbar was not a novice, but he was out of practice. In his ramblings, it had been long since anyone had brought to mind the careful lessons his father had taught him.

He was a second too late in parrying, but he did parry, cursing under his breath that he had not provided himself with a shield, such as Salahan wore.

"So you stole armor and got some sword lessons," Salahan grinned.

Telbar wanted to tell him that he was born to this, and that at least he, Telbar of Denre, had never gone after defenseless young men, already being attacked by someone else. For that matter, he'd also not killed peasants, or raided their simple houses, or taken their offspring captive.

What he said instead was a word, the single word that rose to his tongue in Susapetan: Derir. *Coward*, just that, spit out like a curse. And *coward* served.

In the moment of uttering the word, and knowing what it meant, in the moment between roar of rage and calming, he realized that if he had continued charging, in that insensate, irate way, he would have been killed. Instead, he had made Salahan angry.

The Susapetan roared like a charging bull and came at Telbar.

Once, in Susapeta, he'd put Telbar in a field with a wild bull, and given Telbar only a dagger, telling him that if he wanted to feed his fyhis, he'd have to do it the hard way.

There had been guests, other Susapetans, dressed in silks, resplendent with gold jewelry, sipping wine from jeweled goblets around the low stone wall that separated the space where the bull was kept from them.

Telbar had gone in. And for a while all he did was dodge the bull, while the spectators applauded and laughed. He had been sure, too, that they were applauding the bull.

Until the bull had charged him and, desperate, Telbar had suddenly ducked low, while raising his dagger-bearing arm.

Now, as Salahan charged, Telbar shifted his weight to his back foot, giving the impression that he was going to run. Salahan was an experienced fighter. He must have noticed the movement without even realizing it.

He leapt towards Telbar, sword lifted to split the skull of the Denran.

Only Telbar was not there. He ducked, and came up, beneath the lion shield, his sword aimed.

Partly his movement, and partly the descending of Salahan's body as his jump ended, impaled the prince of Susapeta upon the heavy sword.

The moment seemed to last forever: Salahan's eyes widening in shocked surprise. His sword arm flaying out one final time, and missing Telbar, or mostly missing him. And the sudden, hot spurt of blood coating Telbar's inherited armor.

It must have been only a second, perhaps less, because Telbar pulled his sword free, and jumped aside before the heavy body of the giant from Susapeta fell on the sand.

Around him, the other fights seemed to have ended. He looked around, searching for Kyrva. The Susapetan who had attacked Kyrva lay dead between Telbar and where Kyrva had been. But it was hard to see. There was sweat running into Telbar's eyes, and the goats moved around making the scene seem to change, even when it did not.

In the play of light and shadow, he was sure the place Kyrva had been was empty, and he knew fear for his brother.

And then.... By the boats he saw two silhouettes, barely visible, dark against the darker night. Kyrva. And the wraith that had once been the Lord of Denre.

Clutching his sword, Telbar ran through the melee on the beach, absently striking at a Susapetan who slashed at him, running, to the place of quiet, near the boats, where Kyrva and his father faced each other.

As he approached the creature who had been Lord of Denre turned to face him. It was a horrible sight to behold, caked with the dirt of years, his eyes vacant, his mouth moving soundlessly.

"He came to me," Kyrva said, in a rush. "He tried to touch me."

Telbar grasped his sword, but something in him said not to strike. Not yet. Perhaps it was a whisper from the ruby on his finger, the pendant on his breast. But he thought the thing needed reassurance. It needed peace.

"We've saved Denre, Father. It is safe. And I'm its Lord."

For a moment nothing happened. Then the lips stopped moving, and the blind eyes turned to him. Wraiths could not speak. But there was such pleading in what had once been the noble face of Lord Euridir of Denre, such a request.

Telbar lifted his bloodied sword and swept it in a simple arc.

There was a sound like a sigh. The head and the body of Euridir of Denre fell to the foaming waves, at the ocean's edge. Slowly, slowly, they dissolved and disappeared.

Above, a song of victory had broken out, and someone had lit a bonfire.

Teryon was up the stairs, leading his victorious party back home. They'd gotten the lanterns from the goats, which were climbing the steps on the cliff with them, and there was a festive air to their blood spattered tunics. He turned towards Kyrva and Telbar, and shouted, "May we have wine now, my Lord?"

Tired, and half laughing, though he felt tears salty and cold on his face, Telbar shouted back, "You can have what you very well please."

And then he looked up at his city, lit by fire, rescued by sword. "Sweet Denre by the sea," he said. "The city of Horse." It was a prayer.

WRITING DO NO HARM

IF YOU'VE READ THIS story in the first Black Tide anthology, Black Tide Rising, you'll be surprised it's longer here. Well, there is in fact a reason for that. And the reason is that 2015/16 were their very own slog through h*ll. We moved... five times in less than twelve months, in the process selling our home of thirteen years. One of our closest friends died of cancer. I also had major surgery. And there were other things, most of which I can't even remember anymore. But it was a very bad year.

In the middle of this, John Ringo invited me to the anthology at Liberty Con, in person. Afterwards the editor contacted me and asked my address for the contract.

In all this what no one told me is that the anthology was supposed to be ONLY the fall, not the recovery and the coming back. So when I turned in the story I was told they could only use the first half of it.

Ah well. Here's all of it now. (For the first time together and live!)

Thank you to Toni Weisskopf and John Ringo for allowing me to publish this in my collection.

Do No Harm

The String's Already Broken

Bethany realized she was watching the end of civilization when Dr. T. zombed out on her COW.

Yeah, she knew she wasn't supposed to call the second stage of the H7D3 virus *zombing out*, but that's what all the Emergency Room scribes had been calling it, since it had overwhelmed all the ready beds at the hospital and got a designation and everything.

For that matter, she wasn't supposed to call the Computer on Wheels a COW. Administration was very clear that it should be called WOW for Workstation On Wheels, but it was black and white and had four legs, and it was best not to get too attached to it, because sooner or later it would die on you. So everyone in ER called it a COW and Dr. T – because no one could quite figure out how to say Tomboulian – was one of the cool docs. A little green eyed porcelain doll with an infectious smile, she had attached longhorn horns to the front of her COW and a bell beneath the screen, and she ran around with it every shift doing most of her own data entry, which was cool from where Beth sat because it was one less thing landing on the overworked scribes, most of them pre-med students.

The scribes were paid for by the doctors out of pocket, and in return were supposed to handle all the crazy paperwork the bureaucrats dumped on the docs. Some scribes were trained to deal with only one doctor, and that seemed relatively simple, but Beth hadn't been able to promise she'd stay more than one year, and therefore couldn't take that training. So she was supposed to handle other doctors, and most doctors weren't so easy to deal with or so nice. Which is why Bethany was trying to take dictation on a patient disposition from Doctor Barfuss when Dr. T. zombed.

Dr. Barfuss had a bad habit of whispering to something other than the poor scribe following him around, and had just mumbled something about giving the patient hot sitz baths which couldn't be true for a case of pink eye, and was now whispering confidentially about – Beth would swear it – playing tiddlywinks, when Dr. T. yelled, "What is this? What is all over me?" and started ripping at her clothes.

Before Doctor T. started biting, there were two doctors and a patient on her, trying to hold her. The signs had become that well known. The bell around her COW's neck tinkled like mad as they tried to hold her, and she fought them, and her teeth started snapping at them, and Dr. Hayden yelled, as she got bit.

Dr. Nikhil Pillarisetti whom no one called Doctor P. because he'd say "psych, not urologist", must have been in ER for some psych eval because he yelled, "Hold on, now," in his Texas accent and plunged across groups of people, to hold Doctor T. in a headlock. He yelled calm orders to bring him restraints, and the next thing, Dr. T. was on a cart, her hands and feet bound to the railing and two people from transport were taking her away to be evaluated, not that anyone doubted what the diagnostic would be.

Beth tried not to look at Dr. T's face, as all personality and sense had gone from the doctor's eyes, and there was nothing there.

She had a strange sense something had broken, that something had left the doctor and it wasn't going to come back.

The world was coming to an end. Bethany couldn't say it had been wonderful before. Sure, life with Mom and Dad on the ranch had been pretty great, but the ranch being kind of far from civilization meant she'd never had that much of a social life.

And it turned out that wanting to be a doctor needed glib social skills. She'd volunteered at hospitals since Middle School and she really wanted to heal people. But the applications for medschools all wanted you to say how you'd overcome adversity, and how you had some story of hardship.

Just wanting to heal people and do no harm wasn't enough. Beth was starting to suspect she'd never get in when H7D3 hit. And now none of it would matter. She'd be a scribe until she caught it and then--

"Did you get the disposition for the patient?" Doctor Barfuss asked.

But Beth caught at the sleeve of Doctor Pillasiretti as he walked by. "Doctor?" She said. "Doctor T. is not going to be all right, is she?" And as Doctor Pillasiretti looked back his lips tight, she realized he'd understood "she's going to be all right?" and hastened to correct, "She's not coming back, is she?"

He opened his mouth, and closed it, shook his head, and walked away, while Doctor Barfuss insisted, "Ms. Arden, did you get that dispo?"

"No, I'm sorry, doctor, I couldn't hear through the noise," she said meekly, by habit avoiding mentioning that he dictated to the floor and his left sleeve, and sometimes his foot, but never to the poor scribe following him around.

He made a scathing sound at the back of his throat, and pushed his glasses up. He was a little, mostly bald man, who clearly thought he'd become a divinity the day he'd got his medical degree. There was a way he had of looking at people that gave them the impression he was looking down on them, even though for that he'd need a ladder. "The patient is to give his eye saline baths, or rinses, and put in the antibiotic drops, and observe proper hygiene in the future. And call us if anything changes for the worse."

She typed the notes quickly into her tablet, while an irreverent voice at the back of her head said, *Like it matters. He'll probably get his face eaten on the way home, pink eye and all. Why did Doctor T. have to zomb out? Why couldn't it be Doctor Barffy?* Then she shuddered, because really she didn't want anyone to zomb out. One moment there was a person there, and then nothing. Just a feral critter with human shape. But the person was gone, as effectively as if they'd died. And it was worse that the body stayed around to bite and spread the virus.

She knew that it had been transmitted by fake air freshener units with an ecological slogan put in the bathrooms at international airports. She wondered if it was really the enviros who had done this. It seemed to her there was a branch of them who was sure that the Earth would be better without humans. Better for what she didn't know, but they seemed very sure.

Dr. Hayden was dictating a dispo, and Beth hurried to take it, because she was the shared scribe for the shift and had to take the dictation and do the run around for any of the doctors who didn't have their own individual scribes. Regardless of whether that was a physical impossibility or not at times.

She'd considered getting trained to be an individual scribe, but she was hoping against hope to be in medschool next year, and if she took the training then she would have to work for the scribe service for a year to pay it back. Of course, she was very much afraid she'd fail in the application this year as she had last year and would be here forever.

And on that, she stopped, some inches from Doctor Hayden as her mind readjusted. With the emergency room and all available beds filled, with more and more people, like poor Doctor T, zombing out and becoming mindless killing apes, what prospects did she have in the future? What part of her carefully laid medschool plans was still operative? Would there even be a medical school? Were any medschools still even interviewing?

"Beth?" Doctor Hayden asked. "You all right?"

"Uh. Oh, yes, doctor. I was wondering when this will end, and what it will mean for me. I mean, I was hoping to go to medschool--"

Doctor Hayden snorted. She looked hot, like a fever had come on her suddenly. Her cheeks were flushed, and she was fumbling a bandage on, one handed, where Doctor T. had bitten her. "I'm supposed to tell you everything will be all right, right?" she said. "That if you work very hard everything will turn out all right. Only that's not true, if indeed it ever was except in rare cases. It wasn't ever just hard work, but hard work and aptitude, and contacts and confidence and all that. I don't believe in lying to the young. It might not have been all right even in the past. Oh, thank you," she said, as Beth slapped the bandage over her wound. "I disinfected and all. They say this will lessen the risk of transmission, but I'm not sure I believe it. Not from what we're seeing here." She frowned at her arm. "You know, Beth, I don't believe everything will be all right. I've studied epidemiology. I know this is exponential, and without an official vaccine or a cure, we're ..." She paused and it was obvious she was moderating her language. "In trouble. At the very least there's going to be a serious--"

"You were dictating a dispo?" Beth said, seeing tears sparkle in the older woman's eyes. Doctor Hayden, like Doctor T. was one of her favorite doctors to work for. She wasn't as tech competent as Doctor T. and so wouldn't do her own data entry, but she was always kind to the scribes and didn't treat them like serfs or blame them for her mistakes. She had a daughter about Beth's age, who lived in Seattle and who had stopped answering her cell a few days ago. That Dr. Hayden never mentioned her daughter was part of why Beth knew she was worrying about her all the time.

Beth's parents... Beth's parents also weren't answering their phone, and she hadn't been able to, or had the courage to drive all the way to the ranch to check on them. She wished she were back at the ranch, as hard as she could, but her name wasn't Dorothy. Maybe she should never have left. "The patient you were seeing when Doctor T. zombe-- came down with phase two of the H7D3 Virus."

"Oh, that," Doctor Hayden said, and blinked her water-shiny eyes. "Yeah, admitted and restrained for H7D3 Virus, second phase. We're down to carts on the corridors, Beth, and I don't know where we'll put the next zombie." She smiled, a wry smile. "Even if it's me."

"Some people don't catch it. It happens."

"Yeah, but everyone I've attended for bites has caught it, and some caught it in hours," Doctor Hayden said, as Beth copy-pasted the normal dispo for H7D3, second phase on her portable work screen. She no longer bothered to even try to type it individually. "The odds aren't good, and I never even won a cent on the lottery."

Beth opened her mouth but said nothing. What in hell could she say? The doctor was right of course. The chances of her still being herself in a few days were about none. And Beth didn't want to lie to her.

"If I zomb out," Doctor Hayden whispered, urgently. "Kill me?"

"Doctor—"

"Yeah, I know, murder and all, but Beth I've autopsied Zombies who died. There's nothing there. All the parts of the brain that make us human are gone. I don't want to live like that and be a danger to others. Shira... Doctor Tomboulian, and I have been friends since medschool, and it's harder to think of her as a zombie than to think of her dead. So— Just put an end to me."

"Doctor, I want to go into medicine," Bethany said. She didn't want to talk back, but it was important to make Doctor Hayden understand. "I don't-- I don't want to kill people."

Doctor Hayden gurgled with laughter at that. "Sorry, if you get into medicine, I guarantee you will."

Beth felt herself go red. "No, I know," she said. She tried to explain. It was the same trouble as medschool interviews. She could never explain properly and it came across like she didn't care. Last year an interviewer had actually asked her if she was only doing this because of prestige and told her to go back to the farm. She struggled for words, "No, I know you kill people accidentally and all. But I mean I never wanted to kill people on purpose."

Doctor Hayden looked intently at her and sighed. "Of course not. But with H7D3... Don't you see that you have to kill to save? Look, I never believed in all that crap about *community medicine* they gave us. It seemed like an excuse not to do the best you could for the patient, with some nebulous social justification. But in this case, you can do nothing. Once the patient zombs out, he or she isn't coming back. There's nothing in there to come back. All you can do is save other people from catching it. If we'd started killing them when we realized that, Doctor T. would still be fine, and I ... I wouldn't have been bitten." She took a deep breath. "I too never wanted to do harm, and I don't want my body to do harm after my mind is gone. I need to know someone will stop me before I spread it. You're a ranch girl. You're practical."

Beth wanted to say that it wasn't as easy as all that. She'd killed deer in season, but they needed culling or they'd destroy the crops, and she'd killed chickens. Of course, being made into nuggets probably raised a chicken's intelligence. Killing a person or what had once been a person was something else again. And then there was *how* to do it. Living in Denver, she'd left her guns at her father's ranch, and at any rate, the hospital was a no-gun zone. And what else was she supposed to kill someone with? She wasn't even supposed to come near patients. She supposed she could beat someone to death with a computer, but really-- She met Doctor Hayden's eyes, and nodded.

Later, in the doctor's lounge, they gathered around the TV.

The doctor's lounge was really just a small room, with a loveseat in a corner, a TV on the wall, and a table where people tended to throw whatever sweets they'd brought from home. It was a dirty little secret that doctors and most medical personnel in the ER lived on sugar, like some form of bee. In what Beth was starting to think of as the good old days, before H7D3, there weren't many people in the lounge. There weren't many people in the lounge now. For one, the nurses had been failing to come in when scheduled and didn't answer their phones, so it was anyone's guess whether they'd zombed or hightailed it out of Denver. Which, Beth thought, was arguably the sane reaction.

The few nurses that were in just used the doctors lounge anymore. And the Physician's Assistants who kept coming in did the same, as did the scribes. The weird thing was that other than about five percent of the doctors that were known to have zombed every doctor dragged himself or herself in, by grim determination, as though their presence there could stem the tide of the infection. As Doctor Clithero, a beautiful Samoan woman with an inability to suffer stupidity gladly -- or indeed at all -- had said that night, in desperation at the seventh H7D3 patient, "I feel like I'm trying to empty the sea with a conch shell."

But that hadn't stopped her coming in, and now she was munching on a brownie and drinking coffee, while about ten doctors, half a dozen scribes and a PA took a break from the mess in the emergency room.

From behind the break room came the low-grade growl-screams of the infected, housed in all the rooms of ER and in all the hallways. Since all their space for H7D3 was taken up, St. Thomas the Martyr hospital had started a divert to the other hospitals in the city. Which meant there was a lull that allowed doctors to gather and socialize for the first time in days. Weirdly there weren't many patients otherwise. Not even frequent flyers or drug seekers. Then again, maybe it wasn't weird. After all, if you got eaten on the way to the hospital, it was not that easy to get in for that pain in your left foot that had bothered you for three years but was an emergency now that you were bored.

The TV was set on news and all the anchors sounded hysterical. Though seeing Emerson Cuiper go full zombie on camera before chasing the other CNN anchors around trying to eat their faces had been completely worth it. And it was a sign of how jaded they'd got in the last few months that it warranted no more than snorts from a couple of the doctors and Lucas Fiacre, one of the Physician's Assistants saying in his best camp voice, "Oh! That is nothing to brag about," when the news anchor tore all his clothes off.

And another called out, "First time Cuiper chased women in his life."

"The thing is," Dr. Pillarisetti said when laughter died down. "When do the lights go out?" He spoke without drama, in a grinding, flat voice, that made his words seem more scary than if he'd shouted.

Beth, leaning against the door frame of the room was so startled she said "What?" aloud, even though normally she tried to stay quiet when doctors and other trained professionals discussed things. It was okay, because hers wasn't the only "what?" Just about everybody else said it too.

Dr. Pillarisetti swept the room with a concerned gaze. "Seriously? None of you has thought of that? An advanced technological society needs a certain number of personnel with knowledge and ability to keep it running."

And Beth spoke in a gathering of doctors for the second time, somewhat shocked to hear the words coming out of her mouth, "But wouldn't a small population be better for everyone? It seems like after the black plague in Europe—"

Dr. Pillarisetti's ancestors came from the Indian subcontinent. He had very dark eyes and an unnerving way of bringing his heavy eyebrows down over them made it look like he was contemplating where to hide your body after he was done ripping off your head and beating you to death with it. Now he turned the full force of his glare on Beth and said a word that, if everything weren't falling apart, would certainly have got him a process open with Human Resources. "Is that what they teach you kids these days? Well, they're wrong. The black plague did not hit an advanced technological society. Remember your first year classes and how many people dropped out of bio or chem or engineering to take a humanities degree? And that was from the ones who got into college in the sciences to begin with. The pool of people who can handle math and science is limited. It's not even an intelligence thing as much as the type of intelligence they have. Not all smart people can handle science. Given the morbidity – or at least the *zombidity* – of this virus, leaving maybe 10% of the population untouched, how do you think technological civilization can survive? The virus is not selecting for intelligence."

Beth bit her lip to make sure she didn't say anything more. The certainty that Dr. Pillarisetti was right sank in, even as the TV flickered with dramatic timing, and then an announcer said, in an eerily calm voice, "Folks, we're getting reports that the lights went out in New York city." The TV flickered again. "And now our lights have gone off and we're working with backup generators." There were screams behind the man, and the sound of breaking glass, and someone yelled "Turn the farging lights off. Zombies are attracted to light and sound." And the man on the screen who couldn't be a regular announcer because he was wearing sweatpants and a stained t-shirt that read *You Can Have My Coffee When You Pry It From My Cold, Dead Hands* said "They're tearing into the station now. Folks, stop listening to me and save yourselves. It's the end of the world."

The TV went out. Doctors, nurses, physician assistants and scribes had just the time to look around at each other with horror, when the lights blinked. Then the back up generators hummed, and the lights came back o n.

They looked at each other, each as pale as he or she could get.

St. Thomas Martyr was not quite downtown, but was set right off Colfax. If the city was dark, and the uncountable population of zombies out there *were* attracted to light and sound, the hospital had just become a magnet for a horde of Zombies that would submerge them all.

How do I get out of here? Beth thought. And read the same thought in everyone else's gaze. She heard glass break from down the hall, at the emergency room. Then there were very distinct human screams. Of course, the hospital was modern and the façade was mostly glass. Beth choked on a chuckle at the thought that if they'd known what was coming they'd have built like the middle ages, with narrow windows and small doors. She gave herself a mental shake. Hysteria was one thing she didn't need right now.

"We can't go out the door," Doctor Barfuss said.

"The roof," Lucas Fiacre shouted.

"Why the roof? What do we do after?" Cody, an older scribe yelled.

"How the hell do we get off the roof?" one of the other PAs asked.

"Helicopter-ambulances," Lucas said. "Bound to be some at the rate they've been bringing us patients."

It made sense. St. Thomas Martyr serviced all the southern suburbs and all the outlying areas up to Aurora, whatever wasn't covered by the medschool hospital there, so it had six helicopter ambulances, donated by a kind benefactor, which brought in the stroke cases, the heart attack cases and the alcohol poisoning cases of a Saturday night.

"And who the hell is going to fly them?" Doctor Barfuss asked, in his annoying, superior manner.

"Well, I can fly one," Fiacre said, grinning over his shoulder. "Flew helos in 'stan."

"And what about the others? We can't all fit into one!"

Doctor Sarah Clithero, who had been looking out the door of the lounge said, "Oh, I can fly another. Learned to fly them when I was young." As though anticipating the question, she said, "Was bored."

"But the ambulance helicopters—"

"Are designed to be an easy to fly vehicle," Fiacre said. "How does it look out there, Sarah?"

"From the sounds, they broke the front glass panes, and anyone who wasn't a zombie in the waiting room is dead. We're going to have to fight our way up. Grab whatever you find that can be used as weapons," Doctor Clithero said.

It gave Bethany a little shock, and it was stupid. Of course they needed weapons, unless they just wanted to be Zombie chow.

"It might surprise you," one of the other PAs, Albert Schoen, a tall, blond man, said, "But the emergency room and this lounge weren't designed to have a lot of impromptu weapons on hand."

"Grab what you can," Dr. Pillarisetti said, pulling a fire extinguisher from the wall. "Just try not to get bitten."

"Gait belts," A nurse said. "You know the things to help obese patients walk. Attach something heavy to the end and you have a mace," She ran out of the room, then back in and started distributing seven rainbow colored gaits around. "We had some in the nurse's lounge." Some of the men were taking their belts off and attaching things to the end of them. Others attached things to the end of gaits.

Beth didn't have a belt and she didn't get a gait. In despair she grabbed a standing lamp, by the lamp end, holding the weighted base in a defensive position. As a weapon it sort of sucked, but not as much as the others. It was fine. She wasn't sure she could look into a human face and smash it, anyway. She hadn't been made for the world as it was now, and she was afraid she wouldn't last long.

Just then, she heard, at the back of her mind, what her dad had said, when she failed the first round of medschool interviews, *Of course, you'll try again. If you're sure that's what you want to do, you try again. Life is trying and failing and trying again and sometimes succeeding. If you stop trying for something you really feel you should do, you might as well be dead, Beth.*

"Come on," Lucas Fiacre said. He hadn't got one of the gaits or a belt. He'd grabbed the curtain rod and tied a knife to the end of it with strips of curtain. He probably wasn't supposed to have that knife in the hospital which was a weapon-free zone, but she was damn glad he did. His grin looked entirely feral. "We have to get higher. We'll go to the second floor and bar the stairs. "Come on."

Beth wondered why Lucas seemed more alive than she'd ever seen him. She knew a lot of P.A.s, Lucas included, were war vets. She wondered if learning to survive under fire changed you, if it made you even like it.

She wondered, if she survived, would it change her the same way?

And it won't last for long

It all turned surreal very fast. Beth had gone hunting with Dad since she was about five, and, being a farm kid, she'd seen animals killed. In the hospital, too, as a scribe, she'd seen her share of bleeding and dying.

But all that was different. Now they were killing people, or at least hurting them very badly to escape. No. Not people. She remembered what Doctor Hayden had said. Zombies. Vectors, who'd infect people. The back of her head screamed that this was a dangerous slippery slope, but damn it, they knew you couldn't come back from Zombie. Not to kill them just meant they took over the whole world.

Her mind was torn between *Do no harm* and *but it's self-defense*, but all she knew was that as the zombies tried to come in, they fought back.

The first time Bethany hit a zombie and heard the sick crunch of a breaking cranium and got splattered with blood and brains was bad, but she couldn't stop. She turned her head not to get splatter in her eyes or mouth, but there was so much gore flying, she had to just hope. Her mind said *vector. Save people from the vector*. She argued with herself, *that's a slippery slope.* But then she looked at the vacant eyes, the gnashing teeth. There was no human there. There was no coming back. They were vectors. *Just vectors.*

She swung the lamp. Somehow they cleared a space so they emerged into the hallway. She found herself in the front lines, swinging the lamp as a mace at zombies' heads, as they gnashed teeth and whined and tried to reach them. If you swung the base with sufficient force it killed a zombie. *Vector.* She was saving people.

A zombie grabbed for her and Dr. Pillarisetti's fire extinguisher swung on its gait and broke its shoulder and then its face. The hand let go of Beth's arm, and she swung her lamp at a zombie trying to bite.

She and Lucas -- probably because they had long range weapons -- back to back, managed to clear the cluster around the lounge enough to get to the hallway that led to the service stairs up to the second floor.

They were stepping over zombies' still-twitching corpses and she was glad she was wearing her ankle boots, otherwise she would have been bit thirty times over. Fortunately the zombies slowed long enough to eat other fallen zombies. As was, as they reached the second floor, Lucas looked over his shoulder and said, "Stop. How about the patients?"

"What patients?" Doctor Barfuss asked. "Good God man, you can't mean the zombies."

"No, the other patients," Lucas said. "Second floor." He squinted. "Oncology?"

"Mostly," Doctor Clithero said. She was splattered in blood and gore, and held a blood splattered reinforced computer case nonchalantly. "Right now. Usually anyone we need to do a lot of tests on, but right now mostly oncology. I don't know how many patients we have, or how many are ambulatory."

Lucas looked at the door to the ward, then down at the door to the first floor they had locked in their wake.

Beth heard the glass on the door break and knew it was a matter of time before the Zombies either squeezed through the door, or broke the handle. "I'll go in," she said. *Save people.* If they just let people be eaten, what was the point? "I'll see how many of the patients here are ambulatory and how many we can rescue." She didn't say *and how many have zombed out.* But she thought it. Just because you were a cancer patient, it didn't mean you couldn't catch the zombie plague. In fact that had been their biggest problem: people admitted for other things turning and wreaking havoc in their units. Even in maternity.

And that night had been bad. That much was obvious as they stepped out of the elevator. Whoever had been on duty in the hallway nurse's station was dead. Even from a distance that was easy to tell because people are rarely alive with half their face missing. A trail of blood led deeper into the ward. As they got deeper in and checked the first room, where a man tethered to the bed and to machines that were making a long, continuous beep, was also very sincerely dead and partly eaten on the blood-soaked sheets, they heard from the end of the hallway the moaning growl of the zombies.

They rushed forward, side by side, while Beth hoped that the people they'd left by the door would keep the zombies from attacking them from behind. The hospital smelled of blood and feces, overlaid on the normal disinfectant smell, and the polished tiles of the hallway were spattered in blood, which made it hard to run without falling on her face. Once she almost fell, but Lucas grabbed her shoulder, without ever slowing down, and hauled her upright and back into the run.

At the end of the hallway, they were faced with a knot of people, all wearing hospital gowns. It was clear a lot of them were zombies, covered in bite marks and groaning-moaning.

But the thing was, when formication – the sensation of something crawling all over their skin – hit, as people were zombing out, they ripped all their clothes off. With the hospital gown that was either not easy – their being tied behind the back – or, their being so skimpy the zombies ignored them.

Which posed the problem.

"Shit," Lucas said as he came to a skidding halt. "Is it just zombies fighting?"

"Oh, hell no," a voice said from the middle of the melee. "About time you guys got here. I'm going to give this hospital a very bad review in my patient satisfaction form!"

He Left Yesterday Behind him...

Zachary Zodiac Smith had been having a bad day long before this. Actually if you really wanted to be specific, he'd had a bad decade. Maybe a bad life. But he balked at that idea. His life hadn't been bad. At least not until Mom had decided to off herself, when Dad hadn't come back from Nam. But even then there had been intermittent good times. Hell, yeah, very good times. Like Rosie.

But he turned his mind away from his first wife, Rosamund. Damn good thing, all things considered, that Rosie and the baby had died. Otherwise now he'd have to worry about her, and about a twenty year old son. Okay, maybe it wasn't a good thing they'd died, but at least they hadn't zombed out. Thank God. Until now ZZ hadn't understood *a fate worse than death.*

Now he did. Even if a part of him still longed to know that when he died he left something of him behind. But how many people would be able to do that now?

He stood with his back to the wall. He'd wrapped his arms in blankets, haphazardly because he hadn't exactly had a lot of time when the patient on the bed next to him had started screaming there was stuff crawling on him and throwing the bed clothes around. ZZ wasn't an idiot, no siree. He knew damn well what that shit meant, and he was out of his bed, wrapping his arms in sheet and blanket with a lot of it trailing, and grabbing the nearest defensive weapon. Which wasn't a very good weapon, being the tray on wheels that they'd put next to the bed.

Given he'd come in for throwing up all his food and catastrophic weight loss and the stomach cancer and all, he probably wouldn't have been able to lift that tray like that normally, but fear, like love, makes a man stronger. He was swinging the tray table around, and caught the guy getting up from the other bed, teeth gnashing and hands groping, on the side of the head and sent him flying.

Of course he came back. ZZ had seen zombie videos on youtube. There was a reason people were calling this the zombie apocalypse. The damn things just. Wouldn't. Stay. Down.

He tried to forget the guy had been named Bill and that he had cancer of the bladder, and that he had a two year old grandson and a granddaughter in Arizona. There was no Bill now, only a Zombie, chomping and clawing as it dragged itself upright, and lurched towards ZZ.

Who, this time, managed to catch him harder on the other side of the head, and, when Bill dropped, rush him and smash his head flat with the tray table.

Of course ZZ was out of breath and winded, but zombies came to the sound, and apparently Bill was not the only one to have turned, because there was the sound of chomping teeth in the hallway and someone rushed in, running like a gorilla, on feet and knuckles, and dragging a mess of tubes and an IV stand behind her. ZZ had smashed her against the wall, hitting out with the tray and catching her head between it and the wall. Her head went crunch and then splat, with a sound not unakin to a cabbage getting dropped from a great height and he turned his head just in time to avoid being splatted with blood and brain matter.

But there was another zombie. Right about the third, he realized that they had to be coming from somewhere, which left him with the question *where in hell are all these zombies coming from?* It was impossible they'd all zombed out at the same time as Bill. Okay, not impossible, but not likely.

Before he could think to investigate, he was surrounded by Zombies, and then it was crunch, smack, hit. And he realized after a while they were going to get him in the end. There was only one of him. Which meant that they'd kill him and—

And he heard two young people talking, a man and a woman.

He called out to them. Then he thought that even as they waded into the fray they might have trouble telling the zombies from the not-zombie, to wit, himself.

As the young lady – and she was a looker too, with that braid of red hair – deployed the mace in her hand – was that a floor lamp base? -- it occurred to him she might select his head for crunching. And like that, unbidden, came to his lips the song his mother had sang when they went walking when he was a tot, and he found himself singing aloud. "Rocky Mountain High, Colorado."

The young lady redirected the mace, the young man stuck his lance in someone else, and ZZ made to help them with the table.

In a moment – seemed like – they were panting and covered in sweat and blood, the zombies were down, and ZZ said, "Thank you."

The man, a dark haired guy, lean with a sort of sharp face, which made ZZ think of Caesar's line about lean men said, "No prob. But stop singing hippie songs, okay? I can still change my mind and stab you." He moved like someone who'd known war before.

"Hey, it was my momma's favorite song, youngster, and besides get off my lawn."

And then there was the sound of groaning and of teeth from the hallway, and zombies poured into the room.

"Where in Hell are they coming from?" ZZ asked.

"I don't know. We have the emergency stairs blocked and we—" the guy said, as he turned to stab zombies. Fortunately this set was easier, as they stopped to eat their fallen comrades. But not too easy as there were at least twenty of them.

"The other emergency stairs," the girl said.

"Shit. There's more than one of them?" the guy yelled, putting his lance into a zombie's eye and twisting.

"Fire regulations or something," the girl yelled, swinging her mace and spraying out brains. "I can't believe we forgot."

"Why not? I always used the elevator."

To show willing ZZ stepped up to stand with them and slam his table into zombies.

"But that means," the girl said, and it was weird that she looked even better, like that, splattered in blood and fighting. She reminded him of Rosy is what it was, and he shouldn't be eyeing a girl young enough to be his daughter. Particularly not when he was dying. But ZZ had never felt less like dying. He had trouble concentrating on the rest of her words, as they all killed zombies and she said, "That means the people we left blocking the stairway from the Zombies below—"

"Might be overtaken?" the lean man said.

"No, might be lapped," the girl said. "I mean, when we get to the other floors, there will be zombies there ahead of us."

"Shit," the lean man said. He turned to ZZ "You—What's your name?"

"Zeezee," ZZ answered because he'd be damned if he was going to tell a stranger his name was Zodiac. Besides, his grandfather, where he'd gone after Mom died, had shaken his head at the name and just called him ZZ.

"Right. I'm Lucas Fiacre, and that's Beth Arden. Is there anyone else alive on this floor? Not Zombies?"

ZZ eyed the door. "If there were they're probably eaten. "Going to sue the fucking hospital for not issuing fucking guns to fucking patients when this fucking Pacific flu started."

"Tell me about it, man," the lean guy said, with a feral look. "I fucking hate that we have nothing designed to kill these sons of bitches on hand."

"I'm going to run down the hallway and check. Just to make sure."

"Don't be a moron," Beth said. "Just call out."

"It will attract zombies."

"We are anyway."

Fiacre stepped forward, stab zombie, stab zombie, stab zombie, while Beth and ZZ lent support, and as soon as they were through the door, Fiacre shouted, "So, anyone not a zombie in here? Scream or knock or something."

There was no answer but the gnash of teeth and the groaning. "Allee allee in free," Fiacre said and did the best attempt at the hundred meter dash towards the door to the stairwell while slaying zombies – now that would have been a game for the Olympics – stab zombie, run, stab zombie, run, trip over zombie that Beth killed, almost fall and get eaten except ZZ caught him up and pulled him forward.

Then both trip on still live zombie – stab, scream, smash head with table. Beth saved them from falling and pulled them along.

By the end of the hallway, they were all fighting with one hand and holding the other up with the other, while jumping, dodging, tripping over fallen zombies.

I've Seen It Raining Fire In the Sky

When they got back to the landing there was pandemonium. Doctor Hayden was alternately opening and slamming the door, managing to catch some zombies in it each time, while Doctor Barfuss wanted to know precisely what this meant and why they were not going up as promised.

People recoiled from Beth and Lucas and ZZ as they came in. Doctor Barfy said something about contagion. Yeah, well, he should try killing zombies without getting it all over himself.

Lucas told them about the other staircase.

"Does that mean there will be zombies up ahead of us?" one of the nurses asked, dismayed.

"Yep. We'll have to fight all the way up."

"And where are we going once we get to the top?" Doctor Barfuss asked. "Bet you haven't thought of that young man. Even if we can fly the helicopters—"

Do no harm, Beth told herself. It was weird, because with adrenaline pumping through her, she could have smashed Doctor Barfy in the face, like a zombie. She realized she'd have to control it. *That's the slippery slope,* she thought. *Kill zombies because they can't come back and are just vectors, and then start thinking of people who annoy you as better off dead too.* And she was almost sure it wasn't true. Dr. Barfy might be an annoying paper pusher, but what Dr. Pillarisetti had said about the collapse of civilization. *If there aren't enough people who can learn, who will be doctors?* They might need even Doctor Barfy.

Lucas was saying something, answering Doctor Barfuss ".... Can. We'll go to Plynth. You know, the new hospital, which was supposed to open on Monday. They're fully stocked. They have generators. They're empty."

"They won't be empty once the generators start and they have light and sound," someone said.

They were going forward, up the stairs. Beth looked back at where doctor Jonna Hayden was still holding the door. "Doctor, do you see any way to secure that door? To delay them? This stairway seems to be free of zombies."

"Only because they're eating people in the wards," ZZ, the man they'd rescued said. Though he was wearing the hospital gown, he looked in pretty good shape. Middle aged, sure, but trim, and tanned. Black and possibly native American and white and who knew what else, Beth thought, looking at him, so that tan might be built in. It wasn't displeasing. Whatever he was, he was a scrappy fighter, and he still had that table clutched in his ha nd.

Beth chose not to argue and inclined her head. "Probably. But all the same. If we can get to the top with a minimum of fuss."

"Okay," Doctor Hayden said. She'd taken something off her white coat and seemed to be jamming it under the door.

"What was that?" Lucas asked, as she started up.

"My cell phone," the doctor said, grinning. "Figured end of the world, didn't need it."

They started running up the stairs, but Lucas stopped at the door to the third floor.

"What are you doing?" A woman asked.

"Going to see if anyone can be saved."

"That's insane. The zombies will just get ahead of us," Doctor Barfuss said.

"Fine. You go ahead, then, run on up. You and whoever wants to go with you. I'll go see if anyone needs saving," Fiacre said.

"I'll come with you, son," ZZ said.

"And I," Beth said, surprised to hear her own voice as she said it. But after all, she was here to save people, right?

Third floor yielded three people, all women, one coughing violently with the early stages of H7D3. For a moment Beth thought it would be faster to kill her now and easier on everyone, but after all you couldn't. There was a chance she wouldn't turn. Slim but a chance. Fortunately the woman was wearing a mask. And all three survivors had been blooded in combat with the zombies. The coughing woman was holding an IV stand as a mace. People who really did fight as cornered cats were probably as valuable as normal doctors and twice as valuable as Doctor Barfuss.

Fourth floor, Maternity, wielded a desperate woman clutching a baby in one arm, and a jagged, part broken flower vase in the other. The vase had blood on it, and there was blood sprayed up her arm and on her hospital gown. The problem hadn't so much been rescuing her, as stopping her from stabbing them as they approached. She'd become a proverbial momma bear defending her cub and momma bears were almost as rational as zombies. But in the end, she'd staggered and sobbed, lowering the arm that held the vase, and sobbed, "My husband. He was visiting. He—"

"Turned?" Beth said.

"I had to kill him, I had to."

"Of course," Beth said. "Proper thing to do." She said it because she needed to comfort the woman, but her brain told it was right too. "Can you run?"

And they ran.

By the seventh and top floor, as they emerged onto the terrace that held three helicopters, they'd gathered fifteen people in addition to their starting-out two dozen.

Beth almost expected to hear Doctor Barfuss greet them with "That's too many people you idiot. You'll never take off."

But he didn't because Doctor Barfuss was dead. And Ron, the helicopter pilot, was happily tearing pieces of flesh off Doctor Barfuss and eating them.

"Oh, hell," Beth said, and brought her mace down hard on the head of the helicopter pilot, again and again and again, beating head and face, and neck to pulp long after he'd stopped twitching.

"Stop," Doctor Pillarisetti yelled, and grabbed her arm. He was covered in blood and unidentifiable fragments and had just come from the stairway. "Stop, Beth. Stop. He's dead."

And then Beth had started crying. ZZ, the patient, had kind of gathered her in and said, "It's all right. It's better than freezing up, kid."

He only let go of her as they were apportioning people between helicopters. He'd let go of her, leaving her feeling cold but not alone, because, she realized, the others would look out for her. He patted her shoulder as he called out, "Oh, hell, yeah, I can fly one of these. Better than the crap I flew in Desert Storm and at least no one will be shooting at us."

When they were trying to cram more people than should be possible into each of the rescue helicopters, Beth found herself next to Dr. Pillarisetti and asked, "Where did you get all blooded? You weren't on the stairs."

"No," Nikhil Pillarisetti said. "I doubled back, to go... to euthanize those people we left behind strapped in carts."

"But they were zombies!" Beth had said.

"Yeah, but some of them were our friends too. And at any rate, leaving even a zombie strapped down and helpless to be eaten by other zombies felt wrong. Don't look at me like that. It just seemed awful. So I cut their throats. Well, those I could reach. Definitely Doctor Tomboulian. I couldn't leave her."

"Thank you," Doctor Hayden said quietly. "If it were me, I'd hope you do it for me too."

"Yeah, it was hell managing to get back here, though. Someone had jammed a cell phone under the bottom floor door," he said, and grinned as he handed it to doctor Hayden.

When Doctor Hayden zombed out, as they rose high over the city – which was burning, flames licking up to the sky – it was Beth who strangled her, quickly, efficiently, and before Doctor Hayden could bite anyone in the press of terrified people. *She would have preferred it*, Beth thought, as she held her friend and felt her spasm and fight and finally go limp. There was no Doctor Hayden left, not really. This was stopping a vector. And doing no harm.

"I'm sorry, Beth," ZZ told her as he got to her, just too late to help.

"It was a promise," was all she said.

But His Heart Still Knows Some Fear

Plynth wasn't paradise but it sure felt like it, after they'd flown in over burning Denver. Beth saw Lucas greet his friend whom he introduced as the guy who'd been making sure the facilities had the right supplies before opening. She noted he kept his arm around this guy – Mark – as he introduced him. She thought it fit, but she didn't really care much one way or the other. Whom people chose to sleep with was sort of their problem. She'd never slept with anyone. Her shyness had effectively kept her from even being kissed.

What she cared about was finding out that the wards had beds, that they were clean, that she could sleep. Though she did take a hot shower with disinfectant soap, first, and inspected herself for bites, not sure what she'd do if she found one.

Then she dressed in scrubs, because they were the only washed clothes around, and went to bed.

She ended up crying herself to sleep, not sure for whom she was crying: for herself, for Doctor Tomboulian, for Doctor Hayden, or for her parents, in their ranch just outside Denver. Were they far enough away to have escaped? Somehow she doubted it.

She woke up to a bang bang bang sound and followed it to find Lucas Fiacre and Mark shooting zombies out a window in a hallway.

Lucas turned back and grinned at her, and she realized the bang, bang, bang came from upstairs too. "That's Doctor Pillarisetti," Lucas said.

"That guy, ZZ, whom you guys rescued? He's also shooting. Experience in Desert Storm, apparently."

"Where can I shoot?" Beth asked. "Are there more guns?"

"Oh, sure. In the daylight, Mark and I scouted around, and found a couple of empty houses with complete arsenals. We really should see if we can get to Cabela's outside Goldport because—" He leaned out and took another shot.

"Wait, in the daylight?" Beth said.

"Yeah. Oh, yeah, you slept all day. We all sort of let you. You were out of it." He gave her a doubtful look. "Are you sure you want to shoot zombies? Have you ever shot?"

She made a scathing sound. "I used to go hunting with my daddy from the time I was five." And they needed to stop the vectors, to save as many people as possible. "What have you got?"

Lucas evaluated her. "We got nineteen elevens. Owner seemed to like them."

"Gimme! And yeah, I want to shoot zombies. They destroyed civilization. Okay, it might not be their fault, but it will be my fault if I allow it to spread. Yeah, I know I'm not supposed to do harm, or I wouldn't be if I could ever become a doctor, but sometimes you have to think about it and realize that the real harm is letting zombiedom – totally a word – take good people, rather than stopping it in its tracks."

Lucas half laughed, delighted. "Yeah, sometimes it's hard to tell what real harm is, isn't it? Go grab some coffee and something to eat first. There aren't many zombies. I didn't think there would be, because Plynth is so spread out that they'd have to walk miles to go from place to place. But Doctor Clithero said we should turn lights on – it's okay, this is powered by solar as well as backup generators, and the outside lights are all solar. They store during the day and glow at night. – to attract them, because if we kill all the nearby ones, then we can relax a little and not risk being overwhelmed. And maybe stop them from spreading it. Go grab food and coffee. You'll shoot better."

"And you'd shoot better if you weren't talking," Mark said, shooting a zombie that Lucas had missed.

She'd gone in search of coffee – following the smell – and found that someone had warmed up some frozen cinnamon rolls. She wondered how much food they had. She must ask someone in charge – she wondered who that was – and push the Cabela's idea. First, because she figured they'd need ammo, but she figured they'd also need as much survival food as they could muster.

Afterwards, she went around. There were two pairs of shooters in each floor, except on the third floor where Doctor Pillarisetti and a nurse were shooting out the windows on the north side, but there was only ZZ on the South side windows.

She took up position next to him, and he – now wearing generic green scrubs, like hers – gave her a wide grin. "There's nothing like a fine woman holding a fine gun, and baby you're all kinds of fine."

"That movie," she said, sternly, as she took up position, and prepared to shoot a zombie, "Sucked, though the Whole Nine Yards was pretty good." She stopped, because the Zombie couldn't be more than seven years old, tottering around looking lost. But it was naked, and even from here, you could see his movements were that of a zombie. ZZ sighed as he shot it. "Sorry, kid. It's not easy."

She shot the next zombie attracted to the lights, a young man who stopped to eat the kid. "Why were you in the hospital?" she said, trying to pretend that she wasn't nauseated by the cannibalism and the horror. "I mean, you were in the oncology area, weren't you?"

He hesitated. "I was in the hospital," he finally said, in a voice that brooked no dissent. "To find out the secret of my insane attraction for all people of the female sex."

Beth shot a zombie "If you say Woof! and slap your own butt, we can't be friends."

He shrugged. "Stomach cancer," he said. "They told me the tests were positive yesterday afternoon and were talking chemo. They said I might live as much as ten years with chemo. I suspect my chances are as gone as ... civilization."

"I'm sorry," she said, and meant it. Weird that in this massive collapse a small tragedy still mattered.

But that's how humans were wired. Who had said that one human death was a tragedy and a million was just a number? Someone. She suspected some communist. It was the sort of thing they liked to say, to make it sound like their actions were completely normal when they killed millions of people.

"Don't take it so hard," ZZ said. "After all, this is the most fun I've ever had in a hospital."

By the end of the day, they were in fact friends, and he'd told her all about his childhood, and how his Cherokee mother had killed herself when his "probably mostly black, though there was Italian and Greek there too" father had died in 'Nam. He said it without sadness, then talked about being raised by his rancher grandfather in Oklahoma. "But Momma loved

Colorado. She used to sing *Rocky Mountain High* all the time. So after Desert Storm, when I came back, Rosie and I came back here. We were gonna save and buy a ranch. But then she died and the baby with her, and I..." He shrugged. "I learned computers, and I married... but no one was like Rosie. Ah well. I guess it's been a good life. Girl, how could you miss that shot?" he said, as he shot the young female zombie running up. She shot the big guy zombie who might have been chasing her. It was a clean shot through the head, and ZZ said, "That's better. I was beginning to think I'd been wrong to like you."

Seeking Grace In Every Step He Takes

"Hell," said the priest. Father Lyon had been the chaplain assigned to St. Thomas Martyr, which had after all been a Catholic hospital. They'd found him in the chapel, in the fifth floor, holding the sacrament against his chest and killing a zombie with the leg of a chair.

The first words he'd said to Beth had been a whole speech, "I suppose I should have let them martyr me, but the Pope can't have been serious when he said the zombies were still human. I looked in their eyes. If there's a soul in there, it is one that longs for release from the demonic body holding it." He'd paused a moment and said, "Then again that wasn't a statement of doctrine, and there's a good chance the pope is no longer alive and we have no pope."

Then he'd stowed the sacrament in his coat, and had fought his way cheerfully back to the rest of the group.

So his exclamation shouldn't have surprised Beth, but it did. Her parents were Catholic, and she'd never heard a priest swear like that.

But it was the general meeting. They were all sitting around tables in the cafeteria and Doctor Clithero, who had assumed leadership, Beth supposed under the principle that in danger everyone wishes they had a mother at their back, had allowed one of the nurses to get up and speak. She was talking about how to make the hospital really safe.

"Hell," the priest said. He got up. "Brothers and sisters," he said, in a voice that took Beth back to childhood. "I say we weren't put in this world to be safe. The last few days have shaken my faith to the core, but that's something I'm absolutely sure of. We weren't put in this world to hole up in a comfy place, being safe, and let the rest of it turn into hell on Earth."

"It's already hell on Earth," someone shouted.

"Maybe. Then our goal is to make it better."

"How?"

"I suggest we make expeditions during the day," the priest said. "Some have already been doing it," he looked towards Luke and Mark, "And clear the area of zombies, but also look for survivors, holed up."

"What if there are no survivors?"

"Well, then we won't find them," the priest said. "But the thing is that if there were survivors in the hospital, there will be some here, holed up, trying to survive, fighting, maybe."

Doctor Clithero took the podium from the nurse, "Likely, Father, and I agree with you that we should save them. But I'd like to see the area a lot more secure when we do that. I mean, it's somewhat safe, but there are only fifty nine of us. It's too few, and I don't want to lose any more." Other than the woman who had had the cough, of course, and who'd gone zombie this morning.

And that was when Beth had remembered her childhood and how they often set traps on their land, for the rabbits. And she thought they should trap zombies. And next thing you knew, she was talking about the No Hope Mine which had first been the cause for the existence of Plynth, but which had played out before the silver crash. "It's deep," she said. "We could play music and have light down there, and then when zombies came— Well, if we can find dynamite we can blow up the entrance and trap them in there." She realized she'd spoken, aloud, clearly, and no one was laughing or asking her who she thought she was. Instead, people looked impressed.

"After which we'll open the mine in three months, and find a really fat zombie," Doctor Pillarisetti said. He had started asking people to call him Nikhil because, he said, at the end of the world, formality was insufferable.

"Maybe. Or we could not open it," Beth said.

"Yeah," Nikhil said. "The only issue is that people who built hospitals never seemed to remember a good gun powder or dynamite supply."

Which had led them finally on a raid to Cabela's, a trip far less eventful than expected, since it was outside the medium sized city of Goldport, and there was almost no water around. Something they'd started to learn is that water equaled zombies. They could survive on water so foul no human could endure it and live. But they needed water.

On the way to Cabela's, they'd gone by Beth's parents' ranch. She'd found no one. She'd have felt better, if she'd found someone dead. As it was, all she could say is that she didn't know where her parents were. Everything in the house looked like life had been interrupted early morning, with cereal bowls on the table, the food in them now black and shriveled. Someone had remembered to open the gates, and the horses were long since gone. But since Beth's guns and her father's were still there, she couldn't believe it had either been robbers or her father, knowingly leaving the place.

She'd got her guns, and given her dad's to ZZ.

And that night, she'd refused to sleep alone.

More People

And they'd found people. Holed up in houses. Isolated on roof tops. They'd saved a couple of intact families, but most of the people they'd brought in were mothers who'd killed their whole families, fathers who'd strangled wife and children after they turned, or the occasional child someone had managed to lock away in safety before turning.

The weird thing was how soon all that became normal. The death, the dying, the horror, yeah, but also the forming of new connections, the helping, the new loves and new children.

ZZ knew that he should never have allowed Beth to seduce him. Okay, maybe she hadn't exactly seduced him, but what do you call it when a lovely young woman crawls into your bed and tells you she can't sleep alone, and then tells you she's never been kissed and kisses you something fierce. He wasn't made of stone. He was all too human.

They'd found some drugs and equipment here, and Doctor Clithero had found a drug regime that seemed to be keeping the cancer kind of under control, but they'd told him, and he knew anyway, that it had metastasized before he came in to have it checked out, and that he couldn't survive this. Even if they had top surgeons, as they used to, and not just a couple of people who had other specialties but were good at surgery, like Nikhil, he couldn't have been operated on and saved.

He shouldn't have slept with Beth. And he shouldn't have dragged her in front of the priest to get married. But now he was kind of glad he had, because she was pregnant, and he wasn't feeling so well, but he wanted the kid to know his parents had been married.

"Deep in thought?" Nikhil said.

"Sorta," ZZ said. "I was hoping that the trap we set yesterday will have caught some zombies, but also wondering if there's a lot of them how you're going to get their spines without them eating you doc."

"Well, that's why we have armor," Nikhil said. "Courtesy of Cabela's." He nodded. "And anyway, you're along. We'll shoot them, before I climb down to ah... anatomyse them. But you know, I'm a psychiatrist. I should analyze them before killing them. Just to make sure, you know, there's no humanity remaining."

"Humanity? In a zombie? Oookay."

"There's always a first time," Nikhil said, and grinned. "Seriously. You didn't even smile. You volunteered to come out and help harvest the spines, so what is wrong? Are you disgusted at the idea of making vaccine out of ground up spines of zombies? It's our only chance to help the survivors of the military bases in Colorado, and we kind of need that, not just to help protect us against Zombies, but against marauders. Because as soon as things stabilize a little there will be marauders, you know? Also, if we're going to be a proper hospital and get patients in, we need to protect our people. Otherwise we're hosed. We could be killing half our people every time we take an unknown in for treatment."

"I know. I've been listening to the short wave, since we got it off that cabin." He paused. "Let's suppose I got much worse, and I died. You know Beth is due in three months."

"Yeah. Are you feeling—"

"No, doc, no time for my symptoms. Thing is, Beth wanted to be a doctor, and I think she'd make a damn fine doctor. I think we'll need all the doctors we can get, too, because—"

"Because we've been treating people over short wave, giving instructions blindly. I get that. Medicine will be needed if the human species is even to survive at all. There's less than one percent left, and we can't afford to die of stupid things, but ZZ we don't have medical schools anymore."

"So? Before fancy medschools and certification requirements, and quotas and all, doctors took apprentices. I'm asking you to take my wife on as an apprentice. Teach her the doctoring thing. That way she can make her own way in the world, and look after our son." The ultrasounds showed a boy, and ZZ thought it was funny, because he'd been supposed to have a son who'd died, so it was like he was being given back something. He hoped Rosamund would understand. He wasn't replacing their baby, but there was a relief in knowing he'd leave a son in the world, behind him. Maybe it was an atavistic thing for all men. Even when the world was falling apart.

No, as he'd told Beth last night, particularly when the world was falling ap art.

Nikhil paused, then nodded. "Makes sense," he said. "I've been thinking. The Catholic Church preserved civilization and learning in the middle ages and—"

"I ain't Catholic," ZZ said. "Beth is, and the padre was the only one who could marry us, but—"

"No, no," Nikhil said. "But we have a high concentration of medical knowledge, which is one of the basis of civilization. And we have a few engineers we've rescued. I was thinking that the Plynth hospital could be sort of like an old monastery, and a city could grow around us of people we taught the fundamental sciences of civilization."

"I won't live in no monastery either," ZZ insisted.

Nikhil snorted. "No one would expect you to. And yeah, ZZ, I'll teach Beth if she wants me to. To the best of my ability."

"Thank you, doc," ZZ said, even if later, he doubted the doctor's sanity a little as Nikhil yelled down at six zombies in a pit: "I see you're all trapped. So how does that make you feel?"

The zombies groaned and chomped.

"Yes, we've covered that. But it's time to stop hiding behind your aggression. Anger is always the second emotion; we need to find out what's beneath it."

Groan.

"I know this is tough for you. It's tough for anyone in this situation, but you're just not anyone are you?"

Chomp. Chomp. Chomp.

"Very good. Let it out buddy."

One of the Zombies made a desperate scramble and almost got out of the pit.

Nikhil stepped back. "I know you crave flesh. You know, sometimes the things we crave are really stand-ins for an inner feeling of emptiness. Do you think that's what's going on?"

Chomp. Chomp. Chomp.

Nikhil sighed. "Okay, no one home." He pulled out his gun. "Let's shoot them."

Shooting them was easy. ZZ had more trouble chopping them up to remove the spines. Thank God they were all male. Even so ZZ had to stop and vomit a couple of times. More than normal, that is. Nikhil meanwhile was all cheerful about it, and took the spines back to the lab where Doctor Clithero had worked and turned them into vaccines.

Which is how they'd ended up as a proper settlement, of sorts, because with the vaccine, they'd been able to protect themselves and the military men who'd joined them. Plynth, in the mountains, was easier to protect than the installations in cities, which had been cannibalized to make Plynth into a fortified town serving a scattered population. A remnant of civilization in the middle of barbarism. A light in the dark.

ZZ wished heartily he could see it when it was bigger, when his son was a young man. But he knew his days were numbered.

The Shadow From The Starlight Is Softer Than A Lullaby

The day President Stabba, former vice-president, former Lt. governor of Oklahoma, visited Plynth was a red letter day for everyone, including the president herself.

She had heard all about the hospital, functioning and modern, protected by what remained of military forces in Colorado. She'd heard about the people who'd joined the small core of doctors and medical professionals who'd started the settlement. She was impressed with their ambulance helicopter system and had heard stories of daring medical rescues, and of one woman who'd given birth in the helicopter.

So while the inhabitants of Plynth were honored to see her, she was eager and interested in them and in figuring out how many people they could put through their mentoring program and how fast. They needed a lot more doctors. A lot more. They were losing people to stupid injuries. And they couldn't afford to lose people.

But first of all she had to inspect the troops, in parade uniform, and looking very proud of it, who lined up to the sound of the Star Spangled Banner.

And afterwards, she watched the people come out of the hospital, in scrubs, in an orderly fashion. They weren't military and had never been, most of them, but they were trying to preserve order and dignity. One of the young women in scrubs had a baby in arms. Others were very obviously pregnant. As they came out, *Rocky Mountain High* started to play.

She'd been told about this. She'd heard it from their helicopter rescue man, Lucas Fiacre, who'd met them the day before to brief them on the situation. One of their initial people had died last night of cancer. He'd become sort of a father to them all. And he had lived just long enough to see his baby born. *Rocky Mountain High* had been his favorite song.

There were tears in the eyes of the medics, but everyone, even the young woman with the baby had a smile for the president.

A Samoan woman, Doctor Sarah Clithero, in blue scrubs, explained as she shook the president's hand, "We're hoping it's a beginning to the return of civilization. We know we won't see it fully restored, but maybe our grandchildren will."

The final strains of Rocky Mountain High climbed into the fiery sky over the Rockies, and in the sunlit, bright clouds, there seemed to be suggestions of cities and of lands that would eventually exist. And a hope for the future.

Writing Dead End Rhodes

THE FOLLOWING STORY CAME into being from a DAZ rendition of a woman dancing with a cyborg. Then I got invited to an anthology (Parallel worlds) which was about "different types of heroism." As part of it we were supposed to write an essay about what type of heroism this was and why we admired it. These essays were later ditched from the anthology, for reasons I didn't understand, but probably valid (I was in the middle of moving. Everything is a blur.) I think because their prompt was actually "a different type of hero" not a different type of heroism, and we ALL misunderstood it. Anyway, having been written, the story spawned a world. There is a short novel Other Rhodes out, and another started and will be finished, I swear (the last few years have been "fun".)

Anyway, below in its entirety is the essay that was supposed to go with the story:

This was a difficult story to write, because my favorite hero is the one that Heinlein describes in Stranger in a Strange land when talking about the Fallen Caryatid, by Rodin:

"But she's more than good art denouncing bad art; she's a symbol for every woman who ever shouldered a load too heavy. But not alone women—this symbol means every man and woman who ever sweated out life in uncomplaining fortitude, until they crumpled under their loads. It's courage, [...] and victory." ...... "Victory in defeat; there is none higher. She didn't give up[...]; she's still trying to lift that stone after it has crushed her. She's a father working while cancer eats away his insides, to bring home one more pay check. She's a twelve-year old trying to mother her brothers and sisters because Mama had to go to Heaven. She's a switchboard operator sticking to her post while smoke chokes her and fire cuts off her escape. She's all the unsung heroes who couldn't make it but never quit."

Not only is this the type of person I try to write my characters to be, it is also the type of person I try to be. Someone who keeps towards the goal, even though he/she knows it's impossible to do it and survive.

It's very difficult, of course, to write a short story specifically about this kind of hero, (instead of letting it shine through over the course of many stories and novels) since most of it is "uncomplaining fortitude" which is not something that translates well to fiction.

And then I remembered "Stella D'Or" and "Nick Rhodes which have been haunting my mind for some time and I realized she (and he, but in a different way) fit the bill.

Dead End Rhodes

Of all the criminals in the known universe, borgers are the worst.

They are the worst both in law and in my own mental hierarchy of crimes. I loathe murderers, kidnappers, slavers and all those who treat other humans as objects for their convenience.

But borgers *make* people into objects. They steal the brain, discard the body, and entrap all that remains of a living human in a glassteel body, cut off from its normal senses. They murder the person and keep what remains entrapped in a body so unlike humans that the poor creature goes insane. As far as we can tell, and of course, the operation is so highly illegal that our statistics are probably flawed, borgers end up wasting seventy five percent of those they take, because the resulting cyborg is too crazy to function, even for limited purposes.

Borging is so heinous, and so severely punished, that if you are even caught near a cyborg you haven't denounced to the authorities so they can give the poor soul the peace it deserves, you'll be executed as a borger. Even if you had nothing to do with the making of it.

Why do the borgers do it? Profit. Money. There are certain asteroids and moons in which the atmosphere will eat through skin, the radiation kill any human, the temperature boil anyone not encased in layers of glassteel. Cyborgs are powered by batteries created by an alien race. They don't eat. They don't sleep. They don't excrete. Many of them can't even think in any sense. But they can do the repetitive and boring actions needed to mine rare metals. And they do.

I'd cross the galaxy – and have – to kill a borger.

So you'll wonder why I live with a cyborg, and why he's technically my boss in my mobile investigations business.

Sometimes so do I.

The poor soul who is the head of our investigation business calls himself Nick Rhodes, which is not his name. He assumed Nick Rhodes' identity, after being borged. I think the self-identification came from watching too many sensis in the series. He believes that he is a veteran of some ancient war on Earth called World War One or The Great War or The War to End all Wars, and that he lives in a city called New York, in a country long forgotten, in a world that was the cradle of humanity and like all cradles ultimately abandoned. He believes he's a private investigator. That last is re al.

As I said, most people go insane when borged. But at least he can think. Boy, can he think.

To keep him happy, the inside of our spaceship – a serviceable two floor Flitja of ancient model – is set up as the house of Nick Rhodes in the sensi serial of the name.

I slept in the front bedroom upstairs, and he in the back. Yes, I know he didn't sleep, but I'm not sure he knew. Our office was in the front of the spaceship, just off the airlock he insisted on calling "the foyer". In back was the kitchen, which baffled him, until he'd convinced himself all kitchens in New York in the 20th century came with automated cookers and huge refrigeration units as well as dried food storage with foods from all the human worlds. He'd written these into the memories of Nick Rhodes' from the sensis and would now regularly cook for me, since he could not eat.

Awareness of his condition remained, but in his mind it was Nick Rhodes who had been set upon, in a back alley, and turned into a cyborg. Fighting the condition would only distress him.

I came into the office, early morning, before him, and took my place at the desk that, in *Nick*'s memory belonged to his secretary Stella D'Or. My computer carefully disguised as a typewriter, I set about reading the morning mail, answering it, confirming appointments, charting our course when we left this world, when the current case was – hopefully – solved.

Nothing in my background had prepared me for this. I'd been a socialite in interplanetary society, known for my dancing. Sensis of myself dancing with some gallant or other had graced the press of all the human worlds. I'd lived without a care for money or survival, until I got married. But my father had disapproved of my marriage and disowned me, and this was now how I must earn a living. I managed, more or less.

Nick came into the office while I finished the last of the correspondence. He wore a suit that would befit the 1930s in New York city, this one in a soft brown, with a pale yellow tie on the immaculate white shirt. The surfaces of his cybernetic body left exposed, as between his hat and collar, gleamed, soft golden glassteel. He removed his hat and hung it on the coat tree, and though his face was, of course, motionless, I imagined he smiled at me as he rumbled "Good Morning, Stella," in a voice that sounded less electronic every day.

I said, "Good morning, boss," as he sat at his desk and turned on the privacy shielding.

He had no need to sit, of course, just as he had no need of wearing clothes to disguise his sexless body. But he did anyway. The shield, that made the area in which he sat into a nebulous, swirling, impenetrable confusion, not unlike wind-blown clouds, was a necessity. And like everything else, Nick had rewritten it into his memory, deciding that Nick Rhodes – the fictional hero – had used this shielding to disguise the horrendous facial scarring from The Great War and avoid scaring his customers.

The ringing of someone at the outer entrance to the airlock – not functioning as such while on the ground in a planet with Earth atmosphere -- announced the arrival of the client who had brought us here: the man who had paid enough for the services of our detective agency for us to come to Peura Planet and land in its paltry spaceport and endeavor to solve the client's problem.

Because Nick's brain had become renowned throughout the galaxy, people assumed his pseudonym was a nod towards the old serial adventures by some recluse celebrity or genius. There were speculative articles on who he really was, but despite my presence, right there, and my once-well-known looks, no one had landed on his real identity. Perhaps because I'd changed so much these last five years, living with a cyborg.

Just as well.

The client was middle aged, prosperous – he would have to be – wearing a relatively fashionable one-piece in blue-grey with dark red accents. For this region of the galaxy practically avant-garde. My father had worn a similar one twenty years ago, but we'd been in a far more populous and wealthy area.

He was well built, with steel-grey hair and eyes, which seemed to coordinate with his suit.

He rushed into our office, ahead of me, and stopped, staring at the privacy shield. Then turned to me. "What is this?" he said. "I thought I'd paid for an audience with Nick Rhodes. How am I to know—"

"If you know who we are," I said. "You know Mr. Rhodes always meets clients from behind a privacy shield. Please, won't you sit down, Mr...." I faked hesitancy but of course, I remembered the name. Without his wired advance we wouldn't have come this far. As well, though, to make him think he was one of many and unimportant.

"Mr. Peura."

He gave me a half-annoyed look, as though he didn't like to be reminded that he was not special, and wouldn't be the first to meet Nick Rhodes face to face, without the shield.

I saw him consider protesting, and give it up, then throw himself down on the chair in front of Nick's desk as though he held a grudge against it. He glared at the privacy shield.

Behind it, Nick's chair – specially made to accommodate Nick's weight – creaked, and out of long habit, I could visualize him shifting, leaning back, waiting for the client to speak.

It took a moment. Peura was not unusual in feeling uncomfortable talking to the blankness of the privacy shield. I turned my chair slightly so that I could see him, and so that he could see me and smiled slightly, encouragingly.

If he thought my costume of bright, short dress, the ribbon holding back my platinum hair, were strange he said nothing. I presumed he thought I was keeping the atmosphere to match Nick Rhodes sensies. He wasn't wrong. He was just wrong about the reason.

"It's my son," he finally said. "He's gone missing." As though having said it he'd performed a major and difficult task, he took out a hanky in one of those nano-cleaning fabrics out of his pocket and mopped up his forehead. "I don't know what to do."

The chair creaked. The shield shifted and rotated slightly, indicating that Nick had sat up straight, and Nick said, "I presume you've contacted the authorities."

Peura swallowed hard. I could hear the sound and see his Adam's apple move. "There aren't... many authorities out here. Most of the investigators work for me. You see, I own the mining rights to this world, that's why it's named after me. All three cities in this world are built around mines. Hence their names: Mine One, Mine Two, Mine Three. The security are my security guards, who are supposed to keep peace for me. I don't know if you understand that they aren't police as such. More company security."

I understood him perfectly well. He was the local boss thug and all the thugs in the world responded to him. He didn't say that, of course, but it was understood.

"Of course when I realized my son had disappeared," he said. "I had all my security men look for him. Of course..." He hesitated and mopped at his forehead again. "They're not exactly what I'd call brainy, you know. They're more... more."

"More hired muscle?" Nick rumbled, his voice, from behind the privacy shield sounding more gravelly than usual, in a way that disguised the mechanical timbre.

I expected Peura to take offense, but he made a strange laugh-cough sound at the back of his throat, as though he were afraid of laughing, or perhaps unused to it. "You could say that," he said. "You could say that. What they are is convicts, from ... well, from more civilized worlds, who have trouble keeping them behind bars, and so they rent them out to these far flung worlds to act as security. Well, that is no big difference. Most of the miners are too. They're brought here for punishing labor that would give the government bad press in their worlds."

I felt the encouraging smile fade from my face. And I heard Nick shift in his chair. I'd heard of the system, but I didn't have to approve of it. I didn't know if Nick had. I never understood, in any case how he reconciled the fictional ancient New York City in his mind with the real world of multiple human planets with their differing law codes and different ways of getting around those laws. I don't know what Nick thought of this penal arrangement. I knew in the fictional New York, in the long vanished country of the United States, prisoners had done some work, and it was judged not to be slavery, and was in fact paid, if at a lower rate than any other
.

I didn't know if Nick perceived the difference between that and what was going on here. As for how I felt about it, well, I did tell you I hate slavers, right? This was not much different from outright slavery.

Sure, in the more "civilized" worlds these men might be given some limited sentence, but once that became "let's rent convicts to people who desperately need labor in lawless outer worlds" the sentences had a way of being extended, of becoming fluid, of having years added to them arbitrarily for misbehavior or infraction, with no court supervision. If the rumors were right -- and I'd recoiled from verifying them as one flinches from a sore tooth, because when it is something the United Human Planets agree on, it's nothing I can change -- temporary punishment became life-long slavery, and what was supposed to be a quiet way of punishing really bad criminals became the normal punishment for everything from everything, from littering to multiple homicide.

Worlds have different ideas of what is criminal. Some are so barbaric as to forbid means of personal defense to individuals. You can get a hefty sentence for possessing an energun in a dozen of them. Others forbid certain foods and drugs. Others yet reserve punishment for murder or kidnapping or other crimes against others. But all of these worlds rented their "convicts" to people like Peura in distant worlds, where no one would supervise their treatment.

I narrowed my eyes at Peura. He didn't notice. He was staring ahead at the privacy shield intently. He sighed. "You see, my son wasn't... we weren't on the best of terms. He wanted to go off world and study... he wanted to be a starship pilot. I told him no, because he was my only son and would one day inherit all this. But he wasn't happy about it, so he'd often go into town, this town or another to drink. He often came home very late. But one night, a month ago, he didn't come home. And no one has been able to find any trace of him."

"I presume you have traced his movements until he disappeared though?" Nick rumbled.

"Oh, sure. He was out with a group of... well, he'd say a group of friends, I think, from the spaceport. Not locals. People who landed here, you know, we import... That is, not only do my family and I require some luxuries from other worlds, but we import a lot of our food for the men in the mines. Narcis, my son, he was... He didn't like associating with the miners, not that I can precisely blame him, you know. I mean, they are servants and people with a bad past. In fact we discouraged my children associating with them from the beginning.

"So he has friends among the people who do regular supply runs. One such party was in town, young men from one of the companies that supplies food and liquor. We have... well, with men such as the ones we get here, you have to provide some diversion, so we have bars in the cities, and he and his friends were at one of the bars, drinking into the night. Until they all left.

"No one seems to have seen them on the street as such, but the young men he was with said that he had left them at the door and headed down towards the other bar in the town, while they went back to the spaceport. They did clock in at the right time. But Narcis was not seen again."

That was the crux of the case. The rest was summarized. He hadn't been able to keep the young men here, of course. Their employer, a world called Cinzan, had called them back and to their distribution route. Cinzan was mostly an outpost that purveyed luxury goods, anything from mink stoles to liquor to sex bots. You wanted it, and it was sinfully decadent? You could get it from Cinzan.

And whether they were on Cinzan or in their spaceship, or on one of the many isolated planets to which Cinzan shipped, we could call them at Peura's expense. Peura had secured from Cinzan the promise the three men who had been in the ship would be available for our interrogation, if we so wished.

Other than those men, and the miners who had once been convicts, the Peura world contained women – also convicts, and imported as either wives or comfort women, in close numbers to the men, so as to avoid trouble – and the Peura family.

That consisted of Mrs. Analie Peura, a second or third or perhaps fourth wife, who he admitted "Is about the age of my daughter Reelen."

That age turned out to be twenty seven to Peura's sixty or so.

Both women lived in the world "But take frequent shopping and de-stressing trips to other worlds," he said. "You know what women are."

Nick made a rumbling, uncommitted sound, then said, "Did your son also travel often?"

"When he was younger," Peura said. "When he was younger. Of course I sent him to study abroad, see a bit of the universe. Of course. But lately, since he'd become obsessed with becoming a space pilot – of all the crazy ideas – I told him he could not go anywhere, and I gave such orders to the spaceport as well."

"Would there be any chance the Cinzan men smuggled him aboard the ship?" Nick asked.

"No. There was no extra passenger when they arrived to Cinzan. In fact—" He paused, as though evaluating what he was about to say, as though something about it bothered him. "In fact, when they arrived they were minus one crew member, who got sick, and whom they had to space en route."

"I see," Nick said, in a tone of deep understanding.

Something about it must have stung Peura who lashed out, "I'm glad you do, because I don't. If you think somehow being minus one crew member tells us that my son went to—"

"I didn't say that," Nick interrupted. "Only that any deviation from normal routine is interesting in cases like this, that's all."

Peura mumbled "Cases like this," under his breath. "Have you seen many cases of someone disappearing into thin air at a bar door, in a world as thinly populated and controlled as this one?"

"More than I'd like to tell you about."

"Well, then you should have an answer for me very shortly, and my son back home in double time, right?"

"I will do my best. If you could send your wife and daughter to me." I could tell from the creaking that Nik had turned to me, behind the privacy shield. "Stella?"

He always turned to me for hours, as though we had an open social calendar, and people coming and going and only I could keep track of such complex affairs. Or maybe it was that I needed to eat and sleep, and therefore my mortal needs delineated our availability.

"In an hour and two hours respectively would work," I said, crisply.

"Then so be it. In one hour and two hours respectively."

"I don't know if I can get them to obey commands," Peura said. "And I don't know what they can tell you. Do you think if they knew where Narcis was they wouldn't have told me by now?"

"It's possible they don't know they know," Nick said, which is the kind of infuriating pronouncement he was likely to make. "Do what you can to make them come."

The words had the tone of a dismissal, and were, and I can't blame Peura for being put out. He was paying us a lot of money to come out here and find his son, and, to his mind, all we were doing is bothering him and his family.

I accompanied him to the airlock and out to the stairs down from our spaceship. As the outer door retracted, and he left, walking huffily away from us, towards the gates of the spaceship, I caught a glimpse of a red sunset over arid-looking terrain, all reddish soil and low-growing trees. The air smelled hot and spicy, like an open furnace.

I closed the door and went back to our temperature controlled office. Nick had taken down the privacy shield and was sitting back in his chair, with his feet on the desk, his hands crossed on his chest over the creamy yellow tie.

"You know he has a point, don't you?" I said. "He expects us to do more than question his relatives."

Nick made a sound. I wasn't sure what it was supposed to mean. It sounded somewhat like clearing your throat, if your throat were full of gears, I guess. He made it when he didn't wish to discuss something, which usually meant when I was right.

I went to my desk and barely had the time to sit down when he said, "Stella, did you research this world, when we got the request from Peura?"

"There was no time," I said. "Remember we were under way and quite close to here, and if we had delayed. And as you know, the galactic databases are--"

"Yes." He said. He didn't say that Peura had also paid us a very good price for our coming out here, with an extra bonus for coming straight out. And I didn't belabor the difficulty of accessing the galactic data bases while we were underway. I had never fully explored how Nik interacted with modernity, other than asking me to read him things from my "research" which usually meant a quick search of electronic information sources.

"See what you can find out," he said.

I saw. It wasn't much. Peura was wealthy and owned not just this planet but this solar system, which consisted of this large world and a lot of tiny worlds – asteroids really – orbiting closer to the system's sol-type star.

His wealth was inherited, but his father had come from nothing and it was he who had initially bought the system and devoted his efforts to mining rare metals. I skimmed the names of the metals – it's like they're discovering new ones every week – but the important thing is that they were used in everything from building glassteel to making some of the essential parts for the coms that allowed communication across space.

The current Mrs. Peura was the fourth. The first three lived in different – and distant worlds – the last one as a socialite of some renown.

His daughter Reelen had attended some kind of academy in New Oxford, the world where most well-to-do sent their children to school, and managed to get through fifteen years of schooling with completely average grades without betraying either an interest or an abhorrence for any of the subjects.

His son, Narcis, had also attended school at New Oxford, but surprised me by having excellent grades in mathematics and physics. No wonder he wanted to be a pilot. He had an excellent chance of qualifying.

There was a holo with records, and I activated it.

A slim young man manifested in front of my desk. Blond, unruly hair, a charming smile, and the kind of clothes that meant he cared more for fashion than his father did.

"Narcis Peura?" Nick asked, from behind his desk.

"Yes," I said, and reported.

Nick didn't answer. He never did. Sometimes as he sat there, with his feet on his desk, the lights behind his eyes cycled on and off, on and off, on a rhythm. Not quite off, more bright than low, then bright.

I'd just finished relating what I'd heard when the doorbell rang.

I went out and admitted a young woman who smiled at me, eyeing me up and down. "Why, aren't you pretty. Just like an historical sensi. Does he make you dress like that?"

I shook my head, then shrugged. Nick didn't make me dress like that, but I'd often wondered at the contradictory reactions that would form in his mind if I appeared in normal getup. He seemed to handle it well enough from our guests, but the few times I'd tried to step out of character, he'd been confused and hurt. It was not a good thing to make him suffer more than necessary. Even if he was a cyborg.

"I'm Stella D'Or," I said. "And you are."

"The sane one of the two you asked to see," she said, and smiled again. I was no longer sure it was a nice smile. "Reelen Peura. Pleased to meet you, though of course, despite your pseudonym being very apropos, I probably should ask for your real name?" She raised an eyebrow expectantly. I ignored it, stepping around her to close the door, then leading her into the o ffice.

She, unlike her father, obviously kept up with the off world fashions. She wore a one-piece that looked – rather artfully – like a little blouse and a tutu kind of skirt in masses of tulle. Not tulle, of course, nor was the blouse silk, but both some kind of bio-fabric that looked more like the real thing than the real thing could look.

I thought I'd look rather good in that, gliding across a dance floor, but it had been too long, and now it was never going to happen again.

She made for the chair behind my desk. Heaven only knows why. Some people do. Maybe they think my desk is ornamental. I cleared my throat and gestured her towards the chair in front of Nick's desk. She pouted harder, but obeyed, arranging her skirts before sitting down, and crossing her legs in a way that made the semi-transparent pant portion of her costume outline her legs with just the hint of veiling imperfections, to make them look like sculpted masterpieces.

I smiled a little and didn't say anything. Nick was past noticing that kind of trick, but she couldn't know that, and one had to admire a woman for doing her stuff, right?

In fact, she was arching that eyebrow towards Nick and saying in a slightly throaty voice, "Man of mystery, uh? Or too ugly to show your face."

"We'll go with too ugly," he said, which would be the real Nick Rhodes' response of course, since he was supposed to have been disfigured in war. But said that way, in his gravelly voice, it sounded like flirting.

She had a throaty laugh too. She pulled a cigarette from somewhere. I'd never gone for them, but they were popular again with my generation. We were assured that there were no carcinogenic effects of smoking the new, improved cigarettes. Perhaps. They had gone around as a fad several times since ancient times, and then become unfashionable, or banned, or were considered too dangerous. One never knew where the medically approved or disapproved roulette was going to land. All we could do was roll with it.

But I didn't smoke, or drink to excess, or dope, preferring to know that whatever was thinking my thoughts and making my decisions was myself. My husband, who had been the same, used to say that we were the last two sane people in the universe. A thought of Joe came and went. It hardly hurt at all anymore. I twirled the ring I still wore on the fourth finger of my left hand. Inside it, it said *To Lilly From Joe.* And it was stupid to wear it, I know. Both Lilly and Joe were as good as dead.

"Well, Darling," Reelen said, a smile in her voice as she shook the cigarette to light it. "I suppose you want to know about the darling boy's disappearance."

"Yes," Nick said. "If by that you mean your brother. We were in fact hired to investigate his disappearance."

"I think he did a bunk," she said. "And paid the men from Cinzan a rather large sum not to tell Daddy about it. He loathes living here, not that it is a big prize, mind you, and despises the idea of becoming master to a lot of convict miners one day. He's always dreamed of being a pilot, you know, out among the stars."

She looked wry and amused, but shrugged and smiled. "He'd probably make a rather good one, too." She took a puff of her cigarette.

Nick was quiet a long time. Reelen took a few puffs from her cigarette, letting the smoke out in the kind of lazy curl one has to practice.

I could see her gathering herself to leave, when Nick said, "And you? You never entertained dreams of escaping?"

For a moment, for just a moment, I felt as though the façade of the well-composed girl was just that: a mask between her and the world, and it had come down just a little.

Then it went up again. "It is not the same is it? Daddy doesn't care what I do. And because I was never stupid enough to vent my crazy dreams at him, he never restricted me to the planet. I'm allowed to go and shop in other worlds. My allowance permits me to buy all kinds of fripperies." She pinched at the not-tulle skirt with her free hand. "And Daddy could not be happier if I married and went away to another world. He'd probably endow me generously at that. I'm the spare. It is the heir who is to be bound to this world forever, and to supervising our precious mines here and in the asteroids. Daddy says it's no work for a woman." She took a deep pull on the cigarette and exhaled lazily. "At that, he is probably right."

Nick nodded. He got little more from her after that. She laughed at the idea that she felt resentful because she wasn't allowed to pursue a career. "What? A career darling? But I am like the lilies of the field who do not toil, and yet, Solomon, in all his glory was not as finely arrayed. Don't be ridiculous. I am perfectly willing to believe toil is what happens to other people so I get to live as I please. At least, unlike *poor* Anelie I didn't have to marry into it."

If it hadn't been for that brief glimpse of a real person behind the mask, I'd have felt like throttling her before the interview was done. She told us all her favorite planets to go shopping in; the stores she patronized there; the sensis she'd watched recently. I didn't know why Nick wanted to know such things, but I supposed there was a reason. I often couldn't understand why he asked questions, but it always made some sort of sense in the end.

Of her brother, she said only that "I hope he did make it to somewhere he wants to be, and got to try for a pilot. The way he's been going on, going out and boozing it up with anyone who visits, or going down into Mine One City and getting drunk and fighting with the miners over one of their women... It's not healthy. It will end in tears. So I hope he's happy wherever he is. Daddy should stop worrying. Narcis will come home eventually, or make enough money to hire a manager. Or maybe close the damn mines and be done." That last was said with spiteful force, and once again the mask slipped a little, and I thought she was very angry at the mines, and perhaps at her father. Whether this had anything to do with her brother's disappearance, I didn't dare guess.

When she had left I told Nick that. The lights in his eyes dimmed and relit. "Obviously," he said. "What else do you think is interesting?"

"She's not as vacuous as she appears?" I said.

"Obviously also," he said. There was a pause. "We might have to pursue this in the Cinzan end."

I agreed, and frankly, though I couldn't say why, I hoped we did. I wanted out of this world. It felt like something was badly wrong in this world, and it was – for reasons I could never fully identify – making me think of Joe which was always bad, also.

But the doorbell rang and I let Anelie Peura in.

While she might have been the same age as her stepdaughter, Mrs. Peura was quite a different article. She was also blond, but her hair had the kind of sleek, carefully cut look that told me she probably didn't rely to trips outside the world to get it cut. Something like this required weekly if not daily attention. Also, while her step children were blond, she was the kind of silvery blond that required mods. Probably a permanent mod. Nothing so crude as dyes for Anelie Peura.

She wore a severely cut black one piece that seemed simple, but as she moved betrayed that it had probably cost more than some small asteroids.

It made her look like a perfect woman, with an extra dose of "what the boys want."

I realized I was getting irritated with her, and told myself to calm down. After all, it wasn't as though Nick would notice, or care, except particularly, in the sense that he knew – or had memories of – what men liked, and adding it to his estimate of her character.

I made the introductions, and she sat in the chair in front of the desk, folded her sculpted hands in her lap, and looked ahead, not making any comment on the privacy shield. Either her husband had told her what to expect or she understood that someone in Nick's position – or the position he supposedly had – had to have shielding.

"It must be very difficult for you," Nick said, sounding somehow as though he were empathizing with her. "To be out here, with two step-children almost your age."

She smiled. It wasn't a nice smile. "Oh, so Reelen has been little Miss Pleasant, as usual?" she asked. "You mustn't mind. She's very young for her age, if you know what I mean, and was thoroughly put out at my husband requiring she come here and submit to interrogation. You'd think she'd be thrilled at meeting a real life celebrity, but apparently not. And then, you know, she was disappointed in love."

I tried to think back through the public profile of Reelen Peura, and the magazines that had featured her. I didn't remember any man being particularly featured, much less any broken relationship.

Nick obviously didn't remember my reporting any such thing either, because he said, "I don't remember any relationship being mentioned, in the public—"

"Oh, no," Analie said. "It wasn't public, of course. Would you believe, my darling stepdaughter who spends half her waking hours making jokes about how I had to marry for money – as though I would have done so without some real regard for my dear Peura – fell in love with one of the miners?" She laughed, deep in her throat, a laugh that conveyed a sense of derision. "Yes. A convict miner, sent out here to serve his sentence. Mind you, he was not a pauper. Well to do, and educated, a pilot, sent here on a minor charge of smuggling. Chocolate, if I remember, to one of the worlds where it's forbidden. He told her he'd not done it on purpose, that it was just a moment of forgetfulness. As if. Well. He told her once he went back – he was only here for two years – he would send for her to come to his world and they would be married. But he never did.

"And if she thinks I don't know one of her long-drawn out trips all over was looking for him... Well, all I have to say is that when you have the money that Reelen does and you're reduced to pursuing the man who jilted you, you've lost all your pride and possibly need your head examined, too."

Yeah, I definitely didn't like Analie. Which was just as well, since she didn't tell us anything at all relevant. She talked about her life before she'd married Peura and how she very nearly, and almost became a famous international sensi star. But then she'd fallen in love – she said – with dearest Peura, and become his fourth wife, instead.

Judging by her performance, I'd say the sensi world had lost nothing. If she couldn't help sinking her claws into her stepdaughter the first chance she got, I doubted she had what it took.

After she left I told just that to Nick, who pulsed his eye-lights at me. "Her claws?"

"With gossip," I said.

"Well," he said. "Yes. But it is very interesting, don't you think so?"

I didn't see what he thought was interesting in two women forced to live in closer proximity than they found comfortable hating each other, but then Nick was not someone I could really understand. Not having emotions, all his life had become very cerebral. Perhaps he thought that the way women behaved to each other was, in and of itself, interesting. There was no saying. Perhaps he didn't remember what women were like, in real life? Or perhaps he saw us more clearly now.

"I think we're going to call Cinzan to begin with. And then I might need you to break into some records that aren't publicly held," he said. "And find a few things. Would that be possible?"

It was possible. I'm no more a computer hacker than I am a gene designer. Of the two I probably could figure out the later easier, since I'd taken some biology courses in school. But in my five years doing this I'd acquired some contacts who could do my hacking for me and would. Some out of gratitude for Nick's help in the past, some out of the memory of who he used to be. Or who I used to be.

I concentrated on dialing the codes to raise Cinzan and after trading ID and explaining my business with two layers of functionaries was connected, by relay to the *Do Drop In*, the spaceship that had last touched down in Peura, before returning to Cinzan, and which was now en route to some place called Daisy Wheel.

"Well, hello," the man who answered said with a grin. "Why you are a sight for sore eyes."

His name was Richard Doyle. He and his team mate, Ignacio Fontes were the surviving crew members of the Do Drop In. For this trip they'd been joined by a third, Fernan Jones, who stayed in the background while his teammates answered Nick's questions.

Nick had the privacy shield on, of course, which prompted Ignacio to say "Thank you for not just having the sight off on your end. Your secretary sure is good to see after a few months on an all male route."

They looked to be in the middle of our office, two of them sitting down, in chairs that looked like they were riveted to a bulkhead. The third moved in the background, going in and out of focus, depending on where he was.

Nick took them over the events of the night: they'd met with Narcis Peura, who was a nice guy, and they'd gone out and had some drinks.

"Old Peura is smarter than he looks," Doyle said, with a grin. "He runs that world better than most. Instead of handing out rations, he hands out coupons and he has stores that work on the coupons, where they can buy what they want. That allows them to take wives, and believe they're living independently. The lifers at least, those who will never be released. It's better for them that way, I suppose, and Peura hasn't had any of the rebellions that other worlds have had."

"And people who are short termers can also buy on credit," Fontes put in. "So that when they leave, some of the poor sods are indebted to their eyeballs. And have to send him money, after they're released."

The rest was as had been described to us. They'd drunk with Narcis, and then said goodbye to him at the door, never to see him again.

"Then on the way back poor Mike got sick. And we weren't sure what he had, or if it was contagious, and at any rate, we didn't have the room in the freezer, so we spaced him."

"Mike?" Nick said.

"Michael Argon," he said. "Our former teammate. Good old Mike. But it's the life of a spaceman, right? At any time, we too could go."

And that was about all I got from them, which was nothing I couldn't have got from records.

I told Nick that after they left and he said "Sure, and it might end up with you going to Cinzan and looking at their records, to make sure they really didn't smuggle Narcis there. Thing is, Stella, if they smuggled him anywhere, it was with him intending to go to pilot school, so if you can get into Peura's accounts and see if there has been some unusual flow of money out, or some credit extended to someone who sounds like Narcis? I don't think he would have left without taking the money to study. But if he did, it's perhaps a good idea to also look in whether he's been accepted at pilot school under an indenture arrangement?"

Having given his orders, he got up and left his desk, presumably to go to the kitchen to cook for me.

Meanwhile I dialed someone I used to know. James Brighton and I never dated, which in retrospect probably counts as sinfully wasted opportunity. Jim was a slim, dark man, who attended the same schools I did, but didn't come from the same class. In fact, while I was there on Daddy's money, he was there on a scholarship because of brains and native curiosity.

He'd studied electronics and social communication and ... who knows?

What I knew is that on leaving school he'd become one of the news mediators. One of the real ones. The people who take any current event and dig and dig, until they find gold or muck.

Most people who get a name in that field, sooner or later decide the digging is too much work and start just making up stuff, until they're found out and their career crashes and burns.

Not Jim. The average career in the field was three years, but he'd kept at it for eight. And of course, being where he was and what he was, he kept an excellent team of hackers at his disposal.

Nick had saved him from a sticky situation. Well, not Nick, precisely, but the man Nick used to be. In memory of that man, and out of kindness for me and our old friendship, Jim did me what favors he could. Oh, he wanted payment, in the form of whatever we found at the end of the road, the real version of the events, which he could then add to a mind that must be like one of those multidimensional computers they're supposed to be building: in layers and with infinite capacity. But he never pushed and was never grouchy about being asked. I could only imagine that sometimes the cost was onerous enough. I wondered sometimes if he knew what the real situation was, and that was why he kept doing us these favors. But even if that were true I wouldn't dare ask. There is knowledge so dangerous you don't want even a well-intentioned friend to know. It would just endanger him to no purpose.

He materialized in the middle of the office, sitting at his desk in Haven, a town in New Oxford. He'd never left, saying a center of knowledge and investigation was just right for his sort of business.

He'd not visibly aged in the nine years since we'd been at school. There were some silver threads in his dark hair, and perhaps a few fine lines around the eyes, but he still looked slim and youthful as he had in college days.

His clothes were also much as in college days: a loose pair of pants, and a rumpled pullover top. He was sitting at a desk crowded with various coms and other tech I didn't know the name of, and appeared to be typing on a different keyboard with each hand. There was a tall pot on his desk, and a cup by it. I knew both would contain coffee.

For a man known around the human worlds by reputation in one of the best paying and toughest jobs, you'd think he'd at least pay a secretary and someone to straighten for him.

Heck, he probably did. An army of them I should imagine. But I doubted any of them dared try to straighten his work space or moderate his work habits.

He looked up, right after accepting my call, and smiled, "Hello..." a brief hesitation. "Stella. Before you ask, yes, we're private. What do you need?"

I told him where we were and whom our case concerned and asked him for everything he could find on the family, including any unusual money draws from Peura's accounts that might be traced to Narcis. I also asked to find out if anyone of Narcis' description had enrolled at piloting school, including under a false identity.

In these days of retinal scans it's pretty hard to maintain a false identity, but it's not impossible. The trick is to corrupt the records, not to change the retina.

On a whim, I tacked on a question "If it's possible for you to find if a pilot convicted of smuggling was sent here and released in the last, oh, year or so," I didn't think either Analie's or Reelen's memory went further than that. Not as a fresh wound or grievance, at least. "I'd appreciate data on hi m."

Jim grinned. "I'm sure I can get you that. You'll let me know what really happened as soon as you can, right?"

"Of course," I told him.

Just as I hung up, Nick buzzed from the kitchen to tell me dinner was ready. He sat across the little table from me, watching me eat. He'd done chicken in a cream sauce, with asparagus and these little red fruits that people say come from Earth and that have an almost but not quite sweet flavor. It was excellent as always.

My husband Joe liked to cook, but his efforts were more hit and miss, even with the benefit of the cooker. After all, our cooker was not top of the line, and it was necessary, often, to alter the programming on the fly. I'd guess Nick, being mostly machine, himself, had a special sensitivity for when things needed to be tweaked.

He sat across the small table from me, his eyes glowing duller and brighter, which usually meant he was thinking.

I know I said cyborgs neither eat nor excrete, but that's not precisely the whole truth. There was a maintenance routine that Nick performed,

I'd guess at night, while I slept. There is synthetic cerbro-spinal fluid and also a kind of synthetic blood that is used only in extremely rare instances for human patients, and more commonly for cyborgs. To buy that in the quantities needed to replace what is lost to routine cleaning is not... easy, though we'd managed so far.

The process he undergoes every night puts the fluids through a machine that removes the impurities, and reinjects it into the body, with nutrients and whatever is needed to keep his brain going.

I was glad he did that out of my sight, as I imagined it would be rather disturbing to watch. But maybe not. Maybe he just lay down, and hooked himself up, and processed random thoughts while the machine worked.

But he always watched me eat, and though he never asked me how I liked it, he must catalogue my expressions well enough to make my favorites again more often than not, while never repeating the things I'd enjoyed less.

After eating, I processed the dirty dishes. When we returned to the office, he asked me if I could bring up an image of Michael Argon. I wished he'd reminded me to ask Jim about him, but of course, I also didn't think it would be that hard to find a picture.

It wasn't. Minutes later I brought up a hologram of the late Mike Argon. Like Narcis, he was tall and slim, with an unruly shock of blondish hair. The resemblance ended there. It was obvious that Mike Argon had grown up in a rough neighborhood. He had a scarred face, which meant he both fought a lot and lacked the money to regen. He also had a tattoo on his left arm, from wrist to shoulder, which showed a spaceship in full flight. It was so detailed, you could read the name of the spaceship as the Never Late.

Shortly after Jim called back.

There was no sign of any extraordinary money outflow from Peura accounts, and he would bet money – he said, and Jim never bet money – that Narcis had not been in the Do Drop In when it took off from the spaceport at which we currently sat.

I said "Maybe another ship, then? I mean, they have an entire spaceport. They must have more traffic than one ship at a time."

"I don't think so," Jim said cheerfully. "Not from anything I can trace. I think that spaceport exists to bring in ore from the asteroids and send whatever supplies are needed there."

"That is odd," I said. "As none have taken off or landed since we've been here."

The other thing that Jim had found was the pilot, who had been convicted of smuggling. His name was Mars Rosen, and he'd finished his sentence six months ago, "But here's the funny thing," Jim said. "He has never returned to his favorite haunts. The family got a letter from him, but that was all. He said he was going to take a crew job on the By Your Leave out of Cinzan, but they never heard of him. Your Reelen has looked extensively for him, but he hasn't been found.

Later when I reported to Nick, I mentioned that it was weird we'd seen no shuttles.

"Maybe," he said, "Or perhaps Peura doesn't want us knowing about his business."

And then he asked me to look up Doyle and Fontes and tell him if they were only children.

As it happened they weren't, and I whistled under my breath as I found out both of them had had brothers who were convicted of drug infraction on two different planets, and had been put into the rental system. It was harder to find out to whom their services had been rented, but when I reported to Nick, I said, "Do you think that's it? They had some vendetta against Argon? Maybe he was dealing drugs."

Nick shrugged, which is an embarrassing habit for a creature who isn't human. "Unlikely. After all, Cinzan deals in drugs. You just have to be careful where you take them, and I'm sure they are."

Then he gave me instructions. This case had been unusual in that I'd not left the ship much. Normally I am Nick's legs. My husband would have made a joke about what fine legs they are too, but Nick, of course, never does. What I mean is that normally I go out and see and hear and find the things he can't know. I suspected in this case he'd been protecting me, from what was obviously a rough neighborhood. He shouldn't have been. While I'd started out not very good with weapons I could hold my own with anyone now.

Still I dressed to disguise the fact that I was obviously female, slim and young, by putting on a padded suit and boots and a helmet.

"Peura wanted me to send you with an escort," Nick said. "Meaning someone who'd follow you everywhere. But I told him no. Which means he'll probably have you followed. You know what to do."

I knew what to do. The area outside was paved with concrete. There were warehouses in the far southern quadrant. I wondered what they contained. Food for the miners in the asteroids? They must be starving without their regular shipment. What could Peura be hiding?

It's not easy to lose a tail in a miner town with one street. It's also not easy to tail someone. I spotted him long before I got to the outskirts of the town. Mostly because it's really hard to tail someone on flat ground. His attempts to meld with the trees didn't work. He was a tall, well built man. Which meant I was going to have to do something he'd regret.

I did it before I got to the bar that was the last known location of Narcis. I turned into a blind alley and waited long enough he couldn't help following me. And then I'd jumped him and injected him with a heavy soporific that would give him a headache in the morning.

It wasn't something I liked to do, but it would only give him a mild hangover. And I couldn't have him tail me as I headed back to the spaceport from the bar.

I kept in mind what Nick had told me to look for and found it in the vast wilderness, with the low trees. It was a large reservoir, low to the ground, hidden among the trees. I wouldn't have noticed it had I not been looking. It was probably used to collect infrequent rain for watering. I thought if it were for drinking water, it would be guarded, and the cover on it would be tighter.

Climbing to where I could pry the cover off wasn't easy, but shining a light in there revealed exactly what Nick had said. Let's say Argon was none the better for the wear. But his tattoo was visible, and *Never Late* was still readable.

I beat it to the spaceport, but once there, having gen-identified myself past the automatic gates, the curiosity about those warehouses came again.

I heard no sound from them and saw no movement or light, so I headed that way, at a fast clip, keeping to the shadows.

There are instruments that detect and disable security systems, and the systems on those warehouses weren't ... well, they weren't what you'd have in a more heavily populated world.

The first one I got in was filled with barrels. It took a little prybar work to figure out they contained synthetic cerebro spinal fluid and synthetic blood, of the exact kind we used. My first thought is that one of those barrels would avoid the dangerous business of securing it for a year. My second thought wasn't a thought, but something that made my hair stand on end at the back of my neck.

The second warehouse contained parts. I knew those parts. The third warehouse was an operating theater. There were tables, and what looked like an automated crematorium.

To say I beat all speed records back to the ship was to say little. I got in and secured the door, and told Nick all I'd found.

"Borgers," I said. "There's borgers operating in those warehouses."

"Of course," Nick said. "I figured as much. Not every prisoner, but some of them, perhaps the ones he knows won't be missed, or have family that can be fobbed off with letters and some remittances will be borged and sent to the asteroids to mine."

"He being Peura?"

"None other."

"But you can't think he borged his own son."

"Oh, no, not him. That would be Doyle and Fontes. My guess is that both their brothers were borged and they figured it out somehow. I don't think the borging operation runs around the clock. In fact, I'm fairly sure he gets people to come in from outside and do that. Perhaps the two pilots heard rumors. Perhaps Narcis found out and talked. At any rate, what they did was kill their third team mate, and somehow fake his data, so that Narcis read as him going back into the spaceport."

"Corrupting stored data isn't that hard."

"No, it's just one outdated scanner, I understand. They probably disposed of Argon, and went back, got Narcis and convinced him they could take him with them, so he'd go willingly."

"And they borged him?"

"They probably tried. It's not an unskilled job. I think they just killed him. I don't think they made a borg, because if they had they'd have sent him back into the streets, to denounce his father with his presence, and perhaps his words. I doubt a shipment has gone to the asteroids since he disappeared. If it has, then maybe the borging was successful, and maybe he's there. But I bet you they will find traces of his DNA in that operating theater."

We called the authorities, of course, at the same time we took off. There was no point staying there, when they came to town looking for borgs.

Nick was wrong. Narcis had indeed been borged, and was in the asteroids and coherent enough to testify before they put him out of his misery. His testimony was the death sentence of Fontes and Doyle. Peura also met a death sentence for borging even if he'd not done it personally.

Reelen, suddenly the sole heir of the system sent us a fat check. Not for finding her brother, but for finally finding out why Mars Rosen hadn't come back for her. Yes, he too had been borged.

As for us, we stayed away from all worlds for a while, floating in the night of space, bound by our routine.

When we didn't have clients, Nick read in the office. I did my filing, called Jim to report what had happened, and caught up on news and trivia.

Two Earth-days out of Peura system, I woke with my bedroom door open. Nick stood in the doorway, his eye lights dimming and brightening.

"Yes," I said. "Nick? What do you need?" I thought perhaps he'd run out of fluid or something had gone wrong with the machine.

The voice that answered me was curiously hesitant, "Lilly," it said. Nick rushed into the room, fell to his knees beside my bed. He has no expressions, of course, but I got the feeling he was searching my face. "Lilly!" he said. And then, after a long pause, "I remember. I remember. I'm sorry."

"There's nothing to be sorry for," I said, while he lay his hard, smooth head on my shoulder. "You didn't choose to be borged. Someone else did it to you, Joe. There was nothing you could do. And you're still helping people."

"But, oh, Lilly," he said. "You don't deserve this."

"No. But that's not how life works." I ran my palm gently on the hard glassteel surface that hid my late husband's still living brain. "I just do what I can."

He'd forget again. He'd done it before. But for these brief moments I had Joe. I didn't know if that made it all better or worse.

Because he couldn't, I cried for both of us, holding the unyielding mechanical body that held all that remained of my love.

Writing The Knights Of Time

There is a person in fandom known as Tully D. Roberts (not his legal name, but his fandom name.) He's been a friend for some years now, and he spent some months a few years back – the psychiatrist he doesn't have would know why – sending me articles about the longheads and Malta. When I got invited to a Malta anthology, this had to happen.... It's all his fault, and I've told him so. A lot. He laughs, which is not at all the proper spirit.

The Knights of Time

The thing about time, remember darling, when I told you that? The thing about time is that it is not as most people think, a thing that advances, linearly, taking us from cradle and depositing us safely into the grave, to sleep forever.

Eh. So maybe it's that way for most people and most certainly for most places. Most people live like a swimmer who sets out to sea, facing forward and pressing ever onward while around him the current eddies and swirls, rises and falls, and he alone continues on, facing and seeing nothing, till he comes to the end.

For other people – no, other beings -- and in certain places... time is different.

Time winds and twists, erodes and surfaces, like an old nautilus shell played with by the sea, carved, recurved and chambered anew, so there are holes and smooth spots, and places that shouldn't be there. A grain of sand here, a bit of salt there. None of it in places it should be, and none of it, really, part of the place where they are.

And of all the places in the universe where time curls and recurves and flows back against itself, Malta is probably the most prominent. It is certainly the most prominent on the Earth, the umbilicus of the world.

Conquer it, penetrate its heart, wind through its spirals, and you'll own the Earth, past and present, and most assuredly future.

And if you are a species that can work time, like humans work wool, you can do that, and claim it for your own, and make it as if humans never existed.

You can make the green and blue Earth of the humans your own, and make the humans into nothing: maybe only a suspicion of existence, a vague memory as one has of a dream, an image that fades upon waking.

It almost happened once. Remember my darling?

It was in Atlantis, and there we walked, hand in hand, in young love. Our elders were worried and talked long into the night.

The Archons had stopped their politicking and hand shaking, there were no elections, no campaigns, no kissing of babies.

Instead there were late night talks, and pulling of grey beards. Did you pay attention to it then? I did not.

My name was Ptah and I was the son of the chief of artificers. At sixteen, I'd started to learn some of the cunning ways of intertwining current to make machines move, but mostly I had an eye for the ladies, and for drinking in the tavern late at night.

Until I saw you and you drove all thought of others or even of carousing from my mind, you Aglai, with your dark kohl rimmed eyes and your laughter like crystals knocking together in the wind. You, with the skirts like rainbow gossamer whipped in the breeze.

We walked through the golden streets of Atlantis, blind to all, but only thinking of each other and of our love.

Until.... How was it, *in a day and a night*?

The terrible serpent-people, the longheads came in their ships that pierce time, and landed in the middle of our city, and made it as though it had never existed, corkscrewing time around it, and winding, so our elders and the people we loved, all vanished into the vortex of dreams not worth remembering.

Brave Aries, the only one of the Archons to survive, gathered us shivering on the shores of what was Malta, might have been Malta, might always have been Malta, but I remember through the dream mists as the place where the mountains of Atlantis came to a peak, and where you could sit and watch the fields of lavender stretch out to the horizon till the blue of flower melded with the blue of the sea.

There were you, and me, and others, maybe three hundred companions, young and old, and all inexperienced with fighting, because Atlantis had been prosperous and peaceful.

Most, Aries sent into the world, in what boats had been salvaged, and somehow, in the sweeping tide of time ended up on the mountain. "Go, go out into the world, and create a civilization of humans. Be full of life and populate the far off lands, with your abilities. Build, dream and make and someday again maybe the splendors of Atlantis will shine in the land of Man. Forty of us – all volunteers – must stay here and fight.

"Because the strangers fight with time, we fight here and now and for all time. Just us. Forty of us. Here. Forever."

You volunteered because you were brave and beautiful, and full of the certainty that it was your duty, that you must fight and ransom the earth. I volunteered because I had to. Because you had.

We learned to fight and struggled on the blood-slicked golden tiles of Atlantis, while the ships of our friends became distant dots in the horizon, their improvised sails – black and green, blue and flame embroidered, all the fabric stitched from the tunics we'd worn proudly on the streets of our great city – disappearing far into the horizon.

We fought, and bled, and killed many long heads, while the serpents cut at us with their subtle time blades, their piercing time lances.

Did you die that time, or did I? How many times did each of us die? It doesn't matter.

We fought on the shores of Malta, as the memory of Atlantis disappeared into nevermore dream-land. We fought the longheads while around us, the returned descendants of those our friends who had departed into the timeless sea made lives, and loved and bore children, and fought among themselves.

Saracens and Christians. Crusaders and colonizers. Pah. Ephemeral. Discarded husks bobbing on the currents of time, never aware enough of what is going on beneath.

Sometimes, of course, the longheaded weapons hit them, and strange things happen. For a moment an ephemeral glimpses the truth, or perhaps the dream.

And sometimes one of us vanishes. Thrown out of the stream of time by the longheads thrusts, and sent gasping, like a fish, to the shore of mortality.

Perhaps that's what happened to you. I don't know. I know one day you were not there, you were part of the dream. Aglai, a winged maiden who'd flown away from our perch, and left me alone with the memories of walking hand in hand in Atlantis, of making love in the lavender fields, till the scent and love were all one, and us also.

I remember it was a becalmed time. We'd come to a time when the longheads weren't quite so active. Perhaps they, too, get fatigued that we refuse to disappear, to disintegrate, to be just dreams. Perhaps they fight so much that even they, Lords of time, lose too many of their numbers and have to return to the shores of their home to respawn before they can attempt conquest once again.

This lull was after what the rest of the world calls World War II. I remember the fight between humans and humans, more fierce than anything seen since Atlantis, and the planes overhead. Sometimes a plane or a pilot got caught in the time blades whirled by the longheads far above the island.

Some never landed but disappeared into the ethereal ever.

And some – And some appeared many years later living completely different lives in other lands, and remembering this life and Malta only as something they dreamed once, long ago.

At the time you were gone, and I was lonely. You'd been gone long enough my memory of you was streaky and thin, honey washed away by the sea water, disappearing in swirls and amber streaks.

Ah, Aglai, I remembered your honey colored hair streaming in the wind, your kohl rimmed eyes. I remembered the taste of your lips and the smell of lavender, but I couldn't know if I'd dreamed it whole, or if perhaps it was just time winding and covering itself.

And then I went out into the world. As you found out, the locals around here know us. They don't talk of us, of course. The many times children of those we sent out to live in the world as humans do, have forgotten Atlantis, and write many silly books about how it never existed, and even sillier ones about how it was built by aliens, or perhaps how it was just discovered, somewhere in an improbable place. But they're humans still. They know forbidden when they see it. They know taboo and things that aren't good to talk of.

If they must speak of us at all, they call us the Lords, or the Knights, or sometimes – rarely – the forgotten ones.

But they facilitate our movements. During one of the lulls, any of us who wants to go out and stroll through the town – it feels more dream-like to me than the memories of times severed by the longheads – never has to pay for his coffee or his Pastizz. And we can return to our time tunnels by a myriad routes.

The one I used to go out that time came out in the kitchen of an old woman. She was making something on the stove, wearing one of the sail-like black garments they wear, which they can't trace the origin of, but which are of course what the married women of Atlantis wore, my mother and yours, and all your laughing aunts.

Malta is like that, because of being at the vortex of the time attack by the longheaded serpents. Things get swept from the past to the present and back again.

Children disappear with their teacher at the Hypogeum, and their disappearance remains real enough long enough that the papers print about it, but decades later no one can find a trace of any missing children; no local families are missing any children; the whole has disappeared into dream-like never existence.

The woman turned around from her stove when she heard me scrabble from the pantry in which the tunnel ended.

I was wearing current attire, for the time outside. Jeans and a tshirt. But she knew who I was. And what. I've often wondered if we look different to them. If there is something to us, who survived the destruction of time and all the many millennia since that. If anything sets us apart from humans who live now, in time.

Perhaps.

Perhaps there has been.... Selection. Like breeding animals selecting for characteristics – the island is full of a variety of cat that didn't exist when Atlantis fell. Much smaller, and in so many colors, though they remind me of your beloved tame panther-creature Vatayr, and how fond you were of her – and if they have gone noticeably away from us in little ways, ways we can't tell. I've wondered if that's why the locals can identify us on sight, of if it is only that we have in our eyes the tiredness of millennia facing an enemy that never dies, and of having seen time lost and remade over and over again –great cities, great peoples, great thoughts -- all leaving nothing but soap-bubble dreams in its wake.

The woman knew me, and she crossed herself, and mumbled some prayer. I never understood if they think we're demons or angels, but in either case, of all the things that have no effect on us, prayer is perhaps the least effective, because we are just humans.

I nodded to her, and smiled, and slid by and out the door into the brilliant sunshine.

If you asked me what I was looking for I couldn't tell you. All of us got restless sometimes, and the commander, now Mikiel, told me to go out and see the real world for a while, and listen to the people, and know what we fought for.

So out I went into the sun-washed street, the sidewalk cafes crowded with people. I'd learned the languages of these people as we went. Or rather, they were in my head whenever I came to myself, after falling. When I emerged from the womb of time, I had languages, those spoken in that d ay.

I heard Maltese, of course, but also Italian and Greek, Spanish and English. So much English. I remember when the language didn't exist at all, but suddenly it was everywhere. Oh, I knew the history, it just seemed improbable, how a people from a tiny island, in the dark and cold, could endure devastating invasions, and suddenly go out and conquer most of t he world.

There were echoes of Atlantis' own history there, and sometimes I wondered if the time blades of the Serpent people did reach much further than we think, if they cleave time and history and attach a bit of thought here, a bit of memory there, and the fate of far-lost Atlantis is now part of the history of Great Britain, as it sails forth to colonize the world.

I won't know, and neither will you, but sometimes I wonder if one more, just one more, of the Archons had survived to join our number, would it be different, would he know? Aries Mikiel does what he can, but he has no one as learned to talk to.

On that day, I walked aimlessly, enjoying the air and the sun on my skin, and not thinking, just catching here and there a word, a sound, the turn of a head, the look of a man or a child, that made me think of Atlantis. Of someone lost or perhaps never having been. Of memories that seem like they happened yesterday and yet are buried beneath the sands of non-reality.

And then I was at the cliff, and there was a young woman ahead of me.

I remember thinking it was a pity she was wearing the same clothing as I: jeans and a t-shirt. These times leave almost no room for mystery and romance, for the sweep of a cloak in the forward wind, for the grace of your rainbow gossamer skirts. I sometimes wonder if when we turned our beautiful clothes into sails we lost a part of the beauty of the world, and it never returned.

No. Never mind. It is madness. It is too many years in time. It is nothing.

Anyway, I saw her ahead, her honey-blond hair shining, caught back in a pony tail, and her body slim and pleasing, but encased in clothes that neither flowed nor enhanced. And I had a moment of chagrin. She was staring out at the sea, a book in her hand.

And then she turned around. In that movement, I knew you, and your eyes – your dark eyes, though innocent of kohl – looked into mine. I realized I knew you, but you didn't know me.

"I'm sorry I startled you," I said, speaking English with a slight accent no one ever could place. I'd talked to other English speakers, from the British Isles and America, and they guessed me Greek or Arab, Persian or, if tone-deaf, Spanish. "I just came to look at the sea."

You smiled at me, and your smile I remembered. "You didn't startle me," you said. "Well, not really, only I was thinking and had quite forgotten that other people existed, even—" You paused and shook your head, as though you'd caught yourself about to say something that made no sense when you thought about it. It happens a lot to us, those who remain, because the dream and reality mingle, when time gets re-written.

I could have left then. Perhaps I should have left then. You had been sent somewhere by time, erupted from the womb of time in a new life, a new place, a new present. You had a past you remembered, a present, and a future you could plan, and none of it was fighting the longheads in long-forgotten tunnels or bleeding on the dry dusty land that had once been the golden streets of Atlantis.

But how could I? I'd lost you – I thought forever – and then I found you. How could I let you go?

We sat down. You came – or thought you came. These pasts seem to appear fully formed when they do, like the pilots flying to Malta who instead had always been living another life in North Africa – from Tulsa, Oklahoma, in the United States, the colony of Britain they make movies about. I've sat through three movies, entranced, but didn't pay the stories much attention. Just sat in the darkened theater, for once sharing a dream with others.

I told you that. That you came from the place of movies. And that I'd seen three of those.

You laughed, and your laugh was still the same bright tinkling crystal. "Not in Tulsa, Oklahoma they don't make movies. Well, they might, but not as a thing."

You told me of your life. Your mom was a painter; your father wrote books about lost civilizations.

"All a great deal of silliness," she said. "Atlantis and Mu, all that stuff. And how it is all, somehow, tied to astrology, and how..." You shrugged. You handed me the book you'd been reading. "But some of it is entertaining. He came to Malta because of the long skulls in the Hypogeum. He's going to write about it. It's all very silly, but it puts food on the table." You got a faraway look. "He once consulted for a TV program on ancient aliens, and we could afford ice cream for a while. Someone paid him to come to Malta and write about all the strange things."

We talked a long time. Of Atlantis and Mu, and all the theories. You made as much fun of your father now as you used to make of your father the Archon and his deep philosophizing about time.

I remembered your father then talking, one night, in the deep red shadows of sunset, with the smell of the sea all around. We'd been sitting on your parents' portico, and there were grapes and walnuts on the table. Or perhaps my memory has been affected by the slicing and reslicing of time, the dream spinning of what was once real. But I remembered your father saying "Perhaps other creatures live in time like we do in space. Perhaps they have no world, and can't manifest in the world but at a time, slightly. Perhaps those are the people we call gods. What if they should find a path to us, and fight us for our space, so they can take it, and have it for all time."

I remembered this was before the first tremors, and the first signs of longheads. Or perhaps he felt their existence already in the elsewhen.

You looked at me, suddenly, your dark eyes serious "Creatures who live in time? That's stranger than any of the books father writes. Perhaps I should tell him about it. He could probably make a great deal of money. Perhaps he should write it as fiction, for a change, admit it is fiction, and perhaps it will make him ice-cream money."

I realized I'd spoken your long-ago father's theory aloud. "Perhaps," I said. "But enough talk. Come with me. I'll get you ice cream."

You laughed, then, startled, but happy. And all the time inside of me, I was fighting. Should I let you go, release you from our trap of time and let you live and die in peace like everyone else out there? I should. It was the decent thing to do. You could be free, and I should let you be free.

But oh the smell the breeze whipped from your hair had a hint of lavender, and your laugh sounded like the tinkling crystals I'd loved so well. And there was this look, from the corner of your dark eyes, that wasn't like remembering, but it certainly wasn't forgetting either.

I bought you ice cream – for a definition of buying. I did say the locals gave us everything we consented to ask for, didn't I? – and we walked again.

We talked... I don't remember of what.

I found myself talking of the lavender fields, and the multicolored skirt, and the way the sea smelled in spring. I didn't say the word "Atlantis" but I talked of it, my heart in my words.

And you sighed deeply and said, "It sounds lovely."

Cats followed us, and you stopped and petted them. "Always liked cats," you said. "But Father says we can't have any because we could never afford to take it to the vet and look after it, and it isn't right." You paused. "I am going to try to make it into veterinary school, so I can have a specialized clinic and look after cats."

I had an image of you, lying on a silken blanket in your parents terrace, petting your panther, and smiled. "I think you would be good at it."

At that moment, well-beloved, I was determined to let you go. Let you go out into the world, to grow up and grow old, and never remember we, few warriors of Atlantis, who must fight the longheads forever in their trap of time.

At some point we realized the sun was setting, and I asked you if you wanted dinner, or if your parents would be worried by your disappearance.

You said they'd probably not even realize it, because they weren't used to paying that much attention to you. "I've more or less learned to fend for myself," you said. "When Dad is in a writing and research jag and Mom is in a painting mood. They know I won't do anything stupid."

You'd told me the same – that they trusted you not to do anything stupid – about your parents in Atlantis, just before leading me to the lavender fields.

I smiled wanly and took you to dinner at a restaurant that had tables out on the cliff, overlooking the ocean. It was about as close to your parents' terrace in Atlantis as I could find, in this degraded time. And I was determined this should be our last evening together, so I wanted to spend it enjoying your presence in a place much like the one where I'd first loved you. I'd have my dinner salted with tears, while you talked and laughed and thought nothing of it, and then went on to have your veterinary career, and look after cats.

As I thought that, you gave tidbits of your dinner fish to the stray cats that swarmed around your legs.

It was the cats that warned us first. There was a tabby at your ankles, purring, when—

I was about to say I heard it, but it was not a sound. The time blades make no sound, unless you can imagine that the screams of realities as they collapse and rebuild, cut in twain and reassembled, alive and bleeding, are sounds.

There was a feeling. I don't think humans are supposed to coexist in peace with time blades. We sense them. They feel like a cold shiver down our spines, a clenching at our hearts.

The cats sensed it first. The tabby jumped back, hissing, and I turned in the direction it was hissing, just in time to see a longhead, standing there, time blade held in both hands.

I've fought them long enough, I believe I'm allowed to say they're magnificent creatures. We've seen them dead, we've disposed of their bodies – those skeletons found in the Hypogeum, whose number and characteristics keep changing, as time gets reshuffled. We know they are pale, like.... Like shaved cats, with greyish skin. But they wear clothes, or perhaps shells, brilliant and bright, made as though by accreting pebbles and jewels and turning them all into a movable adaptable fabric around them.

And the blade of time is invisible, unless you catch it from a certain angle, when it's white as long-discarded bone, bleached on the shores of ages.

I caught a glimpse of this one. His gem-coat was mostly red and fire color glimmers. His eyes were great and dark green, and filled with… fear? Hatred? It's hard to tell the difference.

His mouth opened to shout. His hands swept out.

The blade cut through a couple at a table. In a moment, like that, they were no longer the same. Where two American men had sat talking, there were now two Italian women, as the Americans faded in glimmers, like the dissipating of a soap bubble.

And the little cat caught the time black in the downstroke, and it hit her hard, killing her, spilling her blood onto the sands.

I never know when you stop existing, and when it cuts you. No one does. Well, except maybe the longheads.

Before the tabby had bled onto the dusty ground, I was moving. I've been doing this a long, long time. I'd thrown you behind me, and I'd grabbed the knife from the table.

They might be creatures of time, existing and living in the temporal streams, but—

But they die just like we do.

I dove beneath the blade, and drove the knife upward, under his sternum, to pierce the strange organ they used for a heart.

The longhead convulsed once, and fell, green bubbling blood pouring out, as his jewel coat lost its luster, and he twisted a moment on the dirt.

People in the restaurant were screaming, but you were not. And I wasn't worried. In moments, it happened. Just like we are buried and decompose in the world, they decompose and are buried in time. He shimmered and there was a sound like what a clock would make if it disintegrated, and then he was gone, gem coat, time blade and all. And people in the restaurant were looking confused, like they do after a time attack.

The little cat was no longer dead, and was now orange, rubbing around your ankles.

You bent down and petted him, but there was a look of puzzled thought around your eyes, a vertical wrinkle above your nose.

"I want to know—" You said. And paused. And then, "I remember, when—"

I kissed your lips, quickly, hoping to distract you. In the back of my mind I was tallying the fact that this longhead had been up here, in the surface, above the Hypogeum. That was bad. Under the Hypogeum time twists and turns, and we've managed to trap most of their invasions there. It's easier to fight them there, to lure them to dead ends, and make them disappear forever, into their shores of time to decay or respawn, whichever th ey do.

"I have to go," I said. "I'll see you tomorrow, maybe."

"No," you said. "No. You—You never told me your name." You held onto my arm. Your hand was warm and firm and very, very real. Very how I remembered it. I took a deep breath, hoping to remember that touch forever.

"It doesn't matter," I said. "I have to go. There's... I have a duty."

And then I was running. Running away from you and the memory of us, running along the winding cobbled streets, for the entrance to the Hypogeum. No point going the secret route now. I had to get there as soon as possible and tell Mikiel that we had trouble incoming, trouble as bad as that terrible night when Atlantis fell and her lights went out forever, trouble as bad as that night during World War II with planes fighting above and the time blades slicing, slicing.

Did I hear you running behind me? I don't think I did. But I heard you call, just as I was about to dive into the supposedly closed off tunnels beneath the Hypogeum.

"Ptah," you called. "Ptah, wait."

There are things the heart can do, and things the heart can't do. And one of the things my heart had never learned was to ignore your voice when you called my name. My real name. The name you'd called me to get my attention when we were both young and innocent on the streets of lost Atlantis.

You caught up with me, out of breath, half laughing, "I don't know how I know your name, but I do. And I remember. I remember you. I remember fighting by your side. I remember that creature. The one that—I remember. Not everything. It's all mixed up. Like... like someone took many movies and cut them and spliced them together, and it doesn't make any sense." You paused on a deep breath. "Am I going mad?"

I could feel the seconds – vital seconds – trickling by on the back of my head. I had to go and warn Mikiel. I had a duty. But I could no more walk away from you than I could walk away from my own heartbeat.

"Oh, Aglai, golden Aglai, my love," I said. "Go. Go and be who you are. Go and be Daphne from Tulsa, Oklahoma, go and be brave and strong, and cure many cats. Leave the dying and the bleeding to us. Forget the defenders and the duty. Why should it be your lot? Go and live, like the ones who left in the ships, and all those who came after them."

I kissed you again, this time hard and with hunger. The hunger of a man who would never again taste your lips.

And I turned into the dark, following the path I knew for millennia, and yet which changed every day, and yet which I woke up knowing every morning.

Like my own hand, like my own skin, like the rhythmic beat of my own heart. My heart that had broken over leaving you.

I could feel the time disruption coming closer, a sense like when your ears drum with altitude changes, only all over my body.

Mikiel knew. What a fool I was to think I could tell him. Mikiel had been an archon and like the archons in the day leading to the first assault, could feel the disruption in the air and taste the coming destruction in his mind.

All of them, all my companions were getting dressed for battle. The armor of leather that stops the time blades for just a breath – and sometimes that is all you need – and our hair bound behind our heads, and the helmets made of the shell of something that hasn't grown anywhere but the shores of lost Atlantis, and which stops the confusion of changing time streams.

And our swords. Our swords, which are their swords we stole from them. When we killed them. And real knives, made with Atlantean steel, the last resort if pulled in close.

I was so used to the movements, to getting ready for battle in the semi dark, that I didn't realize anything was wrong. Until I was aware you were by my side, and getting dressed and ready in quick, practiced movements.

"No, Aglai," I said. "Go."

But you gave me a smile, partly a baring of the teeth, feral and beautiful like a knife glinting in the morning light. "No. I remember. I remember enough. And I swore an oath."

And then they were upon us.

A day and a night of hard fighting, first in ranks, pushing the longheads back, preventing them from reaching the surface, as the other one had. Then in melee, pulled in close, in sweat and effort.

Our blades mowed them like scythes in a ripe wheat field. They fell and bled their green shimmering blood, and disappeared back to be buried in time.

And we.... We lost Kybele and Marija, and tall Pawlu. They were cut and bled away and lay immobile in the dirt.

You covered your mouth with your hand staring at them, and at how we walked around them, dry eyed and matter of fact.

"They will be back," I said. "Or we will be back to them. It's complicated and hard to explain. But tomorrow we might all wake up again in the Middle Ages. Or Atlantis. And fight another battle. Past and future don't matter where time winds."

You nodded, your eyes wide, but I didn't think you knew what I meant. To be fair, I didn't know if I knew what I meant. It was a dream, wrapped in mystery and twisted in strands of ticking clocks, defying the mind and words of men.

"I remember," you said. "I think I remember."

You took off the armor, and you bathed in the woman's pool, and then you joined all of us, eating pastizz and drinking new wine, in the long hall. All the beloved, well-known faces that had died so many times together, and triumphed so many times together.

And then you said, "I have to tell my parents. I have to say goodbye."

I didn't say anything, because what was the point of saying it, when you'd find out all too soon?

We walked out, together, holding hands. There was at least that. I could hold your hand. You were not a dream anymore, and my heart was whole.

Your parents were in a small, picturesque hotel, not very expensive. We were lucky, perhaps, in that we didn't have to go in. They were at the entrance when we arrived. The proprietor had put some folding chairs out by the door, where the guests could sit to while away the heat of the night before they could go inside and sleep.

Your mother looked sweet and soft, and dressed in a loose dress, colorful, such as I hadn't seen since Atlantis.

Your father was tall, and serious, and long bearded, reminding me of your father, the archon of Atlantis. But why shouldn't he? Our brethren went out in the world and reproduced, carrying the genes of Atlantis and shuffling and reshuffling them.

How many times had I found a familiar face, passing by, carrying a camera and speaking Greek or German? And I swear to you I once met the identical twin of Melquart, lord of the fisheries. He was as self important as he was back then, but dressed in somber clothes and talked of financial planning.

The couple looked at us, a little vague.

"Mom," you said. "Dad, I've come to tell you that I must stay in Malta."

They sat a little straighter and looked puzzled, glancing at each other with the look that said "I have no idea either" that passes between long-bonded couples.

"You see," you said, plunging ahead, full of your urgency and your need to deal fair with these people you had a memory of having raised you in that strange land where stories are concocted and made visible. "I have remembered a past life. I am supposed to be a warrior, defending the Earth from the longheaded aliens, who are trying to conquer it for their kind."

Your dad sat up a little straighter, but your mom shook her head. "But..." she said. "Who are you?"

"I told you," you said, impatient. "I am the reincarnation— Or at least, that's not it, but close enough—of a warrior who—"

Your mom swept her hand in front of her face, as though seeking to pull aside a veil. "No. I mean. You called me Mom, but we don't have children. We tried but-- Who are you?"

I felt you shake, even though I was not holding your hand. I felt you shake like someone rudely awakened, suddenly. "You—"

"We never had children," the woman who had been your mother said. "We tried, but it never happened, and we were so busy with our projects, and money was so unreliable, I figured it was for the best."

Your father nodded, looking bewildered. Then said, "But what you said, of fighting aliens who fight with blades of time—"

"It's a book," I said. "It's just a book. She read a book." And I pulled you away.

Later, under the hypogeum, in our bed made of straw and cloth from another time, you nestled close to me and cried, for the memories you had but they no longer did, as though your remembering your true life had erased you from the world outside.

"Perhaps we should have gone Ptah," you said. "Perhaps we should have gone into the world in those ships with their bright sails. How many millennia would we be dead now, and the fight done for us?"

"But the fight isn't done," I said. "And we are needed. We're all that stands between the longheads and their turning humanity into a memory of a dream."

"Perhaps," you said. And you sighed a little. "And perhaps one day we'll run out of longheads, their shores of time empty of their spawning, and then we can go into the world and live and love, and have children."

"You could have gone," I said.

"Not without you," you said. "It would be leaving my heart behind. I can't walk away from my own heart.

The next morning we woke to an attack, the blades vibrating through our quarters, slicing flesh and time alike.

We dressed in the dark, and armed up, and we fought. *A whole night and a whole day*. A whole night and whole day through, and all of them died one by one, until we found ourselves here, the last two, the last remaining.

In this little tunnel, hidden and protected by layers of time accreted and deposited in the thousands of years of time-fighting.

At first you cried. You thought we'd failed; that all was lost.

You didn't remember.

I told you this had happened many times, but we always engaged in battle again, awakened from death in a time and place where we could stop the longheads once more.

It is just what happens here beneath the Hal Saflieni Hypogeum where time coils like the shell of a nautilus, and is battered and beaten like a pebble rolled by the waves of the sea. Here, in Malta, the umbilicus of the world.

Once we stopped crying, we realized you'd been cut, and were bleeding out, slowly, through a sharp rent on your shoulder.

I've held you as your blood trickled out, soaking my tunic as well as yours, and I told you this story, in case you're confused and don't remember at all when you wake up in time.

It's raining now. At least I think that sound is rain, though it might be, yet again, the waves of the sea overwhelming this, our frail earthen barque. Or perhaps doing so for the first time.

In a single day and night of misfortune all your warlike men in a body sank into the earth, and the island of Atlantis in like manner disappeared in the depths of the sea.

It won't be long now, not long at all and you'll walk with me in the streets of Atlantis again, and then we'll fight side by side when the long-headed ones, the serpents, land, trying to take Earth and make it part of their dizzying empire.

Or perhaps we'll be on the cliff top again, young and free, and have time and life before us, before it comes to that night and that battle, and your red blood flowing into the dust of the Hypogeum, blessing life into time-forgotten stones.

One or the other it's all the same. For you're one of us, and we must fight forever or lose forever the green and blue Earth of men to the destroying serpents.

Not so long now, my love, not so long.

And we'll again bleed and be born and live. And love.

Without end.

The Writing of Done With Mirrors

The following is a prequel to a started novel. Well, let's be fair, a started six book series.

If I have a few more years, you'll see it. For now, enjoy the short story.

Done with Mirrors

I woke up staring at the mirror, and something was very wrong. For one, it wasn't my mirror. For another it wasn't my room. And for yet another, it wasn't the world in which I'd fallen asleep. The only thing right in it was you, Katrina Rhea, golden skin and golden hair, and long-limbed clean grace naked among the silk sheets, asleep on your side, your face like that of a very young girl despite your millennia of life.

A quick look at the mirror again. Not only wasn't it my mirror, it wasn't a mirror. Not a functioning one. It had no depths in its innocent reflection, of me, half sitting, looking at it, dark haired, and dark eyed and looking like a suspicious youth of twenty or so, the age at which I'd frozen my appearance. And you beside me. It was simple, untroubled. And it wouldn't do us a bloody bit of good.

I touched you. Just my fingertips on your shoulders. Your eyes opened, instantly, and went from sleepy confusion to alarm. I don't know what you read in my eyes. But we'd been married – well, as good as – for thousands of years, and thousands of times, and thousands of places, and hundreds of children. You knew me as I knew myself, or perhaps better.

You looked at the mirror and your eyes reflected my panic.

We didn't speak. Words weren't needed.

Jumping out of the strange bed, at once, we looked for clothes and, more importantly, weapons.

Our clothes were there, as we'd discarded them however long ago, in a safe world. For the sake of brevity, I'll describe them thus: when you read this you'll have the memories of Terra Prima, of having grown up in Terra Prima, the world of humanity's birth. You might have seen the clothing people wore in the covers of science fiction novels of the early twentieth century: tight pants and a tunic for me, something like an elaborate brassiere for you, and capes for both.

I've always wondered if there were enough of us, or of our children, drawing those covers to make that fashion permanent.

Mine were silver and black, as they always were, and yours gold and shimmering green, like the fields of Terra.

There were no weapons. More indications that someone had brought us here. Someone placed us here. For an ambush?

But why move us? Why not kill us where we were? And who could move us? Of all the Lords of the Mirror only you and I remained, my best beloved.

And yet, we'd been moved. The sky outside was a pale and sickly orange, a sky that did not exist, could not exist in any of our worlds. The mirror was wrong. The weapons were gone.

There was a sound from the corridor outside. We were out of time.

I jumped towards the window, where purple, semi-transparent curtains waved in a hot breeze, catching you around the waist with my arm. You didn't resist.

In my careening run, I paused, less than a breath, to see the landscape out the window. Ocean spread in all directions, barely rippling. The ocean was red like spilled blood, but it smelled of water and salt. In the sky, two dark, dying suns explained the colors.

The pause was barely noticeable. We lost no momentum. Behind us, I head the door slamming open, and voices, too confused to identify.

The ray of burning light blazed above us, as we were already in a headlong dive out of the window.

The water was cold when we hit, and it smelled like the oceans of Terra. Without a word, we plunged, side by side, but there was nothing, except a wall of the palace to left and open ocean to our right. Not even a fish, or a plant, or rocks.

You touched my arm. You flipped around. Using sign language we'd created and used long ago, among the deaf people of Unormach, you told me, "There is no escape. They know where we are."

I flipped around, too, towards the surface, and my fingers worked, fast "They're here. There must be a mirror."

You nodded. Your green eyes were deeper than the ocean and more full of depths, as your eyebrows came down over them. You pointed up. Which is when I realized it must be close to two minutes and my need to draw breath was becoming pressing.

Centuries ago in Rodanancia, that drowned world, I'd perfected my ability to hold my breath to three minutes and past, but I was out of practice. And so were you. Still I pointed sideways and up, along the wall of the palace. First because there was no percentage in resurfacing where we'd gone down. Second because we must see if we could enter this palace at a different point. We had to get to the mirror.

As we swam the way I'd suggested, I thought that perhaps this tower was the only building in the world, and the window we'd dived through, the only in the building, and shivered, despite using all my strength to swim.

If I were setting a trap, I'd set it thus. If I were setting us to be killed, I'd do it this way.

But obviously our antagonist wasn't myself. We surfaced as close to the wall as we could, and you pointed to the left, where a corner was barely visible. We went underwater again – no point making ourselves sitting ducks – and swam around the corner before we resurfaced again. Both of us stared up and for a moment both of us were mute with shock.

The building was, to put it no better, a bare façade, like they did on Terra Prima for old movies. We were shocked, but also puzzled. I had a feeling, though it might be wrong, that there was no one else in this world but us. So for whom had they built this façade, pierced with recurved windows? Only the third floor, from which we'd jumped, seemed to be real though barely more than ten or so meters, jutting out and back, cantilevered, somehow, over the sea. It was there our room had been, but there was more than that, as it ran the forty meters of so of the wall's width.

You pressed close to me, cold in the cold water. "They will be up there," you said. "And the mirror, too."

"Yes," I whispered back. "And they'll be waiting."

I nodded, then grinned at you, the grin you knew. Oh, perhaps we were damned this time. Perhaps the death we'd evaded for thousands of years would catch us now. But perhaps we'd beat it again.

You grinned back, the same reckless grin that had captured my heart on Terra Prima so many millennia ago, and then we were climbing. The wall behind was almost smooth. Almost but not quite. It was no harder than the peaks of Varoumer, those glass mountains we'd climbed easily enough oh, so long ago.

Out of the water, I tied my cloak down around my waist, and you did the same. After all, no point calling attention.

Up and up and up, on fingernails and the tips of our sandals. Up and up and up. In the middle of the second floor, my fingers were bleeding, but it didn't matter. I'd climb up on the stumps of fingers to find out where we were and to jump to salvation.

And you, you must be suffering equally, but my look down at you garnered me a glittering, brittle smile.

That was when the Rodans dove down from the same window. They were wearing the weird space-suit like attire they wore in air. Which made perfect sense, since, though they had hyper-developed fins that could do the turn of arms and legs, they were... well, sardines. And smelled as such, as I remembered. And they were going to look for us. But they were intelligent. Well, as much as humans. And that meant after not finding us at whatever depth they dove, they'd come and look up.

I started up faster, and you followed without asking, you, doubtless, having arrived at the same conclusion.

Up and up, and at the top we realized we'd made one miscalculation. There was no door on this side. But I remembered there had been windows on the other side, and so did you, for you were already climbing to the roof of the box and across it. Atop, it was made of concrete with seashells in it. I wondered if it was made by the Rodans, and if perhaps its existence had another purpose. It still made a trap, but it saved someone the trouble of building it for the purpose.

We ran across the roof and then climbed the wall to the last window a floor up. I remembered our window had been up, and so did you. There was only one problem with this. We could hang from that window, suspended by our arms, and swing into the window in the floor below. It was about the right length from the bottom of this window to the top of the other. They were tall windows, probably four meters in height, floor to ceiling in the room.

But—

"We'll have to go in blind," I whispered. "Anything could be in that room."

You hunched a shoulder and scoffed, as if to say that surely, you knew that, and I was not giving you any news. I nodded. And you nodded back, with just a hint of a smile, but you bit the right corner of your lip just before, holding the bottom of the window, we swung ourselves out.

We had to swing out, then start swinging in, feet together, then let go and jump.

The bottom of our sandals hit the glass, shattering it. We landed on our bottoms amid glass pieces in a large white room.

I didn't have time to take in the details, as a man turned and pointed a burner at us.

It has been said that a gun pointed at one's head concentrates the mind wonderfully, but in that case the only thing I could think was that the man holding the gun on me looked familiar.

He stood tall, and his blond hair, caught back and tied, had highlights of red. His eyes were an odd color: brown but with a tinge of dark red, like well aged liquor.

As always you were ahead of me, in memory. You stood, indifferent to his implied threat, and shook the glass from your pants and untied your cloak, as you said, with withering calm, "Ah, Ermis. I knew it would be one of you."

He threw his head back and laughed at this, "Hello, Mother," he said.

Ermis. Suddenly the face, middle-aged, older than mine though that was arbitrary, fit the expression of a small boy, running happily through a field of daisies, clutching in his hand a half a dozen of them to offer you. Ermis, our clever Ermis, our first born.

He'd known nothing of mirrors, and had no affinity for them when we tried to teach him, but they said – the old ones, the lost ones – that the ability sometimes comes late. Very late. He must be a quarter a millennium, if my memory didn't deceive me. It might, because keeping the count of Terra Prima while rotations away was difficult.

"This is ridiculous," I said. "What do you want from us, Ermis?"

His smile turned subtle and gloating. "You don't know? Why, my dear parents! I want my birthright, the secret of the mirrors."

You and I looked at each other. We'd tried. We'd tried to convey to each of our children the secret of their heritage, to replace the Mirror Lords who had died, to renew the universe. But either they couldn't or they wouldn't or their minds simply lacked the quality to create the jump points and to jump.

Or not...

You sounded confused and appalled, "You didn't need to entrap us for that. And how did you entrap us? It would take troops to break through our security, and it would take suborning our people to—" You must have understood at the same time I did, because you stopped.

"You've allied with some king," I said. "Some republic, some satrapy. You've allied with some world to come and extort the secret."

Ermis smiled. His voice was rich and echoed of joy, of fields full of flowers, of the confidence of one who was raised in a palace, in a designed world, safe and happy and believing himself of divine origin. "Oh, not allied, and not one of them. We – my brothers and sisters and I – have assembled an alliance, that's true, but they're our vassals and we're their Lords. They want the age of the Open Mirror, the time when mirrors were made so anyone might cross."

You said, "No" before I added "I'll see you in hell first."

And he laughed at us, Ermis, our first born, and he told us to suit ourselves. In this empty world, in this empty counterfeit of a building, he'd leave us to wait, with only Rodans for company. Mute Rodans, who hated all humans and all who breathed air.

"I'll take their guns. They're a little quick with them," he said and smiled.

And then he left. I didn't see the mirror, which meant he was being clever, and the mirror wasn't here. He disappeared midair, mid-sentence, which meant his mirror was elsewhere and set to pull him back at a certain time.

I cursed, and you smiled thinly, "My love, you've cursed the Satrapy of Remearuta three times, and the horned kings of Letania five."

"They can't be sufficiently cursed," I said lamely.

You looked out the window and sighed. "And yet here we are. We should have been touching him when the mirror pulled him back."

Which was true, and which reminds me that since all your memories are Terra Prima and the last quarter century, until we unlock your true ones, you'll have to believe I know of what I'm talking. And if you're reading this, you're in desperate need of your true memories and the ability to jump through mirrors.

Doubtless you're very confused by mirrors and mirrors through which you can travel, and which pull...

Well, they're mirrors and they're not. Look, in the history of Terra Prima, your native planet in either your counterfeit life or the real one, the human race emerged much earlier than any of your scientists credit it. Scientists in any world and at any time are funny creatures. Their inquiry and discovery stops once they have a time line that satisfies them. And then that time line becomes revealed truth, unless something very extraordinary happens. But, sorry if you believe it. As Bob Heinlein, whom I knew briefly, back in the heady days of the mid twentieth century, said there are more holes in the history of human evolution than there are bastards in a royal European line. And trust me, that's an awful lot of them. I know, I've been the re.

Humans evolved much farther back than it's believed, and then... Well, it takes about ten thousand years from barbarism to civilization. Again, trust me, I've seen it again and again and again.

Back in that first dawn civilization in the rosy, blushing morning of Terra Prima, when the world – and everything was new and innocent – the play started.

There are those who make, and those who rule. Those who create, and those who can't, and not being able to, wish to control the creators.

Oh, I'm not disparaging some kings, and some satraps, some presidents, some rulers by popular or divine choice. Some of them, not overly interested in power, simply maintain the minimum for the safety of those they govern.

You'll know them, or of them. Their kingdoms take on the nimbus of paradise, the felicitous shine of prosperity and human joy.

In one of those – oh, very long ago, before either you or I were born – in a civilization that by all I've heard resembled the Italy of the quattrocento -- a family of artists -- or perhaps scientists. The distinction wasn't clear back then – created... mirrors. Only they weren't really mirrors, but things that while they could reflect you, could also afford you passage between universes.

They guarded the secret zealously, and gave it only to those they trusted. And that was the secret of travel through the mirrors. Not the secret of making them. That was kept as a precious secret amid those of the blood only.

I want to say everyone was happy then, but I doubt it. They were human and therefore unhappy and striving, which is the essence of humanity.

As the millennia passed and humanity spread, to virgin universes, to undiscovered lands, they took with them their wars, their rebellions, their hate, and their art, their joy, and their loves too.

Ah, my beloved, if you could see them – I want to believe you will again – the golden empires that arose in those other worlds, one mirror turn from Earth. A hundred golden Greeces blooming with philosophy and poetry and art. A thousand shining Romes in white marble. A million boisterous Parises, glistening with lights. All that and more, in worlds that would never have known the tread of human foot, except for our ancestors, the mirror makers.

But golden ages always end, and our ancestors – must be by the time of our grandparents, a million years ago or so. It's hard to know since I believe mirrors also play with time – got tired of armies marching through the mirrors they created, and of Romes burning again and again in the reflections of their work.

And they got more tired of being hunted and chased, and imprisoned, and asked to make a mirror for this king or that revolutionary.

They ended the era of Open Mirrors. Mirrors were locked and broken, till only a very few, remained. Through those only the people also with the ability to create them, all descended from the same long-ago ancestors could pass. From then on, only those approved of by the family could cross between worlds.

Or was that true? No. Of course it was not. Some people, some families, some states kept mirrors. And they chased our people through the immense weave of the universe. We'd give up the secret, they said. And their pets with the capacity to use the science and art and magic of mirrors would make them mirrors, which would allow them, personally, to jump between worlds, and create their very own empire.

The age of persecution started. Here and there, a cousin, a distant uncle, someone would be identified as a Mirror maker, and hounded, tortured, in an attempt to extract from her, or him, the secret.

None gave it. From earliest age we were all told that those who most want the secret are those who will misuse it.

And then, just over a quarter of a million years ago, if indeed time runs straight, the great plague came. Some cunning scientist, in some human colony created a plague – we never found out which or where, or at least no one living knows – it was tuned to our common gene, the one that allowed those in the family to manipulate and create mirrors. So, everyone, everywhere got very ill. And word came down, passed through the family grapevine, that the cure would be furnished to the ones who talked...

You and I survived. I do not know why. We used to think our genes were mutated which was why none of our children had inherited it. My love, we might have to rethink that explanation.

Neither of us was born or raised on Terra Prima. After the death of the First Ones, we set out, looking for—For any survivor of our kind. Or at least anyone who would welcome a Mirror Orphan. Fortunately, the other thing our ancestors had discovered was... well, not immortality, that would be saying too much. We could die, as the First Ones had of illness, of a bad turn, of an accident, of a million different things. But not of aging. Not that. We could choose our age, and not age a day beyond it.

We found each other in Terra Prima. You remember, that beach at dawn, and how we talked the first language—

Amid the worlds we – who imperfectly remember, and who could barely build mirrors – had raised... was it ten families? Or twenty? Without, we thought, producing a single Mirror Lord, a single one who could, like us, create and control the mirrors.

Until that moment, when we found ourselves prisoners in that false tower, in the middle of a hostile ocean populated by a species who hated all air breathers.

"He'll wait," you said. "Ermis will. Until we're hungry. Three or four days, perhaps. And then he'll come back and try again. And if we refuse—"

"We will."

"Of course, but if we refuse, he'll try again. Remember how clever Ermis is. He won't kill us, or yet allow us to die. Until we speak," you said. "Remember Prometheus."

Prometheus, chained to the rock, while the eagles ate his liver. Yes, that was a cousin. He'd helped a rebel group escape the wrath of their so-called sovereign lord and set up their own colony, away. It is not easy, but it is possible to create eagle-artifacts that eat only at the speed our near-immortal flesh rejuvenates. He never gave the secret. If he didn't die in the plague – and I don't know from where the contagion would come – he lives still. If you can call it living. He must have gone mad thousands of years ago.

But we weren't defeated yet, and we came up with a plan. The hard part was finding weapons, but after all these rooms weren't empty, and we could use the windows to travel to the room we'd first awakened in.

There we broke the mirror. Yes, I know, seven years of bad luck, but what is seven years in our immortal lives? And besides, of course, that applies only to the real mirrors not to the counterfeit concoctions of glass, backed with silver and framed with wood. In fact, most of the sayings and superstitions about mirrors in Terra Prima refer to the real mirrors. Don't get caught between mirrors. Mirrors are cursed because they reproduce humanity. Through the mirror darkly, till the mirror cracks from side to s ide.

This mirror cracked inoffensively, but gave us shards which, when a portion was wrapped in strips of the sheets made most effective knives.

You see, the Rodans have a weakness: they cannot breathe air. They just wear what amounts to space suits with a supply of water on their backs.

As we found, when they came climbing through the window, in a flop of tails, and a buzz water jets, water is heavy and makes the Rodans slow and clumsy.

You and I had been in tougher battles, against more opponents. You slashed the first one who came in. I slit the suit of the next and left him to flop and drown in air.

It turns out Rodan tastes like sardine. And sardine isn't all that pleasant raw.

Yes, I do know about the sushi chefs of Terra Prima. I might have invented sushi when I was drunk, long ago. But trust me, big hunks of slowly-getting-more-rotten sardine isn't pleasant.

It is however food, and therefore, we did not starve.

What we did do was take chunks of Rodan over the window into the other room, because we were sure that Ermis would come back to that room.

Look, yes, there was a reason. You see, mirrors can be used to cross through – mirror jump, as used to be called – or to pull someone else through, but more importantly, they can be set and timed to pull you back from a specific place at a specific time. And then they will transport you back, and any living thing you are touching. It used to be a normal thing for our explorers to do. Go and find a new world. Set the mirror to pull them back before something in the new world killed them. Oh, sure, many disappeared, but only because they couldn't find their way back to the right spot.

So, we waited in the room where Ermis had disappeared. There is a slight shimmer, like dust particles in the air, before someone comes through from a mirror jump. You and I slept turn and turn, waiting. Suddenly – either the third night or the fourth, I don't remember – you touched me.

I saw the shimmer in time, and we were ready. As Ermis materialized, and before he could get his bearings. You got your glass knife to his throat; I relieved him of his burner.

And the mirror pulled.

It was a good thing we had the burner as we pulled to the royal room of Thelvenus where the king laughed at our threat of cutting Ermis' throat. He was an old man, crusty and twisted. Probably younger than any of us, even Ermis, but he looked like a tree that has survived one too many storms. And somewhere along the line, a storm destroyed his moral sense, if he ever had it.

"Go ahead and kill your spawn," he said. "I couldn't care." He made a gesture, and his guards – a hundred of them – pointed their burners at us. "You," the king said. "May tell my scientists who are listening in, how to build the mirrors, and how to open them, or one of you will die. I won't tell you which."

Which is fine and dandy, except the mirror was right there, and the mirror spoke in my mind "Jump Honorable Kreios Yirach, jump."

So, I put my arm around your back, and you put your arm around mine, and we leapt together into the mirror, while behind us the burners hit the surface. I don't know what happened to Ermis. He might still be alive. Depends on how the king of Thelvenus feels. Or what his scientists tell him. Of all theocracies, I despise the one that dreams itself scientific the most. Because any group of humans will come up with irrational rules that cannot be broken, and ideas that must be genuflected to, and scientists are only humans, with illusion of infallibility.

And perhaps that applies to our kind, too. I don't know.

We jumped blindly and landed on a world that was all ruins and had been forgotten. A world of our kind, where everyone had died in the plague.

We were there but minutes when the mirror told us to jump, and that there was pursuit. I'm not as good as you are at plugging into the mirror neural net. I don't know if what you told me was true: that hundreds of our children, if not all of them, were in league against us, trying to obtain from us the secret of the mirrors.

I do know we felt ourselves pursued and attacked, with nowhere to hide. Somehow, through our children, everyone had learned that we were the last two survivors, and they would pursue us.

It was the middle of the night, in a cheap lodging, on Terra Prima, in the middle of the territory they call Arkansas, in the nation that calls itself USA.

You couldn't sleep, even though we'd driven away from the mirror near which we'd landed, and no one would look for Mirror Lords in this undistinguished location.

You'd taken a shower and wrapped yourself in a towel. Fortunately, the night clerk of this nowhere place hadn't found our costumes strange. He'd said, in a very odd accent of English, "You two on the way to Comicon?" And we'd said yes, though we'd never heard of the world. Or perhaps city, since I don't think common hotel clerks in Terra Prima know of the mirrors.

Now, in a towel, your luscious golden-red hair down your back, you paced in front of the closed window, like a tigress in her cage. Now and then you looked through it. "They will find us, Kreios. They will find us."

I had showered too but disdained covering up. I came to stand behind you, holding you. "I know," I said. "But I'm not willing to die to stop it."

"Perhaps not die," you said. "Do you remember cousin Lethos?"

I did. Oh, not in person, but I remember my parents and the other First Ones talking about her, before—well, before.

She had a formula, a way to wire a mirror. She would do it so that when you passed through it, your memories were wiped and you remembered only the first thing you read afterwards as your history.

We built yours carefully. First, we spent the night researching a plausible life history for this world in the early twenty first century. The world having acquired an electronic store of information helped.

Then we went to a place that was open all night and – amazingly – sold clothes. I had a cache of money for this place in mirror reach, though some of those were now probably collectors' coins. The clerk was aggravated about having to count the coins, and also at our attire. For some reason our capes offended him. I think. At least he waved his finger at us and told us "Remember what Edna says. No capes."

I suppose Edna is the governor of Arkansas, but I didn't check. We just bought you a lot of jeans and t-shirts, and appropriate dresses. Then we had to jump somewhere where machinery would create a false identity card, and also the means to hack the local electronics, to give you a history.

When we were done, you were Kathy Jones, from Oregon State, headed to college in Colorado, in your very own car, with your very own clothes and books and ... a mirror which you were told, in the history you were given – carefully written – was your great-uncle's, brought from Italy.

I want you to have the mirror. And I know that under stress your memories will come back even for a minute.

Having wired the mirror, I watched you go through it. And I let you read, on your laptop, set to erase the document in minutes, the story we wanted you to think was your biography.

Then, somewhere in another cheap hotel, I made love to you and kissed you goodbye. You thought I was Isaac Yirach, your boyfriend from back home. I'd driven with you partway, and now I was going to fly back.

"I'll call," you told me when I kissed you. You stood at the door to the hotel room, again wrapped in a towel and smiling. "I'll see you at Thanksgiving."

I nodded yes, but I could not speak. You see, I'd felt it on the back of my mind, the sense they were tracking us.

Me? I'm going to draw them off to some other world, as far from you as I can possibly get. If I can get a little head start, I can do cousin Letho's treatment on myself.

And then—Well, we'll hope on eternity.

If you're reading this, you're in dire need of knowing the truth, and I hope this document has reached you in time.

Goodbye Kathy Jones, my Katrina Rhea, my golden-haired goddess with the oceanic eyes.

If the gods and fate are kind, perhaps we'll meet again sometime, in the eternally bifurcating universe, under a kindly sun, by the power of a real mirror.

I shall wait for you.

www.ingramcontent.com/pod-product-compliance
Lightning Source LLC
LaVergne TN
LVHW091146080826
845145LV00008B/2278

* 9 7 8 1 6 3 0 1 1 0 7 4 1 *